I0831930

BLOOD LUST

A BOOK OF UNDERREALM

GARRETT ROBINSON

BLOOD LUST

Garrett Robinson

The author greatly appreciates you taking the time to read this work. Please leave a review wherever you bought the book or on Goodreads.com.

Interior Design: Legacy Books, Inc.
Publisher: Legacy Books, Inc.
Editors: Karen Conlin, Cassie Dean
Cover Artist: Sutthiwat Dechakamphu

1. Fantasy - Epic 2. Fantasy - Dark 3. Fantasy - New Adult

First Edition

Published by Legacy Books

To my family
It's been a long, hard year.
I survived it thanks to you.

To my parents
The only thing I wish you'd done differently
is sticking around to see this

And to everyone who's waited patiently
for this new foray into Underrealm.

You're why I get back up and carry on.

I hope this is worth the wait.

NIGHTBLADE
#1 AMAZON BESTSELLING AUTHOR
GARRETT
ROBINSON

THE BOOKS OF UNDERREALM

THE NIGHTBLADE EPIC

NIGHTBLADE

MYSTIC

DARKFIRE

SHADEBORN

WEREMAGE

YERRIN

THE ACADEMY JOURNALS

THE ALCHEMIST'S TOUCH

THE MINDMAGE'S WRATH

THE FIREMAGE'S VENGEANCE

THE TALES OF THE WANDERER

BLOOD LUST

STONE HEART

HELL SKIN

THE BOOKS OF UNDERREALM

CHRONOLOGICAL ORDER

NIGHTBLADE

MYSTIC

DARKFIRE

SHADEBORN

BLOOD LUST

THE ALCHEMIST'S TOUCH

WEREMAGE

THE MINDMAGE'S WRATH

STONE HEART

THE FIREMAGE'S VENGEANCE

HELL SKIN

YERRIN

BLOOD LUST

A BOOK OF UNDERREALM

GARRETT ROBINSON

ONE

Sun had long ago decided that she would rather be adventurous than sensible. That was why she was wandering the streets of a small Dorsean town in the middle of the night. She had not heard the town's name; she rather doubted anyone in her parents' retinue had bothered to learn it. They had passed through a dozen towns just like it, and they would pass through a dozen more before the end of their journey.

She did not look forward to that end. But then, it had never mattered to her parents what Sun wanted. She was the daughter of a noble family, and she was expected to do as she was told—at least until she herself became the head of her house. That was the cruel joke of a noble's fate. It came in two halves: for the first half, they were utterly subservient; and then one day, the second half began, and everyone else became subservient to them.

Sun wanted nothing to do with any of it. After nineteen years, she no longer had a child's enjoyment of a noble's life. She was old enough to know where it would lead.

It had been over two weeks ago that Sun had first snuck out of the camp, and she had repeated the venture in each new town along the way. Mother never noticed. Even Sun's personal guards had been surprisingly easy to avoid. But the royal procession had been on the road for weeks now, and Sun guessed that the endless journey made everyone weary.

Not often did Sun ask herself just *why* she kept slipping away from the others. She had a vague sense that she was searching for something, but she had no idea what it might be. And so she told herself she only wanted an adventure.

Most of the time, that was easy to believe.

As she strolled the streets, she kept a cautious eye out for any signs of black and gold uniforms—the colors of her house—but saw nothing. She herself had carefully chosen a cloak of muted blue and skins trimmed in the same color. Too, she had worn sturdy traveling boots that would withstand the mud, for the streets of the town were soaked.

Free to wander the town as she wished, she found herself unsure of what to do. At this late hour, there were no shops open. The streets were nearly empty, and the few passersby moved quickly with their heads down against the chill. There were no children playing outside.

Only the taverns were still open. Sun paused in her walk, staring at an open door. Through it poured firelight and voices that floated on the air half-heard, like Elves murmuring in the mist. That thought made her shiver, and she pulled her fine cloak tighter around her shoulders.

Dare she enter? Sun looked uneasily down the street in both directions. She had not gone drinking in any of the other towns. Yes, it would be an adventure, but visiting a tavern in a faraway kingdom might be a bit too risky, even for her. She was no stranger to ale or mead, but she always drank in her family's home, where a host of soldiers were on hand to ensure her safety. She did not have enough coin in her pocket to be worth killing for, but a thief would not know that until it was too late. Then again, mayhap she was safer inside the tavern than out here on the street.

Black and gold flashed at the edge of her vision, and Sun's blood froze.

Two guards in the uniform of her house were walking down the street towards her. At first Sun feared they were hunting for her, but she saw at once that that was not the case. They moved slowly, chatting amiably with each other, clearly off duty. All the same, they would soon pass by, and they could not fail to recognize her.

Sun turned and darted around the edge of a nearby building—and crashed straight into a red leather breastplate.

"Oof!" grunted the armor's wearer—a reedy man half a head taller than Sun. Sun felt a chill as she recognized his red armor: the mark of a constable.

"Sorry!" cried Sun. She spun around him and made to run past—but the constable's hand closed on her cloak.

"Here now," growled the man. "What are you doing skulking about this—"

Before she could think, Sun reacted with instincts honed by her family's master at arms. She spun her arm around the constable's, trapping his wrist in her elbow and then striking his forearm with rigid fingers. The constable cried out and released her cloak, and then Sun was running through the night.

"Sorry!" she cried again, this time hearing the desperation in her own voice.

Dark below, she thought in a panic. *What was I thinking?*

The answer, of course, was that she had *not* been

thinking. But the constable would not care about that. And if her family's guards followed their duty—which they would—they would come running to see what this commotion was about. That meant at least three people were chasing her now, in a strange town far from home.

Her stomach lurched as she thought of being dragged back to her parents. For a mad moment, she wanted to keep running, beyond the town's borders and into the countryside, and never return.

But that was foolish. She would have her adventure, and then of course she would go back.

She turned a corner and reached a low wooden bridge over a river fifteen paces wide, running through the center of the town. Sun took two steps onto the bridge before she thought better of it. She seized the railing and leaped over the side, coming down on the soft bank at the water's edge. Crouching, Sun pressed herself back against a wooden piling, her ears pricked.

Heavy boots came pounding down the street. They thundered across the bridge. Sun heard three pairs of them. Her family guards *had* heard the noise, then, and now they were helping the constable in his chase. But all three of them ran straight across the bridge without pause. Sun heard "She went this way!" in the constable's gruff voice. And then the street faded to silence.

Sun breathed a long sigh of relief. Holding the

bridge for support, she clambered up the muddy bank to the street. She wiped off the mud as best she could, looking down at herself with a smirk on her face.

"You went looking for an adventure," she told herself. "And you found one, even if it was nothing very grand."

And then, past the far end of the bridge, her family's guards skidded into view. It seemed they had grown suspicious and doubled back. One of them thrust out a finger towards Sun.

"You!" she cried. "Stop!"

Sun declined to obey. As she ran back around the next corner, she thanked the sky for her wisdom in not wearing her regular cloak. The guard had not recognized her from so far away—she certainly would not have referred to Sun as "you" if she had known who she was.

A strange feeling suddenly came over her. She skidded to a halt and tried to identify it. Then she realized—she had been here before. She was back in front of the tavern where she had first seen the guards.

She looked back over her shoulder. The guards were still out of sight, but their footsteps neared with every passing moment. She had no time to think.

Sun darted inside the tavern.

TWO

IMMEDIATELY IT FELT AS THOUGH A SOFT, GENTLE blanket had wrapped around her. The room was warm from twin fireplaces, but just as heartening was the low murmur of voices, filling the air with the cheer of good company. Most wore the simple clothing of Dorsean farmers and traders, with ballooning trousers and shirts that billowed at the shoulders, then gathered into tight sleeves running from elbow to wrist. Sun's supple leathers were strikingly out of place.

She had stood in the doorway for a long moment now, and people were looking at her. Drawing her cloak tight, she picked her way between the tables. The furniture was clean but worn with age, a reflection of the tavern itself: faded, but warm; old, but enticingly fresh to her eyes. Conversations were friendly but subdued, and the patrons sat straight, their elbows collected, their posture considered. It was quite different from the drinking halls of Dulmun, where revelers lounged in whatever position they wished, some sitting on or splayed across tables, and more often than not, a fight in one of the corners surrounded by cheering onlookers.

Despite the difference from home—or mayhap because of it—Sun felt a powerful excitement stealing over her. It was as though she was in a skald's tale, and every new face a character within it. The room felt like a place where anything could happen, where adventures lurked, waiting for someone to come and get them started.

And then Sun found a man in the corner who stood out among the rest. He was of an age that could certainly have been called venerable, but at the same time he seemed utterly uninterested in veneration. Contrary to the posture of those around him, this man had kicked his chair back to lean against the wall, and one leg was flung across the seat of the chair beside him. In his left hand he held a mug of beer, and his right arm was concealed beneath an old brown cloak that had seen many leagues and much hard use.

Sun stopped in the middle of the room, studying

the old man—and she realized rather immediately that he was studying her in return. That intrigued her, but strangely, it did not frighten her.

And then she remembered that a constable and two of her family's guards were chasing her, and fear came crashing back into her mind.

The old man put down his mug and curled his fingers to beckon her. Seeing no better choice, Sun moved to stand across the table from him.

"Put this on." The old man reached into a bag sitting at his feet and pulled out a worn brown cloak, shoving it towards her. His voice was deep, and it grated with age, but it had a pleasant, almost musical quality. Sun briefly thought she would like to hear him sing.

She took the cloak and wrapped it around her shoulders over the blue one, sinking into the chair across from the old man. It was not a moment too soon. Behind her, the tavern door crashed open. Sun knew better than to turn around and look. She huddled under the hood of the cloak—it smelled like sweat and ale, but not in an unpleasant way.

Across from her, the old man's keen eyes swung back and forth, observing the front door without staring too long. "A constable," he muttered. "Alone. Do not turn around."

Sun wanted to tell him that she was not an idiot, but she kept her mouth shut. Instead of turning to look at the constable, she watched the barman. He was a portly fellow, with a bald pate above a fringe of hair that stuck out almost a handbreadth in all directions. As Sun watched, he did a very curious thing. He looked at the front door—presumably at the constable—and then he turned to look at where Sun sat with the old man. But rather than alert the constable to Sun's presence, he only looked at the old man, twisted his mouth, and then shook his head as if to say without words, *Not this again.*

"Tunsha," called the constable from the front door. "A girl in a blue cloak is running about. Have you seen her?"

The barman looked towards the front door again. Then, as if deep in thought, he rapped a silver ring on his finger twice against the bar. It rang out loud in the silence that had fallen since the constable came in.

"Not in here," said the barman. His gaze did not waver.

The constable hesitated a moment, and Sun feared she was lost. But then: "Send for me if you do."

The tavern's front door swung shut. Sun released a sigh. The tavern filled with voices again, the patrons resuming conversations as if the constable had never appeared.

"He knocked to tell the others," said the old man in a quiet voice. "When he hit his ring on the bar, I mean. He let the others know not to contradict him, even though most of them noted you when you came in."

"And they listened?" said Sun. "Why?"

"Because this is that sort of place."

Sun took that to mean *a place where people hide from the law.* And yet, she felt just as safe as when she had first entered. But it did not seem wise to remain.

"I thank you for your help, but I should leave you to your night," she said.

"It might not be wise to leave so soon," said the old man. "The constable will remain nearby for some time, I wager. Wait at least a little while."

"I . . . suppose," said Sun, settling back in her chair. She studied the old man again. He was eyeing her fine leathers, and Sun knew he could tell they were not Dorsean. He himself wore a brown tunic under a dark leather vest, and baggy pantaloons that were out of style here. Neither did his face have a Dorsean look. His skin was almost as pale as a Heddan's, but with a tone and features that suggested Calentin ancestry. Weather and travel had stained every bit of him, particularly his cloak. Sun felt that this was a man who could be very, very dangerous when he wished to be. Yet there was nothing about him that seemed unfriendly, and despite his unusual urging that she remain in the tavern, she did not fear any ill intent from him.

"You look like someone who is looking for something," said the man.

"And what do I look like I am looking for?" said Sun.

"That is less clear," he said. "Though I would not

say it is something material. Sometimes we strive hardest for the things that we can only feel on the inside—an adventure, a tale, the thrill of love."

An adventure. "You . . . are not wrong."

He smirked. "I notice that you do not say if I am right."

Lifting his hand, he beckoned to the barman, who nodded and reached for a mug. But Sun had noticed something else. When the old man had waved, his cloak had fallen back slightly. She had thought his right arm concealed beneath his cloak, but now she saw that it ended in a stump just above the elbow. Something about that twinged in Sun's mind. But it was like a thought remembered from a dream, and before she could chase it down, a heavy girl in a faded yellow dress came with a mug of beer. She placed it before Sun and smiled.

"Eight slivers, dear."

"I have it," said the old man, reaching into a pocket.

"No, please," said Sun, grasping for her coin purse. "I can pay for—"

"Of course you can, with clothes like that," said the old man. "But you are a guest here, and I insist. It is my pleasure to share what I have." He produced the copper pieces and placed them in the barmaid's hand.

"Thank you." Sun turned to the barmaid. "And thank you as well."

"Of course, love." The barmaid winked and left. Sun felt blood rushing into her cheeks.

"Have a sip," said the old man. "It is a decent enough brew."

Sun sipped at the beer and found it good. Better than she had expected from a tavern in such a small town, though she still preferred the mead of home.

"That *is* pleasant," she said. "Thank you."

"And even better after a long day on the road," said the old man. Sun must have looked surprised, for he smiled. "Your boots are muddy, and as I said, it is clear you are not from this place."

He did not ask where she *was* from, for which she was grateful, though the question seemed to hang unspoken in the air between them. Slowly she drank another swig of beer.

"The second sip is better," she said. "I imagine the third will be more so."

The old man snorted and leaned forwards. "I love Tunsha dearly, and so I ask you not to repeat my words, but his brew is hardly the best I have ever had. In my youth I knew a woman who could brew the best ale in all of Underrealm."

Sun nodded politely. But again she was struck by a strange feeling—a sense that she was missing something obvious. It was disconcerting. She had never been in this place—why should she expect anything here to be familiar?

As the old man kicked his chair back to lean against the wall again, she studied him more closely. He kept saying how *she* was a stranger in this town, and yet she realized suddenly that he, too, had recently traveled here. His chin bore several days of beard, and his long-worn clothes spoke plainly of travel—not to mention the second, stained cloak which she herself wore over her blue one. And mayhap most telling of all was his money. He had paid for her drink as if it was nothing, and Sun had heard many coins in his purse. Only someone traveling, and traveling a long way, would bear that much coin while looking so shabby.

Then Sun noticed something curious: despite his single arm, there was an unstrung bow leaning on the wall behind him. Sun knew bows, and this was one of the finest she had ever seen. It had certainly been crafted in Calentin, and she had already noticed signs of that kingdom in his features.

Her thoughts came crashing together with the force of an ocean gale. Sun's mouth fell open and went dry all at once, and her fingers clenched upon the mug of beer.

The old man noticed her reaction, and his eyes glinted.

"Yes?" he said amicably.

"You . . . you are Albern. Of the family Telfer."

The old man took a long pull from his mug, returned it to the table, and wiped some foam from his upper lip. "Now, what would make you say such a thing?"

"Your bow. Your face. Your . . . your arm. Forgive me if I am mistaken, but . . ."

He cocked his head. "But do the tales not say that Albern of the family Telfer lived a very long time ago?"

"Not *that* long ago," said Sun. "And none of the tales say that he has died yet."

The old man's smile widened. "Then I suppose there is some worth in them. You have guessed aright."

"But . . . but you . . ." Sun gestured vaguely, having no idea what to do with her hands. "You . . . you fought in the War of the Necromancer, and—and in everything that happened afterwards. You—" Sun's voice fell almost to a whisper. "You walked alongside the Wanderer."

She thought his eyes went a little sad at that. But he answered only, "Take another drink."

Sun did so, downing quite a bit more than she had intended. It struck her gut, and a heady feeling crept into her skull. "I . . . what are you doing here?" she said finally.

Albern only gave her the same sad look. "I did walk beside the Wanderer, as you said. And it is her beer I praised so highly. Is that how you guessed?"

"That was part of it."

"To think that legends of her ale survive to this day." Albern shook his head. "I would give much to taste it now. Those were the days when Mag was happiest—when she lived in Northwood, and ran her inn, and loved her husband well."

Sun gave a start. "Her husband?"

Albern raised his brows. "You know of her ale, but not of Sten?"

"I had never . . . they say she was not a lover."

"They would be more correct to say she was not a bedder," said Albern. "But love? Oh, yes. She loved Sten. And I suppose it is not altogether surprising that he should have faded away from her story. She would hate that he did. Yet talespinners often focus only on the choicest gems in their own treasure. They have not the jeweler's touch, and so they discard the mountings that make the gems shine brighter still."

Sun did not know quite what to make of these words. She tried for a moment to think of an answer, but when she could not, she took another sip of beer instead.

"But now we are unequal," said Albern. "You know who I am, but I know nothing about you."

"What do you want to know?" asked Sun, her pulse skipping.

"Your name, for one thing."

"It is Sun." It felt strange not to give her family name. Her tongue wanted to say it by reflex, and she had to restrain it from doing so.

If the look in Albern's eyes was any indication, he had noticed her omission. But his tone remained kindly. "Do not worry. In this place, you are only yourself. You are not whatever person you left in the street outside."

It was a pleasant thought, that she had left her past at the door like a coat. But she did not entirely believe it. She felt a need to steer the conversation away from her identity, and she had a perfect excuse.

"Is it true what they said about the Wanderer? About the way she fought? All those things she did?" Again her voice dropped almost to a whisper. "Is it true what they say about how you lost your arm?"

Albern smiled. "That is a pile of questions all at once. You know, I imagine, that if I were to tell you all the tales of the Wanderer that I know of, we would be here for months at least?"

"I know that," said Sun quickly. "But . . . but could you tell me the important parts, at least?"

He studied her more closely still, and Sun felt that he was seeing more than her face, more than her fine clothing. She felt understood in a way that she rarely had before, truly seen in a way that no one in Dulmun had ever made her feel.

"The important parts," murmured Albern, and it was as though he was talking to himself. "Yes, I suppose you might need to hear the important parts." Then he spoke in a normal tone of voice again. "But I think the important parts are quite different from what you believe them to be. I will tell you a story if you wish, but not the story of my arm. Not tonight."

Sun could not help the crestfallen look upon her face. "Why not?"

"Stories may belong to whoever knows them, but these are more mine than most," said Albern, smirking a little. "I do not mind sharing some of my adventures with you—but only if you will listen to the ones I choose. Do we have a deal?"

It was not such a bad thing, Sun supposed. Knowing what she did about Albern and the Wanderer, even a simpler tale was bound to be exciting. And the beer *was* good. Glumly, she nodded.

Albern motioned to the barman again—Sun had not even realized her mug was empty—and waited for two more beers to be brought out. When the drinks had been set down on the table, Albern leaned his chair forwards, drank deep, and waited for Sun to do the same.

"Very well, Sun of No Name. These are the tales of the Wanderer."

THREE

I WAS NOT YOUNG WHEN THIS STORY BEGAN, BUT I WAS younger, at least. This was decades ago, and though my temples were just starting to grey, I was still hale.

In those days I lived in the town of Strapa, but I had been hired to guide a party of travelers through the Greatrocks. Leading the party—at the end of our journey, not the beginning—was Loren of the family Nelda. Have you ever heard of the Nightblade? That was her. Then there was the girl Annis, of the family Yerrin, and Gem of the family Noctis—no blood kin of Loren's, yet closer to her than siblings. There was also the wizard, Xain but . . . well, he was less than cheery company.

And there was one other who set out with us from Strapa. But I would rather not speak of him now, for no story should begin on a note of tragedy.

I guided them all through the Greatrocks, across long leagues and through great dangers. We had some dark times in those mountains, and some good ones—both victory and defeat, though not in equal measure.

What you care about is that at the end of the journey—the end of *that* journey, at least—we rode down from the Greatrocks and into the town of Northwood. Our hearts were heavy, but our steps were light. To me, riding into Northwood was like visiting an old friend. I had dwelled there for some time. And Mag lived there. Mag, who would one day be called the Wanderer, and to whom legend had already given other names—first among them, the Uncut Lady. Mag, the mercenary, the barmaid, the wife. Mag, my dearest and oldest companion.

How long had it been since I visited her last? I do not remember now. Too long, I am certain. It is often that way when two people part after their youth. We made plans, we promised we would not lose touch, we thought we would always remain close. Such promises are always made in earnest, but the world usually works to break them, and so it was with us. It had been years since we had seen each other, and though we sometimes sent letters, even those had become more infrequent.

Mag and Sten had built their inn with some help from the townsfolk. It had a second floor, which was unusual in Northwood, but very necessary; Mag's skill with brewing was well known, and she had many visitors from both near and far. But despite its size, the building did not seem to loom over you when you approached. Rather, it stood with welcoming arms spread wide, like an old woman greeting her grandchildren as they come to visit. Sten had fashioned a large sign to hang over the front door; upon it, a great rock thrust out of the land, waves and wind crashing against it.

"The Lee Shore," I said. "And does it not feel like one after those mountains?"

We were eager for rest, so after tending to our horses, I pushed open the door and led our little party inside. Once through the door, I stopped to soak in the feel of the place. It was a sunny day outside, but I felt like I had found a warm hearth in the middle of a blizzard. I imagine you appreciate the atmosphere of this tavern where we are now. The Lee Shore was superior in every way you can imagine.

There behind the counter stood Mag. A figure of legend, though she did not look it at the moment. Her hair was held back by a string, and her arms were streaked with grease and dirt and sweat. But she had washed her face and hands, and as we entered she was scrubbing a glass clean.

She looked up suddenly, and our eyes met from across the room. Her expression broke into a smile that warmed me to the depths of my heart.

"Now there is a face this place has missed for far too long," she called out. "Come here, you great lummox!"

I suppose I should tell you how I met Mag. It was not long after I reached adulthood. I had left my home looking for freedom and an adventure. Great skill at archery had been drilled into me by my family's masters at arms, and my sword work was passable. So when I found a mercenary company that was recruiting, I submitted myself to their trials.

They were called the Upangan Blades, and they were a good lot—for mercenaries, you understand. There were no evil soldiers among their ranks, at least, and they had a code of honor. They treated each other well, and did as little as they could to make others' lives worse than they had to be. It had earned them a good reputation, which I knew even in my homeland, and that reputation meant they were never hired by cruel or vicious kings. That suited me just fine. As it happened, they were in their homeland of Feldemar at the time, and I happened to be passing by.

The master at arms was a hard-bitten woman—I imagine I shall tell you more of her later—and she did not look upon me very favorably. I fear I made rather a fool of myself when they asked to see me ride in plate. But they let me show them my bowcraft, and the head of the company happened to pass by while I was shooting. My acceptance was assured after that.

Still, they had a long period of training for all new recruits, and the master at arms tried her best to break us. We worked hard from sunup to beyond sundown. Many did not withstand the trials, but fled home in disgrace. It was not a pleasant time, but it hardened me for a future that was often even less pleasant.

And then, shortly after I joined the Blades, Mag arrived. My sergeant was a man named Victon, and he called me to him one day while I was in the middle of sparring practice. Mag stood beside him.

"Albern," he said, "we have fresh blood today, and you will see to her arrangements."

"Yes, sir," I said.

I stepped forwards, and Mag and I clasped wrists.

"Well met," said Mag.

"And you. Let me show you the first and most important thing you must know in the Blades, or so they have told me. Latrine duty."

Victon smiled and shook his head. "I will take my leave."

Mag watched him go. "He seems to have heard a private joke in your words. I imagine you make the newest recruits dig the latrines?"

"Nothing so unfair." I fished into my pocket and drew forth a copper sliver. "A thousand decisions must be made every day, and a soldier has no time for arguing. When we must choose between two things, and both choices are equal, we let fate decide. Now—head or moons?"

I flicked the sliver into the air. "Head," said Mag.

The coin came up. The face of Andriana stared up at me.

"Congratulations," I said. "You get to dig the latrines."

Mag scowled. "I said heads."

"And your sign came up. We did not specify if you got to choose who dug the latrines, or if you had to do it yourself." I clapped her on the shoulder. "Here is your second lesson as a sellsword: when you gamble, make sure the other person is not stacking the odds in their favor."

"Now *that* is a lesson I will take to heart."

"Fear not," I said. "It is your first day, and so I will be generous and help you dig."

"I suppose I shall take it," she said, smiling, "since you should be doing it on your own."

I decided that I liked her. After we dug the latrines, I took care of the other little details of her indoctrination, showing her around the camp and introducing her to those who would call themselves her superiors—though as we would soon learn, that was only in name.

FOUR

ALBERN COCKED HIS HEAD. "DO YOU KNOW WHY THEY called Mag the Uncut Lady?"

The question seemed to come from nowhere. "I . . . do not think so," said Sun. "I know they call her the Wanderer because of the way you two crisscrossed all the nine kingdoms."

"Yes, but she was called the Uncut Lady long before that," said Albern.

"I always assumed she could not be touched in battle, and so had never been cut."

Albern smiled. "You are not wrong."

Sun grinned back. "I notice that you do not say if I am right."

He gave a great laugh at that. "Oh, well done. You speak the truth of Mag's name, but you understate the matter. Let me tell you another, smaller tale that will explain further. It happened at the end of Mag's second day with the company. As you know, sparring is sweaty, dirty work. It was common for the recruits to go and bathe in the river Skytongue at least once every few days. Some recruits were more modest than others, and they would find places to bathe alone. But most of us stayed together, stripping down to our skins and flinging ourselves into the water."

Albern paused for a moment as he saw color rising in Sun's cheeks. "Ah. You would have been one to bathe alone, I suppose? I do not need to tell you this story if it makes you uncomfortable."

Sun shook her head. "I am not uncomfortable, and I would not have bathed alone. Just because I have never done it before does not mean I would be . . . squeamish."

He hesitated only a moment before nodding. "Very well. Then, with your permission, I will continue."

"Please," said Sun.

"Well, we were all young, then, and blood flowed in our veins. Recruits often stole glances at each other from time to time—though there is nothing very lovely about bathing, truth be told. But in any case, I got a better look at Mag than most. I will not dwell overmuch on the details. Suffice it to say that she had a fine body. Exquisitely muscled and strong and . . . well, she was worth glancing at, let us say."

Sun's blush deepened, and Albern gave her another smile. "Are you sure you do not want me to stop? I had nearly forgotten about the proclivities of noble children."

"Oh, please," said Sun. "I am not some trembling son of Selvan. I am fine."

"Well, then. It was quite some time before I noticed the oddest thing of all about Mag. She had no scars. None at all. Not on her body, her arms or legs. Not even her hands."

"That makes sense, considering how well she could fight," said Sun.

Albern frowned. "It does *not* make sense. No matter how skilled a fighter may be when they learn warcraft, they still have to *learn* it. And everyone, when they are learning to fight, gets injured. Training accidents are common. Your opponent is trying to strike you with a blade. No matter how blunted it is, no matter how padded your training armor, at some point, everyone spills a little blood. You yourself have scars on your hands that do not look like they came from a cooking accident."

Sun frowned and looked down at a few tiny ridges on her knuckles. "That? That was no injury, only a blister from the back of my shield."

"I knew that before I mentioned it," said Albern.

"Yet what I am trying to tell you is that Mag did not have even that much of a mark upon her. Her skin was perfect. Flawless."

He paused, looking at Sun, who suddenly realized her eyes were wide and her mouth was hanging open slightly. Albern nodded.

"Yes. Do you understand now? Can you begin to understand Mag's prowess? How skilled do you have to be—how *naturally* talented, I mean—to avoid *any* wound at all, even early in life? Even when you are first training to use a blade, or fight with soldiers by your side? And as time went on, we got to see Mag train—if you could call it training. Privately, I thought it was more of a demonstration that she was the best among us, and we were unworthy to march beside her. No one could touch her, no matter how many opponents they put against her in the practice ring.

"That was the beginning of her legend—right there, in the Upangan Blades. How could she be real? Think beyond her skill with a blade. How could she have avoided *any* cuts her whole life, even on her hands and knees as a child, running amid mud and rocks and scaling to the tops of trees?"

"It . . . it does not seem possible," breathed Sun.

Albern slapped his hand lightly on the table. "And yet, there it was," he said. "The evidence of it was plain—it lay right before our eyes. The Uncut Lady. I came up with that name myself, by the way."

Sun felt herself entirely caught up in the wonder of

it. But then the tavern's door opened, and there came the sound of new voices. Sun glanced behind her—and felt her blood freeze.

There in the doorway stood the two guards from earlier, the ones from her family. They looked about the place, and for a frightful moment Sun thought they were still searching for her. But they stood relaxed and lazy, and when they saw an empty table on the other side of the room, they moved towards it.

They were not here for Sun, but only to get a drink. Although her pulse seemed to resume after a long moment of holding its breath, Sun still felt herself far too exposed. She glanced back at Albern, whose eyes had widened slightly.

"I take it you do not want those women to see you," he said. "As with the constable."

"You are correct."

"Then ignore them, and talk with me as if we have been conversing all night."

"If you will promise to keep an eye on them for me."

"Of course."

Sun sighed. "Very well. Tell me what happened in Northwood."

A shadow passed over Albern's face. "Many things, and nearly all of them dark. But it did not start out that way."

FIVE

When we arrived to her inn, I asked Mag to let me pay for the food and lodging of my friends. She understood at once. I had never done so before, and she could see the pain in my eyes when I asked it of her. By those signs, Mag knew we had come to her on an evil road. She never troubled Loren or her friends to pay for their lodgings, and when, in the end, I tried to pay her, she refused me, too.

Loren met an old friend in Mag's common room—a boy named Chet. They went off on their own, and the rest of us ate and talked and simply rested after a journey that had gone on far too long. Shortly after the sun set, I encouraged the party to ready for bed.

I myself did not go to sleep right away, but stayed up to speak with Mag and Sten. It had been years, after all, and I was eager to hear how they had been getting on. Mag and I could never have been lovers, but she and Sten could never have been anything else. You could see it in the way they looked at each other, the little touches on the arm or shoulder when they would speak. They would share smiles that turned into private moments between the two of them, and never mind the fact that I was sitting right there.

First I told them all that had happened to our party in the Greatrocks—of how we had ridden north through the mountain pass, and had been attacked by harpies and satyrs, and had found a growing darkness in an old fortress. Those matters had to do with the Necromancer, though of course we did not know that at the time.

"How under the sky did you get involved in all this, Albern?" said Mag. "I thought you longed for peace and quiet in Strapa."

"I did. But even Strapa is less quiet than it used to be, and less peaceful," I told her. "Has word of Wellmont reached you yet, this far north?"

Sten waved his hand vaguely. "Rumors. Some Dorsean border squabble."

"It is a bit more than that, I am afraid," I said. "I did not witness the battle, but Loren and her friends did. Dorsea seems intent on bringing the city down to its foundations."

"Why?" said Mag. "Surely they cannot think the High King would let that stand."

Sten snorted. "Who understands Dorseans?"

"Well, first I heard of Wellmont, and that weighed on me," I said. "And then that girl Loren strode into my bowyery. When I saw her and her companion, I felt . . . I do not know precisely what I felt, but I knew I had to go with her. There was something about her—and the man she came in with, but mostly her—that told me something *important* was going on. Something I could not ignore. And besides, their road north brought me here to visit you."

Mag raised her eyebrows. "Though you almost got yourself killed along the way. That would somewhat have diminished the pleasure of your company."

I gave her a half-bow from my seat. "I am pleased to hear you value it enough not to want to lose it."

That made all of us chuckle, and we spent a moment or two enjoying Mag's ale in silence. As an aside, whatever tales you have heard about her brew cannot do it justice. It was sweeter than honey, and as bracing as a bear's roar. She would chill some kegs of it in the river, and then it was like drinking a draft of gold pouring from the peaks of mountains. Other times she would serve it from barrels kept in a storehouse, and then it was like pouring the warmth of a good hearth directly into your gut. There are stories of people who have killed each other for a barrel of it. Those stories are not true, but they could be.

"So you took a Mystic and three children into the mountains," said Mag, sighing. "And you thought it would be a lark—a pleasant jaunt, after too many years standing still."

"I had no reason to think otherwise," I said. "And of course, that was before I found out about our fifth, unwilling party member."

Xain walked into the room at that moment, as perfectly timed as if he had waited, listening, until he heard me speak of him. Most people know a few tales of Xain of the family Forredar, once a savior of the Lord Prince, once a dean of the Academy for Wizards, and all the other titles he acquired. But in that room, at that time, he looked far from impressive. He was thin and sickly, and his hair had become sparse upon his scalp. He suffered from a sickness, then, though that is too long a story to tell now. He would have walked right by us, had I not spoken just as he passed.

"Can you not sleep, Xain?"

He paused for the space of a few heartbeats, his arms wrapped tight around himself despite the room's warmth, and surveyed us with shadowed eyes that glittered. Then he pulled out a chair and sat—but suddenly he went rigid, looking uncertainly at us.

"May I sit?"

"Of course," said Mag, ever the gracious host.

"Thank you," said Xain, sinking back into the chair and relaxing—at least somewhat.

Mag turned back to me. "You said that something bigger is going on. What, exactly?"

I suddenly regretted mentioning it. There was a curious light in Mag's eyes, an interest she could not hide. I did not want to further stoke that fire. A darkness *was* gathering, it was true—as we know now, in these later years. But I feared that if I made it plain to her, it might pull her away from Northwood, the place where she had finally found Sten—and thus, found happiness. Mag deserved that happiness more than most people I had met in my travels.

But while I hesitated, Xain did not. He knew nothing of my reason for secrecy, of course, and so he spoke before I could think of an answer that would forestall any more of Mag's questions.

"You have been telling them of the Greatrocks?" he asked me. "*Something bigger* hardly begins to describe it. We found an ancient enemy in the mountains. An enemy of the Mystics, I mean. Our friend and leader, Jordel, perished trying to stop them. Now that he has fallen, it is up to the rest of us to warn Underrealm. I do not know everything, and I cannot say everything I do know. But we stand on the brink of a great conflict. The Mystics must be alerted, and the sooner the better."

"Then where are you bound?" said Mag. "The

Mystics have no stronghold here, and I do not know of any who currently dwell in the city. Will you ride for Cabrus?"

"They make for Ammon," I cut in. Xain looked surprised, and I shrugged. "Did you think I was not paying attention? You and Loren did not take much trouble to conceal the plans you made."

Mag frowned. "You say 'they' as though you do not mean to go with them."

"That is because I do not, as I told them already."

"And we understand that choice," said Xain. "I would do the same, were I in your shoes." But though he spoke the words easily enough, he did not meet my gaze.

"Then what?" said Sten, frowning at me over the mug of ale he had just begun to raise. "Will you stay here?"

"For a time, yes," I said. "It has been too long since we saw each other last. But after a while, I will ride home for Strapa. I have had enough of wandering for a good long while, I think."

Mag did not seem to think very highly of this plan—or of me, in that moment, if I am being honest. She did not scowl, exactly, but I could see a flash of anger in her eyes. "It seems to me that Loren and the others need help. Will you not aid them?"

"I do not mean to, no," I said. "I am not beholden to anyone. They hired me to bring them here to Northwood and nothing more."

Before, I had felt certain in my choice. But I cannot deny I felt a small bit of guilt as I answered. Yet I was sure that I was making the right choice, even if I had my own qualms about it.

In our youth, Mag and I had been mercenaries, fighting on battlefields across all the nine kingdoms. A mercenary's life is not for everyone, and it is especially deadly to those who have a place they call home. A king's soldiers are different—they fight *for* their home, and that is what gives them strength. But in a sellsword company, such a soldier is death to have beside you on the battlefield. They will be the first to break at any sign of trouble. I thought I had learned a lesson in the Greatrocks. I thought my days of far-ranging adventure were behind me, and that I had become a man with a home, a man who would wander no more.

What a fool I was.

Xain did not say anything, but he avoided my gaze as he took a sip of his ale. I wondered what was going on behind his dark eyes—whether he was thinking of what I had confessed to Loren. That secret was too painful to think about now, and certainly nothing I wanted to tell Mag. But if Xain was indeed thinking such thoughts, he kept them to himself, for which I was grateful.

Mag did not speak, either, but she was less adept at hiding her feelings. She fell into a silence full of thought, taking many long pulls at her ale.

Sten, sensing the sudden discomfort at the table,

tried to pick up where the conversation had left off, asking me about matters of small importance. I answered him easily enough, and we carried on that way until Xain, wearying, at last excused himself to go to bed.

When he had gone, Mag put down her mug and fixed me with a look. I steeled myself, for I feared she meant to reprimand me. But when I met her gaze, she smiled at me.

"How would you like to go to the Reeve?"

I balked. "Now? Tonight?"

"Yes, of course," she said. "The moons are right for it, and the sky is clear. Sten and I went just a few days ago, and it was perfect. We meant to go again tonight, even before you arrived."

"If we all go, who will watch the inn?"

Sten waved a hand. "My wife still has reputation enough to keep filching fingers from our stores and our coin. We step out fairly often, especially at night."

"I . . ." My voice trailed off, and I shook my head with a smile. When had I become such an old worrywart? I took a deep breath and released it, and suddenly it felt like we were young again, like we had just come here to Northwood together for the first time.

"I would like nothing more in all the world."

Mag led us out through Northwood's south gate. The city had no reason to close them at night, for the land was untroubled in those days. The guards waved to us as we passed, and then they returned to their game of Moons. The country beyond the wall was open and beautiful, the farms well tended, though of course they were now deserted. A wide road cut in straight lines through the fields, turning with the borders of each farm, but always at perfect angles—and always taking us farther south, in the end. We were on foot, and so the journey took us a little longer than it would have otherwise, but in less than an hour we had reached the Reeve.

I do not know for certain, but I would guess it got its name because it used to be a place of official business. It was easy to see it as a place to deliver solemn proclamations. The Reeve was a large hill, and though it was not really all that tall, it was impressive. There was something in the shape of it that gave a sense of eminence, of importance. If Mag's tavern was a kindly grandmother, the Reeve was an old man, wizened but still hale, his arms folded as he considered you, judging your worth with eyes still sharp with wit.

A footpath cut back and forth across its eastern slope. We climbed it to the top, which was flat but surrounded with large boulders. The boulders looked natural—certainly they had not been cut by any human tools—but they stood about the edge of the hill like a crown, as perfectly spaced as if they had been put there. Mayhap it was something done by ancient humanity, a relic of the time before time. Mayhap that was where the hill had received its name, as well. I did not know.

But I did know what had been buried at the top of the Reeve.

My eyes strayed to the patch of dirt as we passed it. There was no sign it had ever been disturbed—but then, it had been many years since a spade had last touched it. I shivered, though the night was warm. Sten avoided looking at the site altogether, and his beard twitched with a frown as we walked by it. Mag did not seem to pay any attention, either. But I knew her well. I looked closely, and I could see her fingers flexing, anxious to grip something.

"Come, my fine boys," she said suddenly, startling us both in the silence. "Show me you have not grown too old to be useful."

She crouched and sprang, landing on a narrow ledge halfway up one of the huge boulders at the edge of the clearing. It was a leap I could not have made two decades ago, and I had no hope of it now.

"I am afraid we are both useless next to you, and always have been," I told her. "But could you help two decrepit old men make the climb?"

Mag laughed loud at that, and she lowered a hand. Sten seized it, and she levered him up to the ledge beside her. I was next, and each of them took one of my hands to pull me up. I was momentarily shocked by the strength of Mag's pull, though I should not have been. When you looked at Sten, you thought he was a man who *should* be able to lift you off your feet. Mag did not project the same strength, for all her plentiful wiry muscle. And indeed, when it came to sheer strength, Sten outmatched her. But Mag understood something about the way the world worked, and the way the human body worked within it. She knew how to twist, where to bend, and how to leverage every ounce of her strength into something much greater. It came naturally to her, as natural as a tiger stalking the jungles of Feldemar.

But as I said, they pulled me to the ledge beside them. Then Mag made another leap, and then she hauled us up again after her. It was like a game to her, and she urged us to move faster with each climb. Soon we had reached the top of the boulder, where there was plenty of room for all three of us to lie down beside each other. Mag lay in the middle, and Sten beside her with his head close to hers—but I was on Mag's other side, and I lay with my feet near her head. Sten and I breathed heavily with exertion, but Mag's chest rose and fell steadily.

"You were right," I told them. "The moons are perfect."

Sten pointed. "The sisters are returning home. Enalyn leads the way, urging Merida to hasten her steps."

"Enalyn may find that her home looks different than when she left it."

The words came out without my even thinking

them, and they surprised me as much as they evidently surprised Mag and Sten. Both of them raised their heads to look at me.

"You are very thoughtful tonight, and very dour," said Mag. "I gave you ale to fix that."

"Mayhap you are losing your touch, brewmaster." We all three laughed, for that was a plain lie. "No, you are right. I . . . suppose I was thinking of Loren."

"Were you." The words seemed inquisitive, but Mag did not speak them as a question.

"If she returns to her home, she will certainly find it different than she left it," said Sten. "What a long road that child has ridden."

And has yet to ride, I thought. But this time I managed to keep the words to myself.

"Speaking of riding," said Mag. "Do you think we ought to worry about that boy Chet?"

"Sky above, Mag," said Sten. He actually sounded embarrassed.

I laughed aloud. "Though you might have put it more delicately—no, I do not think we need to worry."

"Loren seemed distressed after they spoke," said Mag.

"Likely he brought bad news of home," I said. "But he seemed a good sort, if mayhap a bit foolish. But putting Chet aside, I have faith in Loren. She can care for herself, even if he is of ill intent—though as I said, I doubt it."

"As you say," said Mag. There was a long moment's silence, and then she spoke again. "You do not think we need to tell her of silphium, do you?"

Sten groaned. "If you wish to have children, can we do it the usual way, rather than leaping straight into parenting two people who are very nearly adults?"

Mag slapped his shoulder, and Sten winced. "I am only teasing. Well, *mostly* teasing."

"She has always been this way," I said. "Quite a number of new recruits suddenly found themselves with a mother in their own mercenary company. And once she latched on to one of them—"

"Latched?" said Mag indignantly. "You make me sound like a leech."

"I might not have used that word, but you are not wrong to."

Quick as a flash, Mag leaped to her knees and shoved me. My head slipped over the edge of the boulder, and I was only kept from falling off by Mag herself, for she had seized me by the knees.

"Take it back," she said mildly.

"Mag!" I cried. "If I fall I will break my neck!"

"You will bruise at worst," she said mildly. "You have fallen from here before—on previous occasions when you refused to apologize for your rudeness."

"Mag!" She did not reply. "Sten!"

"You are on your own, I am afraid," said Sten.

"I think I feel my grip slipping," said Mag, whose fingers had not budged whatsoever. "You had best hurry."

"I am sorry," I said through clenched teeth.

"For?"

"For calling you a leech."

"Which I am not."

"Which you are not."

Mag yanked, and I flew back atop the boulder to land in a heap. "There now," she said, dusting off her hands—I did not miss the implication that I was unclean. "Was that so difficult?"

"It is not very fair of you to treat your friends this way," I said. "If every argument comes to a scuffle in the end, no one will countermand you, since they know they will end up losing."

"But that is just the point," said Mag, settling herself down next to Sten again and clasping his hand. "Who wants to be argued with?"

I thrust out a finger at her and opened my mouth, ready to go on. But Sten caught my gaze in the moonslight, and he grinned while shaking his head. "Leave it," he said, chuckling. "Tell us how things have been for you in Strapa."

He was right, of course. I was not going to defeat Mag in our verbal sparring, any more than I could have done if we had had training weapons in hand. Huffing, I lay down again, crossing my arms over my chest. "Very well," I said. "I will have you both know, however, that I am entirely disgruntled."

"I will keep it foremost in my thoughts," said Mag.

And despite my words, my soul was filled with joy.

It *was* just like the old days, and my love for my friends had not waned in the slightest over time. For the first time in years, I felt like I was home—more so than I had ever felt in Strapa.

SIX

Now, none of us knew it, but far away, another three friends had gathered in council—though their aims were much crueler than ours.

The southern arm of the Greatrocks serves as the western border of the kingdom of Selvan. But north of the Birchwood Forest, there is a spur that juts out into northeastern Dorsea, and at the end of that spur is a peak they call the Watcher. And at the base of the Watcher, in the council room of a great and long-forgotten fortress, three people were deep in a conversation that would bring disaster down upon me, and Mag, and everyone in Northwood.

First was Kaita, a weremage and a Shade. She had skin the color of burnished walnut and Calentin ancestry plain in her features, and she wore her black hair in a long braid down her back. Across from her was Tagata, a Shadeborn woman whose name is, thankfully, not widely known. And at the head of the table was Rogan of the Shadeborn, imposing and terrible. I can see by the look on your face that I need say no more about him.

These were the days before the Necromancer and the Lifemage had revealed themselves and done battle. The Shades still lurked in secret across the nine kingdoms, and none knew of their designs—none save for me and my friends, and we knew precious little. The Mystics had long been an arm of the King's law, and they dealt with crimes beyond the norm—with rogue wizards, especially. The Shades were their mirror, dressed in blue and grey instead of red, and as far as we could see, intent on toppling all the nine thrones of Underrealm.

So Rogan, Tagata, and Kaita were hatching whatever secret plots they were busy with, when a heavy pounding came at the door of their council chamber.

Rogan's thick, shaggy locks swung as he looked up at the door, frowning. "Come."

The door flew open, and a Shade ran into the room. Her blue cloak was muddy and soaked with rain, and her black hair was bedraggled and wild. She ran to the head of the table and knelt by Rogan's chair.

"Rogan," she gasped. "I bring word. Dire news."

He looked at her, unsmiling but not angry, either. With one great hand he took her shoulder and pulled her to her feet. "Come, Nian. Be seated. However troubling your words, you can take a moment to rest before you give them, unless there is an enemy pounding at our gates this very moment. But if there were, I think I would have heard of it sooner."

Nian looked at the others, obviously unsure. Rogan smiled and waved his hand at Tagata.

"Come, sister. Make room for her."

"Of course," said Tagata, abandoning her seat at once and motioning Nian into it.

Kaita watched the proceedings silently, her right hand toying idly with her black braid. It grated her to see Nian seated at the table across from her, but by now she was well familiar with the eccentricities of Rogan and the other Shadeborn.

Nian sat silently for a moment, still clearly uncertain. But when Rogan moved to pour wine for her, she tried to stop him, horrified.

"Please, I can do it."

Rogan forestalled her with a raised hand. "You forget your place, as well as my own. I have no more authority than I am granted by our father. I am no king, thinking myself superior to those who serve me. We are all of us siblings, partners in a great cause."

Nian seemed taken aback by the words. Kaita doubted the woman fully understood them. Rogan finished pouring her cup and handed it to her, and Nian took a great swallow of the wine.

"Thank you," she said breathlessly. Her eyes, when she turned them upon Rogan again, were full of a fervent respect that bordered on worship.

"Of course," said Rogan. "Now. What brought you here with such urgency?"

"There has been an attack," said Nian. "In the Greatrocks."

The air in the council chamber seemed to freeze. Rogan's brow furrowed at once. "An attack? By the satyrs? Or have we lost control of the harpies again?"

Nian shivered. "Not by the beasts. Mystics."

Rogan and Tagata sat bolt upright, and each gripped the arms of their chair with pale knuckles. Even Kaita could not pretend to be aloof.

"Mystics? In the Greatrocks?" said Tagata. "How did they know about our stronghold there?"

"We do not know," said Nian. "There were not many of them—only half a dozen."

"Dark take them," growled Tagata. "Rogan, what are we to do? If the Mystics—"

"There is more, my lord—Rogan, I mean," stammered Nian. She looked as though she would rather do anything in the world than say her next words. "There was a battle, and Trisken . . . Trisken fell."

The room went deathly still. Kaita straightened in

her chair, staring at Nian in wonder. Rogan leaned forwards over the table, as if trying to bore through Nian's skull with his gaze alone.

"What do you mean, he fell?" demanded Rogan. "He is Shadeborn."

Nian's voice was like the squeak of a reluctant hinge. "He is dead, my lord. They killed him, and he did not rise again."

Rogan slammed his fist on the table with a cry. Tagata gave an anguished roar and kicked her chair away. It struck the wall, one of its legs snapping off. She went to the wall and seized her greatsword, smashing it into a cabinet without bothering to unsheathe it. The cabinet shattered to kindling, scattering books and scrolls across the room.

For her part, Kaita felt as though the stone floor beneath her had become as shifting and unstable as water. Who could kill a Shadeborn? How was it even possible? The Lord had made them invincible. He had all but promised that his favored children would live on forever.

Slowly, Rogan sank back into his chair. He sagged into it, covering his face with one hand. Tears streamed from beneath his fingers, running into his thick black beard. Tagata stood facing away from them all, her shoulders heaving, and Kaita suspected she was weeping as well. She fell abruptly to her knees, head bowed over her sword hilt as its tip rested on the stone floor.

"Death as my witness," whispered Tagata, "I will kill the ones who did this."

That seemed to bring Rogan back to himself. He uncovered his face and looked upon her, his eyes still brimming with tears. "We will, sister," he said. "I swear to you, we will do it together."

They seemed to have entirely forgotten Nian and Kaita in their grief. The messenger looked terrified, quaking in her seat, and her fair skin had gone even paler. Rogan noticed, and he forced a bitter smile.

"I am sorry for our lack of restraint, Nian. Trisken was . . ." His voice thickened, and he paused for a moment. "Trisken was with me almost since the beginning. He trained Tagata. This is an evil day."

"It is, my lord," whispered Nian.

Rogan shook his head slowly. "I told you. None of that. There is but one Lord, and he is your father as well as mine. We are all equal before his kindness."

Tagata turned back towards the rest of them, hastily scrubbing at her face with the back of her hand. She strode over beside Nian's chair and put a hand on the woman's shoulder. Nian jumped with fright. But Tagata pulled her gently to her feet and wrapped her in an embrace.

"You have ridden hard to bring us ill news. It could not have been easy. Thank you."

Slowly, Nian returned the embrace. She began to quiver, as if she, too, was finally relinquishing her grip on emotions she had long kept within—as though

Tagata's massive frame gave her the strength she needed to let go.

"I could have done no differently," said Nian. "It was my duty."

"And doing one's duty is worthy of the highest honor," said Rogan. "Fetch yourself another chair, Tagata. Let us all be seated and discuss what is to be done."

Tagata gently held Nian's cheek for a moment before finally pulling away. She took another chair from further down the table and brought it next to Nian's before sitting down. Rogan shifted his chair closer to the table and leaned forwards, his shoulders hunched.

"What more do we know, Nian? Can you tell us anything about these Mystics?"

"We did not recognize all of them. But we know the party was led by Jordel of the family Adair."

Another shock went through the room, though far less explosive than the last. There was not a Shade alive who did not know that name.

"Jordel?" said Rogan. "That is ill news."

Kaita slapped the arm of her chair. "Why did you not mention Jordel from the beginning?"

Nian quailed, but Rogan raised a palm towards Kaita to pacify her. "We hardly gave her the chance, after she told us of Trisken's fall."

Kaita looked grudgingly away, tugging at her braid again.

"How could Jordel have found us?" Tagata asked Rogan. "Our agents have worked tirelessly to keep him and Kal off our trail. Hewal sent no word of this whatsoever."

"Jordel has been away from Hewal for some time, and our ability to guide him has lessened the longer he has pursued Xain," said Rogan. "But as for your question, there are two possible answers. The first and far more troubling possibility is that they have been aware of us for some time, and somehow they have kept that knowledge from us. But I do not think that is the case. If they had meant to assault us—or even to investigate and gather more information—they would have come here, and not to Trisken's stronghold. The other possibility is that they knew nothing of us at all, and that pure happenstance brought Jordel's party to our doorstep."

"That seems so unlikely as to be impossible," said Tagata.

"Yet it may be true," said Nian. "For I have still more to say. Jordel died in battle with Trisken."

"Ha!" barked Tagata. "And good riddance. Darkness take him."

But Rogan did not seem to share her elation. "That is good, I suppose," he said slowly. "But what else, Nian? For I sense that you still have more to tell us."

"We did not recognize all of Jordel's party, but we recognized some of them," said Nian. "The Nightblade was with him, as was the wizard Xain, and the children who have been with the Nightblade as long as we have known of her. But they had with them someone new—a guide from the town of Strapa. He is a Calentin archer, unknown to us. It is he who led them into Northwood."

Kaita went rigid in her chair.

"A Calentin archer?" she blurted out, interrupting Rogan's next question.

The rest of them paused. Nian and Tagata frowned, but Rogan looked searchingly at her.

"What is it, Kaita?"

She did not answer him at once, but kept her attention on Nian. "Where did he take them when they reached Northwood?"

Nian looked confused. "We . . . have not learned that yet."

"But how do you know?" asked Sun.

Albern paused and cocked his head. "What?"

"How do you know all this?" said Sun. "You were not there. Yet you are telling me the tale as if you were in the room."

Albern smiled. "Of course I was not there. But it has been many years since then. In that time I learned much of what happened, and I guessed at even more."

Sun shook her head and straightened in her seat. "But . . . but why, then, do you not simply tell me what happened? You are making it part of the story—the words they spoke, this woman Tagata's fit of rage, that other woman Nian and her terror at delivering the message. You cannot possibly know it really happened that way."

Albern gave a low chuckle and sipped at his beer. "Ah, I understand. You are looking for a story you can *believe.*"

"Of . . . of course I am!" said Sun, scowling.

"Then I am afraid you will never find what you seek," said Albern. "If you believe every story you hear, you shall live a false life. The same may happen if you believe *any* story you hear. But if you put your faith in the right tales—if you *choose* to believe in them, seeing how they may be useful—there is no limit to what they can teach you."

His words hardly registered. Sun had a vague feeling she had been betrayed, as though she had come upon some beggar who tricked her into a game of chance that she had no hope of winning. "So your stories are lies, then."

"Lies? Oh no," said Albern. "But even the craftiest storyteller knows better than to trust every word coming out of their own mouth, for they know a story is simply something to be learned from."

Sun could not help herself: she scoffed. "You cannot honestly think that is true. History is a story, too. But what good would history books be, if their authors simply made them up as they went along?"

"Historians are often the greatest liars of all," said Albern. "I have read their tomes. I have seen their version of events that I myself lived through. They were far less trustworthy than I am, and far less accurate, I can assure you. But history is only a story that most people have chosen to believe in, without thinking they made such a choice. Like any tale, we use it to shape the future in the way we want, and darkness take anyone who wants otherwise."

Though Sun had been ready with a retort, those words made her pause in confusion. Albern's words had the sound of a deep wisdom, yet she could not understand them. And something in her still rebelled at the thought of hearing a story that even the teller did not think was true.

Albern studied her, and a small smile tugged at the corner of his mouth, as though he could read her thoughts and found them amusing. He gave her a moment longer to think before speaking again.

"Should I go on?"

Sun nodded, though she was uncertain if she truly wanted to hear more.

Kaita rose and paced back and forth in the council chamber, her mind working. And as her thoughts spun faster and faster in circles, a blind rage began to build inside her, and it grew until it was like a wildfire ripping across her skin.

"Kaita," said Rogan. "What is it?"

"The archer is Albern," said Kaita, meeting his

gaze. "It must be. And he is bringing them—Loren and the others—he is bringing them to Mag."

Rogan paused, lifting his chin slightly as he regarded her. Nian and Tagata still looked lost, but in Rogan's eyes there was a deep understanding.

Kaita strode to the table and slapped her hands down, leaning forwards intently. "Let me go to Northwood. I will . . . I will deliver justice for Trisken, and for all our siblings who fell in the Greatrocks."

"Kaita," said Rogan quietly. "I love you like all our siblings, and with that love comes a profound respect. Return that respect to me, I beg you, and do not lie to me. You do not wish to go to Northwood to deliver justice, but to extract vengeance—and not for Trisken, but for yourself."

Kaita faltered only a moment. "And what of it? I have followed your orders for a long time, because you thought me too weak to seek out my revenge. But the time has come, Rogan. And it will mean the same thing, in the end. I have waited so long."

Rogan spoke quietly. "I know you have. And I have never thought you weak. But that is not the plan." Kaita began to flare with anger, but he spoke again quickly. "The time for lurking in the shadows has ended."

Tagata looked taken aback, her scars appearing even whiter as a flush crept up her skin. "What do you mean?"

"I have had many words with our father of late," said Rogan. "Now I must bring him news of Trisken, but I do not think that will change his mind. In fact, I think it will make him even more resolute. We cannot yet declare ourselves openly, but our period of subterfuge and intrigue is over. The time has come for war. We will strike from the shadows, as we always have—but we will strike with blades and arrows, and no longer with secrets."

The effect on all of them was immediate. Nian looked at Rogan in wonder, her eyes shining. Kaita's hand tightened on the back of her chair, and Tagata seized her greatsword again, as if she meant to march off to battle at once.

"Brother," whispered Tagata. "Are you saying . . . ?"

"Yes," said Rogan. "Nian, you have ridden far and long, but I must ask you to deliver yet another message. Rouse the captains. Order the troops to ready themselves. We make for war, and Northwood will be the first to fall before our might."

"And I will have my vengeance," said Kaita, her eyes shining.

Rogan fixed her with a look. "I do not think so," he said.

She flared with anger. "Rogan, you cannot expect—"

"Unless I am very much mistaken," he said, "Northwood will not be the end of your shadowed road. But you may try, Kaita, so long as it does not interfere with the battle. I only give you one command: stay alive. Our father needs all of us, now more than ever."

Kaita scoffed. "You worry for my safety? It is our enemies who should be worried."

Rogan sighed. "Then you may have your vengeance."

SEVEN

On that same night, near the Dorsean town of Lan Shui west of the Greatrocks, a dark evening had come.

A woman named Zhanu lived on a farm just a few spans beyond the walls of Lan Shui. Zhanu was a veteran of the Dorsean army and had fought in the king's wars. Then, one day, she had retired with much honor and a gift of the king's gold, and she had settled near the town where she had been born. In the years since, she had taken a wife named Shu, who had died old and happy, and had mothered three children, all of whom had grown and left Lan Shui to live their own lives elsewhere. Now Zhanu lived alone on her farm, working the land each day and visiting the town's taverns each night.

Except that recently, she had not been visiting the taverns. Like everyone who dwelled outside the town's walls, she had been spending her nights locked up in her own home, a weapon near at hand.

Zhanu stumped about her house, ensuring the windows were closed and shuttered and the front door was tightly secured. She grumbled as she fidgeted with the lock. It was new, having been added only a few days ago by a blacksmith from Lan Shui. Never in her life had Zhanu felt the need for a lock on her door. Lan Shui had never been that sort of town.

"All the nine lands going to darkness," she muttered. Zhanu had taken to talking to herself sometime in the last few years, and though she despised the habit, she could not seem to break it.

A single candle burned in the main room of her house. Zhanu lifted it and brought it into her bedroom, the only other room in the house, and nothing very grand. She had never felt the need for fancy lodgings—truthfully, even two rooms in her house seemed a bit grandiose to her. But her wife had insisted.

Zhanu set the candle on her bedside table, stripped down to her underclothes, and crawled beneath her thick blanket. It had been a long day in the fields, and she looked forward to a good night's rest. She snuffed out the candle and closed her eyes.

Not quite an hour later, they snapped open as something scratched on her roof.

Skritch, skritch.

She lay perfectly still in her bed, her whole body tense, waiting.

Skritch, skritch.

The sound had moved. Whatever was making the scratching, it was moving from the rear of the house towards the front.

Come for me, have you? thought Zhanu. *Well, you will find no frail old victim here.*

Zhanu slid from her bed, moving as quietly as possible. She lifted her sword from its place on the wall, trying to remain as silent as possible, and crept into the house's front room.

Skritch.

The scratching sound came again, but this time it seemed to cut itself off abruptly. Zhanu paused a step away from the door, listening.

There came a soft *thump,* like something landing on the ground outside. Whatever was making the noise had leaped down from the roof.

Zhanu stole to the wall just beside the door. She gripped her sword in both hands, holding it ready to swing.

All was silent for a long moment.

KROOM

The window behind Zhanu exploded inwards, showering the room with splinters.

With an old soldier's instincts, she whirled and stabbed out with her sword. There was a sharp *shunk* as it slid deep into flesh.

Zhanu froze, staring at her intruder in horror.

The creature would have been as tall as she was if it stood upright, but it was hunched over on all fours. Its skin was pallid white, mottled with light grey, and it wore no clothing at all. Its long, thick limbs ended in claws as long as her hands, and its wide, red mouth was rimmed with sharp teeth designed for ripping and tearing into flesh. It had long, pointed ears, like an Elf's.

Zhanu had buried her sword in its chest halfway to the hilt. Her thrust had been pure reflex. Yet the creature stared at her, and its yellowing eyes were filled with hate, not pain.

"What in the dark—"

Zhanu's words cut off as the creature struck her a heavy backhanded blow. She flew through the air before crashing hard into the wooden floor. Nothing broke, but she bit her own tongue hard enough that she tasted blood.

She pushed herself up on her elbows just in time to see the creature seize the sword by the hilt and drag it out of its own flesh. It hissed with discomfort, but the wound did not seem to slow it at all. And as Zhanu watched, the skin and the flesh beneath began to stitch together, until soon there was no sign there had been a wound there at all.

The creature threw the sword past Zhanu. The steel sank into the wall and stuck there, quivering. Zhanu tried to push herself away, but the creature stalked towards her on all fours, its shredded ears twitching, a rasping hiss sounding from its throat.

"Dark take you," said Zhanu. "Shu is waiting for me anyways."

She spat, and the bloody spittle struck the floor just in front of the creature. It stopped in its advance for only a moment, stooping to lick up the spit.

A hungry gleam came into its eyes. It leaped for her, and Zhanu knew nothing more.

Constable Yue of the family Baolan was summoned to Zhanu's farm the next day.

One of her neighbors had not seen her in the fields that morning and had gone to investigate. Once he had seen the horror inside her house, he had run straight to Lan Shui and found Yue in the constables' station. Even as a dark foreboding seized her, she summoned Ashta and Sinshi, the town's other two constables, and set out for the farm with them in tow.

Yue had no illusions about what she would find. Zhanu's neighbor had been too afraid to describe what he saw, but it was not the first such grisly murder she had investigated in the last few weeks. Zhanu's home looked just as she expected it to. The window beside the door had been broken open by something attacking from outside the house. The front door was still closed and locked; Zhanu's neighbor had not been able to open it, and had looked in through the smashed window. The constables forced the door open, and inside they found a scene all too similar to others they had seen recently. Zhanu's corpse lay in the corner, her head propped up against the wall, her eyes staring sightlessly at them. Her sunburnt skin was unusually pale. There was blood on the floor and on the wall, but not nearly as much as one would have expected, considering how the woman's throat had been torn open.

"Again," said Sinshi, averting his eyes. "Sergeant, is it the—"

"The creature," said Yue. "Yes."

She winced at her own unwillingness to name the thing. It was a foolish superstition. But then, Yue had been born and raised in Lan Shui. She had no illusions that she was anything other than the simple child of a small town, and among such folk, superstition died hard. It was her opinion that such traditions had been started for a reason, and she would not change them unless she, too, had a reason.

"Should we send another messenger, Sergeant?" said Ashta.

Yue looked at her. "Would you go, if I asked you to?"

Ashta and Sinshi both grew visibly paler, and Sinshi swallowed hard. But Ashta lifted her chin. "I would."

"As would I," said Sinshi, his voice shaking.

"Then the two of you are idiotic, if brave," said Yue. "I would not send you even if you begged me to, because you would die—just like the last two. And if I do not send one of you because I do not think you would survive, I have no right to ask another of the townsfolk to go."

"What do we do, then?" said Sinshi, voice thick with despair.

"I wish my answer were otherwise," said Yue. "But we have to keep waiting. I have not sent a report to Bertram for three weeks now—nor the Mystics, for that matter. The king's collectors have received no taxes. That cannot go on forever without prompting an investigation. We may not be able to leave the town, but that does not mean others cannot come here."

"That could take weeks," said Ashta. "And the attacks are coming more—"

"Do you think I do not know that?" snapped Yue. "We have warned the townsfolk, and we have warned the farmers. Many have retreated inside the walls, as we suggested, but others are more foolish—like poor Zhanu here, may she rest in the dark. When you have been a constable for a while longer, you, too, may learn that you cannot protect everyone from themselves."

Sinshi stared at his feet now, chagrined. But Ashta still held her sergeant's gaze. "I have been thinking—"

"When did this start?" said Yue, raising an eyebrow.

Ashta heard the joke in her tone and pressed on. "I have been thinking. No one has tried riding east. A messenger could reach the Greatrocks in less than a day."

"Where do you think it is coming from?" said Yue. "It is far more likely to have its home in the mountains than in the western spur. And even if I am wrong, and a messenger made it deep into the mountains, they would never survive. Satyrs are plentiful there, and harpies, and other, worse things that humans have never named. I have thought of all of this, constable."

At last Ashta averted her eyes, joining Sinshi in his awkward discomfort. "As you say, Sergeant," she muttered. "We will remove the body, and burn her."

"I will write a letter to her eldest son, so that we may send it when the road is safe again," said Sinshi. "He is in Bertram."

"Good. Do it quickly, and return to the station when you are through. And do not despair." Yue looked through the shattered window at the world beyond—too bright for such a solemn day. Too sunny.

"Someone will come. Eventually."

And she was right, though she would not know it for some days yet.

EIGHT

Of course, we in Northwood knew nothing of all these dark events, and so our lives went on quite uninterrupted.

I had thought that Loren and Xain would be eager to leave the city and make their way east. But for some reason I did not know, they remained in Northwood for some time. Loren spent long hours walking in the woods with Chet, the children helped Mag around the inn, and Xain skulked about the place as he recovered from his illness.

Others have asked me, and I have often wondered,

why we all did not feel a greater urgency. We had defeated a great evil in the mountains, but we had not wiped it out. I have been called foolish for being so lax about our situation. And indeed, with the benefit of hindsight, I was foolish. But what I said earlier, about stories, and believing them, is never more true than when speaking of the story we live day to day. And we are always prone to believe that which we think will make our lives easier. I thought, as I am sure Loren did, that having defeated our enemy, we would be free from them for a time. After all, they had been hidden in the shadows for so long—why would they reveal themselves now?

That was our notion, anyway. And so, for my part, I spent much time revisiting my old haunts in Northwood and the lands around it. I visited old friends in the town, for of course I knew more people than only Mag and Sten. There was Len, a distant cousin of Sten's. He was a somewhat shifty fellow, and he often got into trouble with the constables after being found with small valuables that did not belong to him in the strictest sense—or in any other sense, truth be told. But he was always a joy to play Moons with, as long as you did not wager any money against the outcome, for he was both bad at the game and a poor loser. And there was old Elsie, who had been wizened and wrinkled even when I first came to Northwood with Mag. Now she could barely walk, even with her stick, and yet she did not let that stop her from managing her farm, from which came the best butter and cheeses that could be found for a hundred leagues. She had hired hands to help her with the milking and the mucking, for that was quite beyond her, but she oversaw all their goings-on with a sharp eye and an unwavering attention to detail.

One day, over an afternoon snack and more than one cup of wine, Elsie and I fell to talking about Mag. She had long been friends with Mag and Sten, of course, and in the midst of all our talk—Elsie's being mostly gossip—she said something that troubled me, and upon which I thought often afterwards.

"It shall lead to trouble, you see if I am wrong."

"What shall?" I asked, cocking my head.

"You. Mag. All this." Hefting her stick, she swung it around generally at our surroundings, so that I had to duck to keep from being brained. "She has been sitting still too long."

"Not as long as you."

"Hah!" barked Elsie. "Peace and quiet are meant for some folk. Folk like me. Not for your kind, or Mag's."

That made me smile. "And what, pray tell, is our kind? What makes us less deserving of the rest you enjoy?"

"I said your kind, *or* Mag's." Elsie took a sip of wine and a large bite of cheese before continuing around a full mouth. "You are neither of you alike, and neither of you is meant for stillness. And what is this talk of deserving? Deserving has nothing to do with it. A silly notion, if ever I have heard one. It is something inside you that is different, not anything you have done. All the important things about us are on the inside. And what is in you has never been in me. I never was a mercenary, you will notice."

"I shudder to imagine it," I told her. "Any enemy would have thrown down their arms in terror upon seeing you across the battlefield."

"Why do you think I never took up the life?"

I laughed, and she chuckled, and our conversation turned down another path that was not important, and which I cannot remember. But though I did not show it, my thoughts grew heavy, and they remained so for a long while.

Mayhap I could not stop thinking of her words because they echoed what I myself had come to fear.

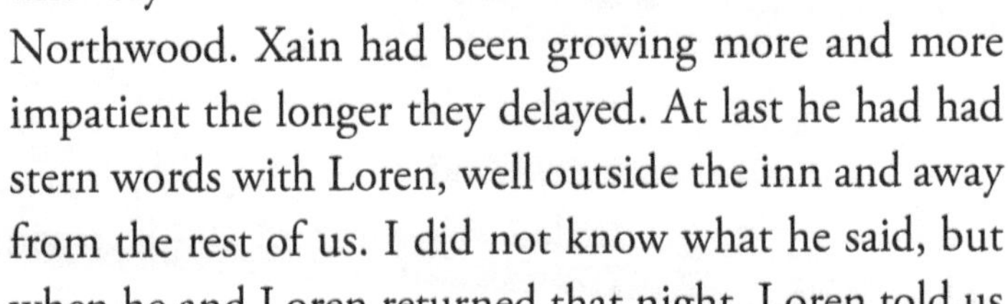

The day came at last when Loren decided to leave Northwood. Xain had been growing more and more impatient the longer they delayed. At last he had had stern words with Loren, well outside the inn and away from the rest of us. I did not know what he said, but when he and Loren returned that night, Loren told us she meant to leave—the next day, if she could possibly manage it.

I have thought often, in the years since, what might have been different if she had made her decision just one day earlier. It is useless to consider such things, of course, and yet our minds will not let us be sensible at all times.

But just like that, our spell of inaction vanished. Mag broke into furious activity at once. That night, though Loren and her party went to bed early, Mag and Sten stayed up late into the night, listing what supplies the children would need, and where they could find them for the best price. The next morning, we went over the needed supplies with Loren and Xain. They agreed to all of it, and they gave us their heartfelt thanks for our help.

Mag waved a hand. "Do not be silly. We are old hands at long campaign roads. It would almost have been cruel of us not to share some of our expertise."

"I will take care of procuring everything," I told them. "I know the town, and if indeed you wish to leave before sundown, you will need to purchase everything quickly."

"Mayhap I will come with you," said Sten. "You shall have to carry a great deal, and your arms are scrawny."

"With shoulders like yours, you could say that to anyone, oaf." I slapped his broad arm. "But I would welcome your aid."

"One of us should help," said Loren quickly. "Let me send Chet."

"You will need Chet's help more than we will," I said. "Be ready to go by the time we get back."

Loren sighed. "Very well. Here." She pulled a few gold weights from her purse and put them in my hand. "Will that be enough?"

"It will. Go see to the horses." As soon as she had left, I turned to Mag and handed over the gold. "Sneak these into her saddlebags, will you?"

"Of course," said Mag.

Sten and I went about our task quickly, and before long we had returned to the Lee Shore with food and many skins of water, as well as new blankets and bedrolls. With the help of Xain and the children, we packed these as well as we could and distributed them between the saddlebags of the horses. Before long, Loren and Chet came to eat with the rest of us.

"I have fetched as many provisions as I thought the horses could carry," I told her. "It should see you at least halfway through Dorsea, though you shall need to stop for more supplies at some point."

"We will stop as rarely as we can afford," said Xain. "The fewer people who mark our passing, the better."

"Once you are deep into Dorsea, I think the danger shall lessen. In the south their kingdom is preoccupied with the war, and in the north they remain as untroubled as ever at the goings-on of the nine lands."

The boy, Gem, suddenly looked past my shoulder and frowned.

"Who is that man there?" asked Gem.

What could have told me that Gem had seen the

first sign of a disaster that would shape not only his life, not only Loren's, but mine, for years to come?

I turned and looked.

At the bar stood Len—Sten's distant cousin I mentioned before. He and Mag spoke in hushed, hurried tones. Mag caught my eye and tossed her head at me. I went to her, and Loren came with me.

"Len, tell them," said Mag.

Len pinched his nose and sniffed. "There is a man. He is wandering about the city, searching for a girl in a black cloak."

You know, of course, that the Nightblade always wore a fine black cloak as one of her hallmarks. There was no doubt in our minds: this man, whoever he was, sought Loren. And I could think of no innocent reason why a stranger would come seeking for her here in Northwood.

Len read the reaction in our expressions. "Aye, that is what I thought when I heard," he said. "Black cloak and remarkable green eyes, he asked for. Used that word, remarkable. Calls himself Rogan."

Kaita followed Rogan through Northwood. Her fingers twitched, desiring to pull at her braid, but it was done up in a bun now. She and Rogan were not dressed in Shade colors, for they wished to remain unnoticed as long as they possibly could. Kaita had on a dark skirt, easy to discard, over grey trousers and a fitted tunic of homespun white cloth with yellow trim. Rogan wore a plain outfit appropriate for a farmer or street vendor. But there was no hiding the sheer magnitude of him, nor the fact that, despite the fact he was unarmed, he looked and moved like a weapon. Everyone who saw him seemed afraid—as well they should have been.

"I know where the Lee Shore is," said Kaita. "Let me go off and find it."

"Not yet, please, Kaita," said Rogan. "Before you strike, Loren must see me. That is very important."

"Why?" growled Kaita. "And why did you not mention this when we were making our plans?"

"Our plan was for you to accompany me," said Rogan. "I did not know you needed a reason, else I would have given it. Loren must see me because she must tell the High King and the Lord Prince about me."

He kept speaking to passersby as they went, asking after a girl "with a black cloak and remarkable green eyes." Everyone they spoke to claimed not to have seen her, but Kaita suspected many of them were lying. They looked upon Rogan with fear and distrust, and she had the feeling none of them would have revealed Loren's location even if they knew it.

But of course, they did not truly need to ask where Loren was. She would be at the Lee Shore. Mag's inn.

Kaita itched for the coming fight. She even considered slipping away from Rogan and going to the Lee Shore despite his wishes. The last time she had fought

Mag, she had been foolish. She had tried to overpower the woman with sheer strength, but Mag was simply too fast. Kaita had learned. She was ready at last.

And then she saw us.

Mag and I had accompanied Loren into Northwood to see Rogan for ourselves. We came around a corner and froze stock still, our eyes fixed on him. I have told you already how fearsome and deadly he looked, and you must have heard stories of him before. So transfixed were we by the sight of him, we did not even notice Kaita standing at his elbow—not that I would have recognized her if I had seen her.

After a few moments, I pulled Loren back, and we retreated into the crowd again. Kaita jerked forwards, one hand outstretched and the other groping for Rogan's arm.

"There!" she cried, pointing. "The girl is with them!"

Rogan's gaze followed her outstretched finger. For one brief moment, he and Loren looked into each other's eyes. And then we were gone.

"Perfect," said Rogan, grinning. "She has seen me, and she knows the fear of my presence."

"Then I am free to go after them?" said Kaita.

"Not yet."

Kaita seized his arm and pulled him around to face her. "What do you mean, no? That is why I am here."

"I said you were free to seek vengeance, as long as it does not interfere with the battle. I need you to fly west of here and order the attack. Then you may seek out Mag."

She wanted to refuse him. She wanted to tell him to order the attack himself. But she knew, too, how much longer that would take, and what that might do to his plans. He had been there for her in some of the darkest times of her life. And despite her unfair words, he had never treated her as anything less than an equal. She could not refuse him this small service.

Still, she did not have to enjoy it. With a frustrated growl, she cast off her loose cloak. Then, right in the middle of the street, she turned. Her eyes filled with brilliant light, drawing the gaze of many in the crowd. They recoiled as her body shrank, her well-fitted clothes sinking into her skin, which soon erupted in black feathers.

In just a moment, it was done. A raven launched itself from the ground at Rogan's feet. Kaita wheeled once in the air. Rogan stood looking up at her, a grateful smile on his handsome features. The townsfolk around him looked somewhat disquieted, even offended, for of course it is not generally considered polite to so brazenly use magic in a public place. But they paid little more attention to Kaita than that.

Fools, she thought. *Useless fools. They do not even see their own approaching doom.*

She turned and flapped hard, shooting east through the sky.

I will bring it to them. And then I will burn down the Lee Shore and kill everyone within.

NINE

Mag, Loren, and I ran back to the inn as fast as we could. Loren and her friends had to leave immediately. I went with her to the stables to ready their horses, while Mag excused herself for a moment, taking Sten with her. Together they went to their room in the Lee Shore, though Sten followed his wife with a mystified expression.

"What is it?" he asked as she closed the door behind them both.

"Danger," said Mag. She went to the bed and flipped it up on its side, scattering pillows across the floor. "I do not know how great the threat is, but from the fear in Albern's voice, it is considerable. The children and the wizard must leave at once, and we are going to protect them."

"What?" said Sten, frowning at the mess she had made. "Protect them from who?"

"I do not know that either, save that his name is Rogan." Mag knelt, seizing the lock of a chest that had been concealed beneath the bed and fishing in her pocket for its key. "You heard Albern speak of the ones he fought in the mountains. I believe they have come here, though I do not know how many."

Sten fell on his knees beside her and took her shoulders, turning her towards him. Mag paused in her hurried movements, looking him in the eye.

"You mean to fight," he said.

"If need be," said Mag.

"It has been a long time since you picked up a blade."

She smiled. "I only wish I had time to go to the Reeve."

His eyes darkened. "You promised," he said. "You swore to me."

"It was a joke. A poor one." The words sounded weak even in her own ears.

Sten looked into her eyes a moment more, letting her see that he did not believe her. But then he squeezed her shoulders, and from his breast pocket he produced the key she had been searching for.

"You always leave it somewhere," he grumbled.

"Thank you," said Mag, taking the key. "Look after the inn."

"Now *that* was a poor joke," said Sten. "I am coming with you, of course."

For the first time in a long while, Mag's face filled with fear. "Sten, you should stay and—"

"I certainly will not," said Sten. "If the children must be seen to safety, then I am coming, too."

"Sten," she pleaded. "If it comes to a fight, I would rather not have you involved."

"You will have to bear it, unless you mean to stay here with me."

"It will be more dangerous for me if I have to worry about you."

Sten laughed, his shoulders shaking. "Do you jest? You and I both know you will be in no danger, whatever may happen."

"But you will," said Mag. "Sten, please—"

"Albern is going. That wizard is going. Even those children are riding by Loren's side. I want to help, Mag. We belong to each other, but you do not own me."

Mag's fingers clenched around the key. But after a silent moment, she bowed her head. "Of course not," she said. Her voice had become quite small and frightened—very different from her usual strong, matronly tone. "But if anything were to—"

The blast of a horn cut the air. Mag's head jerked

up, and Sten met her gaze. The horn faded away, to be replaced with the tolling of a bell.

"An attack," said Sten.

"Yes," said Mag.

"We should go."

"Very well."

Mag's hands quivered slightly as she unlocked the chest and threw it open. Inside were two swords and two shields. She handed one each to Sten before taking up her own. Together they stood, and Mag gave her blade two quick swings.

"It has been some time," she said.

"I wish it were twice as long," replied Sten. "Quickly. The others will be in the stables."

They rushed downstairs. On the threshold of the common room, Mag paused. The customers were stirring, looking around anxiously as the bell continued to toll. The front door of the inn burst open, revealing a woman whose face was a mask of panic.

"An army!" she cried. "An army has marched out of the Greatrocks! They have the west gate, and they are killing everyone they can get their hands on!"

A great tumult burst out in the room, terror rising like a tide. But even as everyone rose to their feet and looked about, trying to decide what to do, Mag raised two fingers to her lips and gave a sharp whistle. The common room fell silent as all eyes turned to her.

"Foes attack Northwood," she said. "If you can

fight, fetch your weapons. If you cannot, find a good place to hide yourselves and your families. But whatever you do, do it quickly, for they will not wait for you to decide. Go!"

The last word cracked like a whip. Her customers jerked where they stood and then began moving with purpose. Mag nodded to Sten, and they made their way to the stables.

When they threw open the wide double doors, Loren and I whirled, drawing our weapons. We relaxed as we recognized them—but then Loren balked at the sight of their swords and shields.

"The city is under siege," said Mag. "We shall see you safely beyond the walls."

"You should go back inside," said Loren. "Wait until we have gone. They will pursue us beyond the city and leave Northwood in peace."

"That I doubt," said Mag. "There is already killing in the streets. And you have no time to convince me otherwise. Mount your horses. Quickly."

Before Loren could argue, I took her arm and urged her towards the saddle of her horse, Midnight. "You are nearly a match for Mag in stubbornness, girl, but not quite. Heed her."

Loren clearly did not like it, but she did as I asked. We rode out, with Mag and Sten on foot, walking to either side of Loren like an honor guard.

We hoped to reach the north gate before the Shades could, but that hope proved to be in vain. We could not avoid the fighting in the streets. Dread and horror came over me as I saw the Shades in battle against the people of Northwood. The attackers were trained soldiers, well armed and armored. The people of Northwood were hardy, but most of them fought with simple clubs and farm tools. Some few of them had old weapons, heirlooms of ancestors who had once fought in the king's army, and there were a few constables among their number trying to organize a defense. But they never had a chance.

It pained me to see Northwood burn. I could only imagine how it felt to Mag and Sten. I watched them as we moved. Mag's eyes darted everywhere, her sword arm twitching occasionally as if aching to be used. We had not yet entered battle, but I knew what would happen when we did. It filled me with the same feeling I had had on the Reeve—that curious mix of trepidation and excitement. But I knew Sten must be filled with dread of it.

Two spans away from the north gate, it happened at last. We came to an open square, and there we found the largest battle we had seen yet. The people of Northwood had assembled into some attempt at rank and file, and they outnumbered the Shades. But though some of the Shades had fallen in the fighting, their victims' corpses outnumbered them three to one.

Mag stopped dead, and I felt the mounting tension inside her vanish. Sten saw it, too, and his jaw clenched as if with pain.

She closed her eyes and took a deep breath, rolling her shoulders.

When she opened her eyes again, something was gone from inside them. It was as though a fire inside her had been hidden behind a heavy black curtain.

I had seen it too many times not to know what would happen next, and I will not lie to you: excitement filled me to see it. But looking into Sten's eyes, I saw his heart break.

"No use," said Mag. "It will be a fight."

Her voice had become a chilling monotone, flat and lifeless. I could see the effect of it on the children, who had only known her for a few days, and had only seen her act motherly. They looked at her as though she were a stranger. I drew an arrow and spoke to Loren and the others.

"Stay behind Mag and Sten. Stay your blades unless you have no other choice, for they will try to seize them and pull you down. Now, charge!"

And Mag did. The battle-lust had taken her. She had seen her fellow citizens cut down without cause, without justice or mercy. Her town burned around her. It filled her with a rage that was white-hot and utterly merciless, and Mag intended to douse that rage in blood, forging it into a weapon against which no one could hope to stand.

The Shades did not see her coming until it was too

late. In a heartbeat she had plunged into the thick of them. Even when they closed in and tried to surround her, they could not pierce her defense. Her shield moved just as quickly as her blade, blocking every attack. Then Sten was behind her, guarding her flanks even though she did not need it. He was a fine fighter in his own right, but he battled to survive, to keep the blades of his foes at bay. Mag fought to kill, to destroy, to cast her foes into the darkness from which there is no escape.

I played my part, of course, loosing arrows as fast as I could—and though I dislike boasting, that was quite fast indeed. I chose my targets carefully, bringing down Shades as close to Sten as I could while being careful not to endanger him. Had there been a hundred warriors like the three of us that day, I do not mind saying that Northwood might not have fallen.

The first fight was over quickly. The remaining Shades quickly turned tail and ran. They had not planned to face determined fighters who knew their way around city warfare. Mag watched them go. She must have wanted to chase them, but the children still needed her protection.

She turned to Loren. Blood had spattered her face. When she spoke, there were flecks of it on her teeth.

"On," she growled. "Do not stop moving, not even for a moment."

Loren and the others obeyed, though I could see in their eyes that they were now almost as frightened of Mag as they were of the Shades. We pushed for the north gate. Twice more we met Shades in battle, and twice Mag massacred them until the rest fled in terror.

I had almost forgotten. The long years since our time as mercenaries had dulled my memories of Mag's battle-trance, the thrill and the terror of it. Thrilling because I felt nothing could stand against us with Mag on our side. Terrifying because when you stand shoulder-to-shoulder with such blood lust, it is impossible not to imagine what would happen if it were turned on you, instead.

Two more turns in the street brought us within sight of the north gate. But there we stopped, for the way was barred. The Shades had already encircled the city. Ranks of them were marching through the gate, swords bared and shields up. It was an army—a far, far greater number than we had seen in the Greatrocks.

"There are so many," breathed Loren.

"Surely not even Mag can defeat them all," said Gem, his voice small and squeaking. "Albern . . . what do we do?"

I hesitated. The boy was not wrong. Mag was the best fighter I had ever seen or heard of in legend. Yet even she could not defeat an entire army on her own. I looked at her. She had stopped in her tracks. *Surely,* I thought, *surely even her thirst for battle is not enough to draw her into a fight against so many foes.*

Loren gripped her reins, pulling them to the right.

"Come. Mayhap they have not reached the eastern gate yet. We can try to—"

"They will have reached it," said Mag. She turned to the rest of us, and there was no trace of a smile on her lips. "Come now, little children. Do you fear so few of them? Come with me, and you shall reach the Birchwood. I swear it."

I heard the words. But I heard what she left unsaid as well. Mag had said the children would reach the Birchwood.

She had said nothing of herself.

Fear gripped me.

"Mag!" I cried.

It was too late. She turned and charged straight into the midst of her enemies, her blood-soaked blade held aloft. Sten did not hesitate, but plunged into the fray just behind her.

Fury filled me then, and though they were not to blame, I turned it on the children. Loren had taken a vow not to kill. She would be no help to us in this fight.

"Make use of those bows on your backs, or give me your arrows, but do not stand here idle while she risks her life for yours."

And so saying, I spurred my mount onwards behind Mag and Sten.

It can be hard to tell a story of your own exploits without sounding boastful, particularly when you accomplish something especially noteworthy. Let it sound like pride, then, when I say that my bow sang a mighty anthem of death that day. I fought like I had never fought for any mercenary company I had served in. This was no warfare for mere coin. For the first time since I had met her, I feared that Mag might fall in battle, and I swore I would not let it happen unless I had perished first. When the Shades got too close, I drew my sword and hacked them down. And I fired arrows as fast as heartbeats, slaying any Shade who dared approach my friend.

Mag, for her part, fought with all the glory and fury that legends have built up around her. Others have been called "one who walks with death," but Mag was death's master on that day. My friend was gone, and a merciless killer had taken her place. She was the Uncut Lady. She was death made beautiful. No matter how many she felled, her strikes never slowed. Her foes could not pierce her defenses, not even when they surrounded her, for Sten was behind her. Back to back they fought, Sten the bulwark and Mag the striking serpent. And I was the vengeful stormcloud that rained death on any Shade who threatened to break their guard.

"Albern!"

Loren's scream pierced the chaos, and I wheeled in my saddle. She sat there with bow in hand, her already pale face Elf-white with fear. But her finger was outthrust, pointing north.

I looked, and I saw what Loren had spotted. The Shades, seeking to kill Mag, had drawn to one side of the wide street. There was an open corridor on the other side, and it led straight to the north gate.

For one moment, hope swelled in my breast. We could escape. We could ride hard before the Shades noticed, and we could reach freedom.

But then I turned back to the battle and saw Mag surrounded by her foes.

We could escape. But she never could.

And then Sten slipped.

TEN

When they tell tales of battle, they never tell you that the deadliest threats are often the most mundane. There are a thousand details in any fight, and the least glamorous are often ignored in songs and stories—like the way a person shits and pisses after you kill them, their bowels and bladder voided as their bodies slacken.

Other details are less crude, but even more vital in the heart of a fight. One is the way that blood soaks the ground. It turns dirt to sticking, sucking mud, or makes a city street slick as a greased board.

Sten knew it. He was never a mercenary, but he had done his fair share of fighting. He tried to compensate, keeping his stance low and wide to keep balance. But Mag had spilled enough blood to bathe in. It was only a matter of time before it became too much.

A blade crashed down on his shield. The shield held, but Sten lost his footing, falling to one knee.

The weapon came around again, flashing in the sun. Sten's head jerked back.

For a moment, I thought he had dodged the blow. And then the skin of his throat parted, and blood poured from the wound.

I felt many things all at once, but three stand out to me now: a surging wave of anger; a heart-wrenching sadness for my kind, gentle friend.

And a rising wave of terror. Terror for Mag, and terror of her.

She did not see Sten at first, for he had stood behind her. She must have thought he merely lost his balance. With her shield arm she reached back, trying to pull him up.

He fell on his back instead, and his blood splashed across the street. And Mag saw him.

I will never forget the way she screamed. I can hear it now, as clear in my mind as it was in my ears then. We had been all across the nine kingdoms together. We had faced many dangers, lost many friends. But

I had never heard her make a sound like the one that ripped from her throat then. It was like the scream of a banshee that strikes the listener dead in the night. It was the sound of a storm ready to break the world. If a host of Elves had gathered and proclaimed the doom of all humanity, they would not have frightened me more.

The Shades fell back from her, their spirit broken for a moment in dismay. But Mag did not let them retreat.

Before her scream had ended, she was killing again. But her movements had lost their methodical beauty of a moment ago. Now she plunged headlong into the fray. When Mag entered her battle-trance, she was cold, emotionless. But now she had removed the leash from her fury, and it burned like darkfire. Now she took no care to guard herself. She sought only to kill. Though she moved too fast to follow easily, I saw blood on her skin that I was certain did not belong to her foes. She would never escape from the midst of that press.

Beside me, Loren kicked her horse to leap into the fighting. I saw a wild light in her eyes. Mayhap she was ready to kill at last, or mayhap she thought she could help Mag escape the melee somehow. But I barked a command before she could.

"No! Fly, while you still can!"

She met my gaze, and I could see the anguish shining through the brilliant green of her eyes. I looked past her to Xain. He gave me a grim look and a slow nod before taking Loren's arm.

"Fly," he said. "Remember Jordel."

Tears streamed into Annis' eyes, but Loren did not weep. After only a moment's pause, she took her quiver from her hip and threw it to me. I caught it and looked upon them all—for the last time, or so I believed. I loved them in that moment, even Xain. We had passed through much peril together, and I hated that it should all come to this in the end. But I thought, at the same time, that there was something very right about it. They had ridden together before I had met them, and they would ride on together after I died. It had been my fault, after all, that we had taken that cursed road through the Greatrocks that had led to Jordel's doom. If Loren and her friends did indeed survive, then mayhap my own death was only fair.

We all think we are the heroes of our own story. But I realized suddenly that I was only a passing figure in a tale that had been about others all along.

I rode for the battle, rode for Mag. And out of the corner of my eye, I saw Loren and the others ride off. They passed the Shades and reached the gate, vanishing out of sight. It was a comfort, if a cold one. No matter what happened to Mag and me now, they were safe. They would warn Underrealm, and evil would be defeated.

Of course, back then, I believed that such a thing was possible.

All my arrows were gone before I reached the Shades' ranks. I fought with my sword from horseback, but then they killed my horse. I managed to jump clear of it as it collapsed. I took Sten's place at Mag's side, and together we forged a path of blood into the Shades' ranks.

And then a chorus of cries broke out behind us. The Shades froze, looking over our shoulders at something to my rear. I risked a look back.

A mass of Northwood citizens poured from the streets and alleys. The people of Northwood had rallied, and they were coming to our aid. There were at least two hundreds of them, and though they held no weapons more frightening than a pitchfork, their eyes were alight with fury, and their screams of rage curdled the blood.

Despite everything, I managed a smile.

They slammed into the Shades. Now it was something close to a fair fight. They had not expected such a fierce battle, that much was certain. And Mag was still there, still cutting them down, covered in blood, the thrill of battle keeping her on her feet.

It was not long before the Shades turned and fled—not forever, I knew, but the respite was most welcome. I fell to one knee right there in the street, planting the point of my sword on the cobblestones and resting my brow on clasped hands over the hilt as I gasped for breath. Mag was on her feet, and darkness take her, she did not even seem winded.

And then I heard a faint croak, and a hand scrabbled at my boot. I looked down, and my eyes flew wide.

It was Sten's hand. His eyes were wide, and his whole front was covered in blood. But somehow, defying all expectation, he was still alive.

"Mag!"

She looked as if she had been contemplating running after the Shades, but she turned at once at the sound of my scream. When she saw Sten lying there, the color drained from her cheeks. Her battle-trance passed in an instant, and she dropped her blade and shield to the cobblestones. Falling to her knees beside him, she grasped one of his hands in one of hers, and pressed the other hard on the wound in his neck.

"Sten, Sten, my love," she pleaded. "Stay here. Stay with me."

"Healer!" I roared. Everyone within earshot turned to look at me, and I gestured at them frantically. "Healer! Now! Sten is alive!"

One of them, a young, bearded man named Taron, managed to gather his wits. "The medica! She is not far. I will be right back!"

He darted off down the street, leaving me thunderstruck. A medica, here in Northwood? That was a stroke of fortune I could hardly have imagined. But Mag had not even looked up—Sten had to survive until help could come, and even then it might be too late.

"Hold on, friend," I said, gripping Sten's shoulder.

I ripped off my cloak and gave it to Mag so that she could press it over the wound on his neck. "We are getting you help. We will not let you go so easily."

Sten huffed through his nose, and a choked sound slipped between his teeth.

"Be silent," said Mag. "Trying to talk will make it worse."

Sten ignored her. He gripped her arm in a bloodied hand and met her gaze. I could not tell you, even now, what passed between them in that moment. When two souls are bonded as theirs were, many things can be said without words.

"I will not let you go," whispered Mag, her voice shaking with grief. Tears dripped from the end of her nose to splash on his cheek. "Not though the Elves themselves should demand it."

He gave another grim huff through his nose.

"There!" I turned at Taron's shout to see him dashing across the cobblestones towards us. Behind him he pulled a younger woman with dark skin and long hair that she had tied back in a tail. Her hands and clothes were stained with a great deal of blood, but her gaze was steady, and as she knelt by Sten's side, she was as calm as if this were a king's garden.

"The throat?" she asked.

"Yes," said Mag. "We thought it was fatal at first, but it must not have been too deep." Sten growled, and despite everything, Mag smiled at him. "You know what I mean."

"I will count to four," said the medica. "Then you must pull away the cloak. This will hurt. One. Two. Three. Four!"

Sten's whole body went rigid as Mag pulled away her hand. The medica's fingers clutched his skin at once, and he tried to seize her wrists by reflex. Mag and I held his hands away, and the medica's eyes began to glow. Beneath her fingers, I saw Sten's flesh start to flow like water. He tried to scream, but only a gurgle came out.

"Try to be silent," said the medica sharply. "It will only be worse."

Sten's guttural sounds cut off, but his eyes were wide and wild. They locked on Mag's, and she lifted his twitching hand to kiss the back of it.

"Almost, my love," she said. "Hold on."

The flesh stitched itself together, sealing the wound. As an ander man, I knew more about medicas than most. This was not true healing—no wizard had that gift. This would only keep Sten from bleeding to death while his body fixed itself from the inside. But as the medica's eyes stopped glowing and she pulled her hands away, Sten's limbs relaxed, and he gave a deep sigh through his nose.

"It is done," she said. "He is not out of danger, but—"

A flash of movement. I saw it from the corner of my eye, and a lifetime of instinct took over.

"Down!" I cried. I dove out of the way, seizing Mag and the medica and taking them with me.

A flash of brown fur streaked through the air where Mag had been a moment before. It landed on Sten's chest. I heard the biting *shunk* of claws sinking into flesh and looked up, horrorstruck.

I recognized the creature at once—yet at the same time, I could not understand it. It was a great cat, the sort one finds in the mountains, larger than a man and with teeth and claws like daggers. This one had a white tail. But what on earth was it doing here in the midst of this battle?

All this passed through my mind in an instant. But before my thoughts could spin themselves into a conclusion, I heard Sten groan, and I realized what had happened. The creature had pounced on us, but I had pulled us out of the way. It had missed us and struck Sten instead. Its razor-sharp claws had pierced his chest many times over.

For a moment, Sten's fingers grasped for the mountain cat's throat. And then his whole body slackened as he died—truly this time, his sightless eyes staring into a sky streaked with the smoke of burning buildings.

"No," said Mag. Not a scream this time. No battle-lust protected her from the pain now. She had dropped all her defenses, and nothing stood between her and her grief, no bulwark against the sharp, crushing reality. Sten was gone. This time he would not return.

"No," said Mag again. She rose to her feet, and her hands curled to fists at her sides. Her sword was nowhere to be seen, but she did not seem to care. The mountain cat growled at her.

“No,” she cried, and she ran for the beast, even as I scrambled to my feet, even as I went after her, tried to drag her back.

“No!” she shouted, as the cat roared and leaped for her. She stepped to the side, but her hand flashed like a knife. Rigid fingers struck the cat in the eye, and it yowled in pain. I barely scrambled out of the way in time as it sailed past.

“No!” she screamed, and flung herself at the beast. It had curled its neck and was pawing at the eye she had struck. Her heavy boot caught it in the jaw, and as its head came up, her hands struck twice, thrice more. I saw blood gush from a wound in its other eye, and as it staggered back, one of its nostrils gaped where she had ripped it open. Mag tried to press the attack, but the beast yowled and leaped back out of reach.

And then its eyes began to glow.

That struck all of us motionless, Mag and the medica and all the onlookers, and me as well. As we watched, the cat’s form began to change, to shift and melt. It was the transformation of a weremage, and in a moment, there she was. A woman, not much older than I was, with nut-brown skin and dark hair worn in a short braid. She had on tight-fitting trousers of grey and a white shirt with yellow trim. Blood still ran from one of her eyes, which continued to glow as she tried to heal the injury.

“Sow!” she screamed, staggering back away from Mag. “You feckless sow!”

Mag did not answer, but merely stooped to pick up a fallen pitchfork. She crouched, readying to leap after the woman. But then there came a great roaring on the air, and another contingent of Shades burst out from between two buildings, rushing to support their master. For the weremage was their master, of that I had no doubt.

"Kill her!" cried the weremage, thrusting a finger towards Mag. "Kill them both!" But rather than help them, she turned and vanished into the press. I saw another flash of light from her eyes, and in an instant she had become a raven. It wheeled up into the sky, heading west towards the Greatrock Mountains.

For the second time, I saw Mag alone amid her enemies. My sword lay on the ground nearby. I scooped it up and launched myself towards the fight with a battle-cry.

Before I could even strike one of them, a club struck my temple. I fell into blackness and knew nothing more.

ELEVEN

"Are you all right?"

Sun blinked. "What?"

"Your eyes," said Albern.

Raising a hand to her cheek, Sun found it wet. She did not know when she had begun weeping. The tears had come slow and silent, wending their way down her face.

"I am fine," she said, scrubbing at her eyes with the back of a hand.

"We could enjoy silence for a moment," said Albern. "I do not mean to distress you."

"It seemed so unfair," said Sun, keeping her voice low for fear it might betray her and break. "For you and Mag to think Sten would live, only for that witch to . . . Sten did not even want to be there."

"None of us did," said Albern quietly. "That is sometimes the way of it. You find yourself somewhere you never thought you would be, and great tragedy or great fortune befalls you, unlooked-for. And then, too, things are not always what they seem. Sten was hardly the first friend I lost that way. I had a friend who I saw struck down on a battlefield in Wavemount, but he lingered on for three more days. One of my captains in the Ruby Crowns took a scratch on his cheek from an arrow. He laughed at the time, and led us to victory. The wound became infected, and he died a month later. Then there was young Bowtin, a foolish boy I met in Dulmun. He fell from a ship into the Great Bay during a sea-battle, and we thought him drowned. We mourned him and moved on—and then we met him in a Dorsean tavern two months later, for he had fought his way to shore and survived. Loren, our friend who rode from Northwood? She thought us dead in that battle. She mourned us for a long while. Our deaths helped shape her life for a good deal of time afterwards—and then she discovered that we had never died in the first place. Life and death are never so clean as we imagine them to be, especially when it comes to those we love. And they have not moved."

Sun frowned. "What?"

"Your friends in the corner," said Albern. "You keep glancing at them as I speak, as if you are afraid they are watching you, or looking for you. But they have not moved since they arrived."

"I know. Is that not odd?" Sun scowled into her beer and took another sip. "They have not even risen to relieve themselves."

"Nor have you."

Sun glared at him. "I would, but I am afraid they will take notice of me."

"I can take you outside if you wish," said Albern. "But if I do, you will have to move when I tell you to, and do exactly as I say."

Sun blinked. "What?"

"I can take you outside. In fact, I think I should."

She did not understand, but his words were earnest, and his eyes held no trace of a joke. "I . . . yes."

Albern lifted his hand, and Sun noticed for the first time that he wore a silver ring on the middle finger of his left hand. It bore a symbol she had never seen before, and it was part of no tale about Albern that she had ever heard.

Curling his knuckles, Albern rapped twice on the wooden table—just as the barman had done earlier in the night. Then, whispering, "Come," he abruptly stood and strode through the back door, snatching his bow up as he went.

Sun dared not glance at the guards in the corner as she leaped to her feet and followed him, but she guessed they must have noticed the commotion. She hid her face under the hood of her borrowed cloak and tried to get through the door as quickly as she could.

In the brisk night air, Albern stood with his face raised to the moonslight. He looked as if he was listening for something, or mayhap sniffing the air. But when Sun emerged into view, he turned at once and smiled at her.

"You will have to make a bit of a climb," he said. "But if I can do it with one arm, I am confident you can do it with two."

So saying, he jumped atop a small crate beside the tavern's back door. From there he took a large step up another two that were stacked atop each other. Sun saw that a pile of crates, which she had thought were stacked at random, actually formed a little mountain leading up to the edge of the tavern's roof, and Albern was scaling it like a satyr.

She hurried to follow him, and soon they had both reached the solid ceramic shingles. There was a little platform there, with two piles of soft cushions. Albern kicked off his mud-covered boots with some difficulty and sank down on one of the cushion piles, and after a moment's hesitation, Sun took her place on the other.

"What is this—" Sun began, but Albern shushed her and pointed down at the ground.

Sun watched as the two guards from her parents' retinue burst out the back door of the tavern. They stopped in the alley, searching left and right. One of them spoke, and the words drifted up to Sun and Albern on the rooftop.

"Where did she go?"

"I do not know. She vanished."

"Our lord will have our heads."

"Not if we find her. Split up. And if you see that useless constable, enlist him into the hunt."

They ran off, one to the left and one to the right, and soon they were lost from view.

"They knew!" hissed Sun, who feared to speak too loudly.

"They did," said Albern.

"They followed me to the tavern!"

"So it seems."

"My parents sent them," said Sun. "Curse them. I thought I had snuck out without detection."

"Our parents often like to let us think we are alone and independent, but they watch us more closely than they allow us to see. Royal children especially."

That drew Sun's attention. "Not royal," she said.

Albern smiled. "Noble, then."

She turned her gaze from him. "You have not asked why I am hiding."

"That is your business," said Albern. "It has nothing to do with me, unless you wish it to."

"What if I am a criminal?" said Sun. "I could be a thief or a murderer."

Albern chuckled. "Those women are guards. Retainers of a noble family, or mayhap hired hands to protect a merchant's caravan. If you were on the run, you would not be afraid of them, but of redbacks."

Sun frowned. "What?"

"Forgive me," said Albern. "It is not a polite term. Constables with their red armor, and Mystics with their crimson cloaks—those who fear the King's law call them redbacks, collectively."

"And how would you know that?" said Sun.

He grinned at her. "I, too, could be a thief or a murderer."

That forced a laugh from her, though she quickly hushed it and threw another nervous look at the street below. "The stories say many things about you, but they say nothing about being a criminal."

"I suppose they are not entirely worthless, then," said Albern with a smile.

Sun chuckled.

"If you still need to relieve yourself, climb down and do it quickly," said Albern. "That shed built against the back wall is an outhouse. I will wait here."

Sun nodded and did as he suggested. After she had climbed back up and settled herself on her pile of cushions again, she looked at him expectantly and waited for him to go on.

Then she nearly jumped out of her skin at a loud *thunk* behind them.

She tensed, ready to run—but then a hidden panel swung up from the rooftop behind them. The barmaid from earlier climbed halfway up through the hole, and in her hand was a tray with two full mugs of beer.

"I am glad you found your way here safely," she said to Albern. She put the tray with the mugs on the roof between the two piles of cushions. "Anything else? Some food, mayhap?"

"None for me, thank you, Morled," said Albern. "Sun?"

"No, thank you," said Sun, who suddenly found her fingernails very interesting as a flush crept into her cheeks.

The barmaid only smiled at her. "Sun. A lovely name." She leaned over and planted a quick kiss on Sun's cheek. "Bear no worries tonight. No one here will let you fall into the hands of the constables—or anyone else who looks for you."

With a final bright smile, she retreated back through the roof hatch into the tavern. It was quite a little while before Sun realized she was frozen staring at the hatch, one hand gently touching her cheek where she could still feel the warmth of Morled's lips.

"Have another sip," said Albern. The moonslight was not bright enough to show it, but Sun could hear the smile in his voice.

"Yes, thank you," said Sun distractedly. She seized the mug and drained half of it in a single pull.

"You are clever," said Albern. "If you finish it quickly, she will have to come back."

"I—that is not why I—"

Albern's smile widened and turned into a grin. "I know."

"Does your injury still pain you?"

He frowned. "What?"

"Your injury. The blow that knocked you unconscious in Northwood. Does it still hurt you?"

Albern raised the stump of his right arm. "This one does, on occasion. But the knock on the head I took in Northwood . . . no, that does not pain me any longer."

"And Mag?" said Sun. "Her injuries—were they very bad?"

Albern's mouth twisted. "Mag suffered greatly at Northwood. But her hurts were of the mind, not the body."

Sun frowned. "I thought you said—"

"I said I thought I saw her injured," said Albern. "In the thick of battle, I was sure of it. But war turns a mind to madness. Soldiers often think they see things that never happened. It is one reason you must be very wary of believing stories—and war stories in particular."

"Do you mean they did not hurt her, even in Northwood?" said Sun. "Even in the press of all those Shades?"

"They hurt her," said Albern quietly. "They hurt her more deeply than she had ever been hurt in her life. But she was Mag. She was good at getting back up and carrying on. We both were, then. And Kaita, the weremage, had always been good at it."

Even as I lay unconscious on the ground, Kaita was winging her way west over Northwood as it burned.

Unarmed, she thought. *She beat me unarmed.*

Again.

Beyond the city's western outskirts, she found Rogan in council with his captains. They had gathered atop a hillock, from which they could observe most of Northwood and the progress of their troops through the city. Kaita landed and resumed her human form. Once he saw her growing out of the bird's shape, Rogan bid his captains away with a wave of his hand and went to speak to her alone.

"I need more troops," said Kaita. "I know where Mag is, but I need more to overwhelm her."

"We cannot spare them," said Rogan.

"Rogan—"

"We cannot spare them, Kaita," said Rogan. "I must ride north after Loren, and I must take many of our siblings with me. And I need you to lead the rest of them back to the Watcher."

"No!" cried Kaita. "Mag is still in there! She defeated me, but I must try again. Who knows when I will get another chance?"

Rogan tilted his head and looked upon her with a kindly expression. "What happened?"

Kaita scowled. "She . . . she was too fast. I had taken the form of a mountain lion, but she still outmatched me." She did not mention that Mag had done it unarmed. She spat. "At least I killed her steer of a husband."

"Sten is dead?" said Rogan.

"He is, and darkness take him."

Much to Kaita's annoyance, Rogan's lips twisted in a soft smile. "I told you that I did not think you were destined to defeat her this day, Kaita."

"You did," said Kaita, avoiding his gaze. "And how did you know that?"

"I have some of our father's sight, though I cannot see as far as he can," said Rogan. "Do not despair. I have made you promises, and I intend to keep them."

"You promised I would defeat her," said Kaita. "How do you mean for that to happen while I am leading your army to the—"

"Your army as much as mine," said Rogan, his tone betraying a rare note of admonishment. "And I have changed my mind. You will lead our siblings into the Greatrocks, but you will not take them to the Watcher. When they turn north, you should continue west. Make sure you leave a trail they can follow. I have been led to believe that Albern is an excellent tracker."

"I suppose," said Kaita through gritted teeth. "And where would you have me lead them?"

"To where it all began. Between the two of you."

Kaita's eyes shot wide. "Home."

"Yes. And not just for your own personal reasons. I need to send a trusted captain there to hurry things along. For some time now, I did not know who it would be. Now the answer is obvious. I trust no one more than you. Lead Albern and Mag there, and help our siblings accomplish their mission. You can claim your vengeance at the same time."

Kaita stepped towards him and smiled. "Yes, this . . . this is better. This is far better. Sky above, Rogan, why did you not tell me this was your aim in the first place? I would have done as you asked."

Rogan shook his head. "This was not my plan. Many things are not clear to me until it is time. Even an hour ago, I would never have considered it. I am sorry, Kaita. It frustrates me as much as you."

Many emotions warred within her. But her fear was still nearly as strong as her excitement. She shook her head slowly—not in refusal, but in thought.

"If I do this," she said, "I want a guarantee. I may need more strength than I currently have."

"You are strong beyond—"

"That is not what I mean," said Kaita. "I want a guarantee, Rogan. If I do this, and yet I cannot take my revenge alone, I want our father to grant me the power he has long denied me."

Rogan's eyes narrowed, filling with . . . not fear, but something akin to it. "That is too dangerous."

"I am no simpleton."

"The risks—"

"The risk to me, and to my mission, is also great," said Kaita. "Promise me, Rogan."

Rogan sighed. "Kaita, if things go ill, we will have to—"

"I know."

"I have no wish to see you harmed."

Her expression softened. "I know that, too." She went to him then, and she laid her head against his chest. "Whatever you may think of me, I am our father's child. My heart is true. But I need this."

"Then you shall have it," said Rogan. His tree-trunk arm wrapped around her shoulders. "If you cannot vanquish her alone, you will have every power our father can grant you. And I only hope neither of us has cause to regret it."

"Thank you," Kaita whispered into his chest. Then she drew back, out of his reach, and looked up into his eyes. "Go after Loren. Bring our father's vengeance to those who call themselves our rulers."

"I will. May death stay its hand from you."

Kaita smirked. "I would wish you the same, but in your case, death has no choice. I will contact you when I can."

Rogan gave her a final smile and left. Kaita took a moment to gather herself before finding the captains to order the retreat.

TWELVE

I woke with a splitting headache to find Elsie kneeling over me, bathing my face with warm water.

"Mag," I groaned.

"You are alive," she said, her brows rising. "The healers told me so, but I did not believe them. Neither would you, if you could see yourself."

"Mag," I repeated. I tried to lift my head, but a spike of pain nearly drove me senseless again. I fought to remain conscious. "Where is she?" I whispered.

"Puttering about the place," said Elsie. She rose and went to fetch me water from a bucket by the wall.

"Alive?"

"No, she died, but that has not stopped her. Of course she is alive, you dolt."

I let myself relax, at least a little. "Everyone else?" I said. Each word came with great effort. "How many survived?"

Elsie's brisk demeanor seemed to fade away. She looked over at me, and for a moment her eyes sparkled with tears. "Not enough. Though I suppose each one is a blessing."

She had been there when I first fought to defend Northwood against invaders all those years ago. I could see from the sadness on her face that this time was far, far worse.

"I am sorry," I said.

Her resolve returned at once, and she turned back to the water, ladling a cup full of it. "You should not be. You fought like a champion. Not as well as Mag, of course, or she would be lying here and you would be the one walking around. But you did all right, I suppose."

That forced a weak chuckle out of me, and with it, I felt a bit better. Strength had been creeping back into my limbs. I tried to lift my head again, and this time the pain was not so bad.

"No," said Elsie at once, coming towards me. "You are to stay—"

"I want to see the town," I told her firmly. "And I need to see Mag."

Before she could reach me, I sat up, and I gently batted away her hands when she tried to push me back down. Despite her protests, I sat up from the straw pallet where I had been laid.

It was not till then that I realized I was in the common room of the Lee Shore. Mag's inn could not have looked more different. All the tables had been cleared out, and the floor was covered with four rows of pallets holding the wounded. Healers and helpers moved down the line, providing more pillows, fetching water, and seeing to their patients' needs.

"Are these all who remain?" I said as I fought painfully to my feet.

Though she clucked her tongue at me, Elsie at last abandoned her attempts to force me back to bed. She took an arm and helped me rise to my feet. "Of course not," she said. "Every tavern and inn throughout Northwood has been turned into a sickroom. Those that were not burned down in the attack, anyway."

"Help me to the door," I said.

"You mean to go *outside?"* she said, horrified.

"I told you I need to see Mag. If she is not in here, then yes, I need to go outside."

Elsie glared up at me and did not budge. "I am not sure how else to tell you this, and I do not understand why I have to, but: *you nearly died, you great idiot."*

I smiled at her. "I am no stranger to injury. I will be fine."

"No stranger indeed. You seem well acquainted

with head injuries in particular." But she sighed and moved forwards, helping me hobble towards the inn's front door. With her help, I pushed it open.

And there stood Mag.

She stood across the street, leaning against the building opposite. Her head was tilted back, resting against the wall, and her eyes were closed. Dirt covered her face, her arms, every scrap of her clothing. A great deal of blood was mixed in with it. But as I looked closely, I could see that none of it was hers. There were no rents in her skin, no angry red wounds. Not even a scratch.

I stood there for a long moment, staring at her, entirely dumbfounded. And as I stared, Mag opened her eyes and looked at me. A small smile tugged at her lips.

"Mag," I said. "You are alive."

"Albern," she said. "You are up. That is good, I suppose."

Gone from her voice was the lifeless, heartless monotone of her battle-trance. This was the Mag who was my friend, who did not mercilessly cut down her enemies, but who provided beds and food and rest to a band of children who had come down out of the mountains with her old friend.

I walked towards her. Elsie tried to help me, but I had almost forgotten her, and I pulled away from her grip. The pain in my body, even in my head, was forgotten. I went to Mag and put my hand on her shoulder.

"I am sorry, Mag," I said. "Sky above, I am so sorry."

Mag shrugged. "It was not your fault, nor mine. Blame the ones who did this." She gestured vaguely at the town. "Something is happening, Albern. If that was not clear to both of us before, it should be now. It is bigger than either of us, bigger than poor Loren and her friends. All we can do is try to weather the storm and pull the ones we love through it with us." She turned her gaze away, looking into the blood-soaked mud of the street. "And sometimes fail."

"Mag—"

"Leave it," she said. There was just a hint of sharpness in her tone, enough to make me obey.

After a long moment, I spoke again. "Before I went down, I saw you surrounded. I thought I saw you wounded."

That seemed to bring her out of the darkness her thoughts had cast her into. For a moment she smiled, and it was like we were on the campaign trail again, trading boasts around a campfire. She stepped forwards and held out her arms. "They did surround me. I fought my way free. Do you see any wounds?"

I did not. I sighed. "You are frightening sometimes, Mag."

"Only sometimes?"

"But . . . but then what happened?" I pressed. "How did we drive them away from Northwood, in the end?"

Mag frowned. "I have only an answer that is both poor and troubling. I do not know that we *did* drive them away. They simply turned and marched into the mountains. No one knows why."

My jaw clenched. "I would like an answer. And I would like them to answer for other things as well."

"As would I," said Mag. "But now that you have risen, many things need tending to—and one of them, in particular, was not one I wished to tend to until you were awake."

My shoulders sagged. "Sten."

She had cleaned him already. I helped her wrap him in cloth. But when I moved to lift him, she shook her head.

"I will take him," she said, and her expression brooked no argument.

She lifted him into her arms. Now, Mag had always been strong and well-muscled, but Sten was a large man. She was breathing hard before she reached the southern gate, and her steps began to falter before we were a span away from the walls. But she did not stop, not even once, and despite her staggering, she never seemed close to dropping him.

Close to the bottom of the Reeve, she laid him down at last. She had prepared the place in advance, and a neat pile of wood lay there to receive him. His final resting place. I could not help but think of how

Loren and I had buried Jordel in the mountains. I had not known him nearly as long as Sten, and I had loved him less well—but not by much.

"Too many," I said quietly.

"Too many," agreed Mag.

She struck flint and steel upon the heaps of dry branches, and they caught with little effort. We stood back, watching as the flames licked higher. The wood burned bright, and soon it caught upon the cloth we had wrapped Sten in.

I sang, then. I have been told I have a fair enough voice, though I did not think it sounded well in that moment, for my words were thick with tears. But I had learned a number of songs in my travels, and many of them were songs of mourning, for this was not the first time I had lost a friend.

To all of you, come all of you
No tarrying, I call to you
The darkness calls, the fall of you
It bids you come to rest

It welcomes you, and all of us
The years will pass, the fall of us
And you below, will call to us
And bid us go to rest

The wind is cold, and hollow too
All joy has passed, and sorrow too

The children weep, and follow too
They bid you come to rest

Now mourn no more, and we as well
Sit by the fire, and heed as well
One day they call for me as well
And bid me go to rest

"Will he truly rest, do you think?" said Mag.

"No one knows the darkness," I told her.

"I asked what you think."

"I hope so. He deserved it. More than either of us, at least."

"Truly said."

Her frame was steady, but I could see her hands shaking. I put my hand on her shoulder for a moment and then took it away. We stood a long, silent vigil, watching as the fires burned away the last evidence of my friend and her husband.

When the flames were only coals and the last of the drifting smoke was nearly out of sight over the trees, Mag turned to me.

"Will you come with me?"

I looked at her in surprise. "Where?"

"Atop the Reeve."

A thrill coursed through my heart. "Mag . . ."

"Something has weighed on me ever since the battle," she said. "I did not know exactly what it was. It was like a sense that I should be doing something, but I do not know what. Do you feel the same?"

"I do," I said. "What *would* you do, if you could?"

"Only one thing," she said. "Kill the weremage."

The words hit me like lightning. I straightened, balling my hands to fists at my sides.

"Yes."

Mag's eyes blazed with fire. "I want to find her. Wherever she may have run to. Wherever she may be hiding. And I want to end her."

"As do I."

Mag balled her right hand into a fist and slammed it into her hand. "Then let us do it. Come with me. Let us have vengeance for Sten."

"She will be nearly impossible to track down," I pointed out. "We do not know where she has gone."

"I have nothing better to do with my time," said Mag.

"Even when we find her, she could very well have an army at her back."

"Let them try to stand before us," said Mag. "Will you come?"

I grinned and thrust out my hand. "Even if we must ride into the darkness below."

Mag seized my wrist and pulled me into an embrace. My head, still tender, swam for a moment, but I held her. Finally, I gently pushed her back to hold her at arm's length.

"We will need horses."

"There are some in my stables," she said. "Come with me to the top of the Reeve, and then we will fetch them."

"And then into the Birchwood."

It was as if a cold snap rushed through the air, piercing us both in an instant. I felt the thrill inside me vanish even as I saw it disappear from Mag's eyes.

"The Birchwood?" said Mag. "Why the Birchwood?"

"To go after Loren, of course," I said. "Wherever this weremage has gone, she will come into conflict with Loren in the end. And she and the others will need our help, in any case."

"The weremage went west," said Mag.

"And who knows where she turned, after she entered the mountains?" I said.

"I do not know, but the mountains are the best place to start."

"But Loren—"

"The way she and the children rode from here, I doubt we could catch them even if we wanted to."

"We could try."

Mag frowned for a moment—but then her expression softened. "Latrine duty," she said. She pulled a copper sliver from a pouch at her waist. "I say heads."

"We are not new recruits," I told her. "This is not—"

"I say heads, Albern."

I sighed. Half a chance was better than none—better, indeed, than an argument I knew might not end. Any soldier knows the virtue of a firm, clean decision—even if it is a poor one. "Very well."

Mag flipped the coin. I think I knew, even as it flashed in the air, what the result would be. She flipped it onto the back of her other hand, looked at it, and smiled.

"West."

THIRTEEN

MAG LED ME UNSWERVINGLY UP THE REEVE. I HAD TO take its sloping path carefully, for I was still tender. But it was not long before we stood on the flat top. The boulders around us now loomed like old, wizened councilors, bearing witness to some grim business of their king.

Mag went to one of them and crawled underneath it. She emerged with an old spade and pickaxe. They looked as though they had been there for many years, untouched. Part of the wood had rotted, but for the most part they were still solid. She took the spade and dug into the ground—the flat patch of earth that I had watched so closely last time, that Sten had tried to avoid completely. The soil was hard, but Mag attacked it with fury, and it broke before her onslaught. I wanted to take the pickaxe and help her, but I did not move. Something told me that Mag had to do this alone.

A pace below the surface, Mag's spade struck hard rock. She dug the hole wider until it was big enough for her to stand in, and then she fetched the pickaxe. She made no remarks about the fact that I did not aid her. As when she had carried Sten to his pyre, there was an unspoken agreement that this was something she had to do alone.

Mag attacked the stone, and it shattered before her. Shards of rock flew from each blow, but Mag hardly seemed to notice.

At last she broke through. Beneath the stone were two bundles, wrapped in oiled leather to protect them from the elements. One was long and thin, the other wide and flat. Mag lifted them out and placed them on the ground outside the hole, then climbed out after them. With steady hands and a reverent bearing, she unwrapped them.

A spear, a shield, and a shirt of scale mail came out. Without pausing for even a heartbeat, Mag took them up and began to clean from them any traces of dirt.

I had not seen that spear in years. Sten had made her bury it here. It was part of the promises she had made to him when the two of them wed.

These were not the heirlooms of Mag, tavern owner and brewmaster. These were the arms of Mag, the Uncut Lady, the most feared warrior in the nine lands. These were for a quest where only death waited at the end. But not Mag's death, I was certain.

I was certain of so much, back then.

Mag had been fierce from the day we met. With any blade in her hand, she was a living weapon. But with that spear and a good shield, she was a walking incarnation of death.

Still I said nothing. I only waited. When she had finished her task, she rose to her feet and donned the mail. She gripped the straps of the shield and hefted the spear, giving it a few experimental thrusts.

As though she needs to practice, I thought. *As though she does not remember how it feels in her hands. As though she and the spear are not two parts of a whole.*

It was not often that my fear of Mag eclipsed my love of her, but I feared her then, for just a moment.

And then she looked at me. "Time for the horses," she said.

We walked back to Northwood, Mag now clad in her armor. When we reached the Lee Shore, I fetched my bow, my sword, and my travel pack before meeting Mag in the stables. They had remained largely untouched during the battle, and the masters of several of the horses had perished in the fighting. Mag went to one of them, a large mare of light grey, and began to saddle her. My horse had died in the battle, so I went to one of the other stalls, where a tall roan gelding snorted at me.

"That one has something of a temper," said Mag.

"Coming from you, that says something," I replied. But I ignored her warning and fetched a saddle from the wall. The gelding stamped a hoof when I stepped up beside him, but I clicked my tongue at him.

"Easy, fool," I told him in gentle tones. "If you throw me, I will butcher you for the townspeople to eat."

He gave me no more trouble as I made him ready to ride, almost as if he understood the words. Mag led the way out of the stable, where we mounted. The gelding shied at once, shaking himself lightly as he felt my weight on his back. But I kept my balance. My family had owned many horses, and I had learned to deal with all sorts of them.

"I am not going anywhere," I said, as the horse began to calm. "You had best get used to it."

"Indeed, it is hardly possible to get rid of him," Mag told the horse. "I have tried." Our gazes met, and I smiled.

As if it understood her, the gelding settled down, though he gave a disgruntled snort. Mag's mare nickered, and I was reminded of one of Elsie's disapproving *harrumphs.*

"Lead on," I told Mag.

She guided her horse over next to mine, holding my gaze. "Thank you, Albern," she said quietly. "For all your many years of friendship, and for your company on this road. It is going to be a long one, and it will grow dark before the end. Yet I would have no one else beside me."

"Nor I."

She nodded, and then she nudged her horse. We rode west out of Northwood, breaking into a canter as soon as we passed the western gate.

High above, far too high to hear, a harsh croak sounded as a raven circled and flew towards the mountains.

The raven sped on, far faster than our steeds. It rode the warm currents of air, drifting through the lazy smoke of the last fires in Northwood, fires soon to be extinguished as the people left their homes forever. Before too long, it winged its way over the peaks of the eastern Greatrocks.

In the valley on the other side, a small party of riders waited, clothed in blue and grey. The raven descended towards them in wide, sweeping circles. When it was less than a span above them, one of the riders took notice of it. He was a large man, with shoulders like cornerstones and a thick, bristling beard. His name was Ertu.

The raven landed on the ground before the man,

and its eyes glowed. Kaita emerged from its form and stepped forwards. The man handed her the reins of her horse.

"They are coming," she said.

"I am glad to hear it," said Ertu. "All this waiting grates upon me."

Kaita frowned sharply at him as she climbed into the saddle. "You serve at our father's pleasure."

"Of course," said Ertu. "I will always obey him. But I am free to wish I was with the rest of our siblings."

"So long as it is only a wish," said Kaita. "Their march north went as planned?"

"As far as we know, yes," said Ertu. Then, curiously, he nudged his horse, walking it closer to hers, and he held her gaze as he went on in a quieter voice. "Some of our furred friends have been watching us for the past few days."

Kaita almost looked over her shoulder, but she restrained herself at the last moment. She knew he meant the satyrs. "Have they caused trouble?"

"They have not. I think they want to know why the six of us have been left behind when all the rest of our force has ridden on."

"They will find out soon," said Kaita. "We are to ride west. I am going to Lan Shui—and so are the rest of you, but after a stop along the way. The satyr elders have not heard from us since Trisken's fall. Father wishes for you to visit them and deliver his . . . displeasure."

Ertu's beard jumped as his lips twisted in disgust.

"I have visited the satyrs once. I do not relish the idea of repeating the experience. They are foul-smelling creatures."

"Father has—"

He shook his head to cut her off. "Sky above, Kaita, I have not refused your orders. I am only grousing. Father deserves our obedience, but you act as though we are supposed to be his unquestioning slaves."

Kaita steeled herself. Even after so many years, she was unused to the way the Shades conducted themselves, the way they treated each other. But then, Kaita had been raised in far different circumstances.

"Of course not," she said at last. "Forgive me. The changing . . . it tires me."

"I imagine," said Ertu graciously. "Fear not. You will be able to rest well, now—or at least, as well as one can when on the road. Let us set out, for the glory of our father."

He turned in his saddle and motioned for the riders to set off. They went west at an easy walk, and Kaita fell into line with the rest of them, her thoughts uneasy.

FOURTEEN

"So she was following you," said Sun.

"Leading us," said Albern. "But you have the idea."

"Why did she wait? I am certain the people of Northwood guarded against another attack, but you left Northwood. Did she not think to wait until you were sleeping, and creep into your camp, and kill you in the night?"

"I am certain she thought of it," said Albern. "But we always set a watch. And I think she well remembered the injuries Mag had given her. But I could not tell you for certain. Many things I know about what Kaita thought in those days, but not everything."

"And how do you know this, again?" said Sun.

Albern smiled at her. "That is another story entirely, and not one I intend to tell you tonight."

"What about the two of you?" said Sun. "You knew you were after a weremage. Were you not frightened? I would suspect every shadow. Any beast could have been the weremage, or anyone you met on the road."

"They could have been," said Albern. "But remember that we thought we were chasing the weremage—we did not know her name, then—and that she was fleeing with the Shades across the kingdom. We did not know we were being led. Not until much later."

Albern stared into his mug of beer for a long moment, his brow furrowed and his lips pursed. Sun studied him. The tale had thrilled her, she had to admit. When he had spoken of riding off from the Reeve, she had felt a sudden desire to rise to her feet and start a journey at once—though she knew not where. Yet the same words that had excited her were obviously disturbing to Albern. She waited in respectful silence, not wanting to agitate him further.

And then, all of a sudden, he drained the rest of his mug and rose to his feet. "Well, I have to be taking care of something."

Sun drew back, blinking. But before she could answer, Albern took up his bow and climbed rapidly down from the rooftop. He reached the ground and passed around the corner of the tavern without so much as a backwards glance.

It was another long moment before Sun thought of standing up. She stood there, staring stupidly down at the empty alley behind the building, until she realized he was not coming back.

Not knowing what else to do, Sun clambered down after him and ran around to the front of the building. Albern stood by a horse that had been tethered to a pole. It was already saddled, and he was checking its straps.

Anxiously, Sun approached the old man from behind. "Albern?"

"Hm? Yes?" said Albern. He glanced back at her and gave a brief smile before raising one foot to the stirrup. With impressive grace considering his age and his single arm, he vaulted into the saddle and took up the reins.

"Where . . . where are you going?" said Sun. The question seemed too obvious to need to be put into words, but she felt as driftless as an unmoored ship.

"I have an errand to take care of," said Albern, looking down at her. Then he seemed to notice her expression for the first time, and he smiled. "Forgive me for not mentioning it sooner, but I had rather hoped you would come with me."

"But . . . but where?" said Sun.

"Oh, this errand is not too far away," said Albern.

This errand? The wording was not lost on her. Nervously, Sun glanced both ways down the street. Two of her family's guards were searching for her even now. She thought of her mother and father, of their caravan beyond the bounds of the town.

"But I need to be getting back soon," whispered Sun. She had meant to say it aloud, to say it to Albern. But she spoke quietly, as if to herself, and Albern did not answer.

She *did* need to get back. Her family expected her. She was supposed to ride on with them tomorrow. On to their final destination, there to remain for a time before returning home. And before long, they would take her somewhere else, and then somewhere else. All part of a plan, a great dance that had always been determined for her, the steps laid out before she had first set foot on the floor.

Sun turned back, looking up at Albern. "You will keep telling the story if I come with you?"

Albern's smile widened. "Until the tale's true end."

Her pulse raced. Her breath seemed to catch in her throat, and she was not sure she could feel her fingers. But she stepped up next to Albern's horse, and as he nudged it to a walk, Sun followed.

She expected Albern to continue the tale immediately, but as they left the town heading south and passed into open country, still he remained silent. He only made gentle noises to the horse as he nudged it one way or another. Sun gave the steed another glance, half expecting to see the roan gelding from his tale.

But that was ridiculous, of course. That had been decades ago. This horse was a deep chestnut brown.

"What are you thinking, child?"

Sun had been thinking many things, but none seemed like the right answer. So she asked him the question that had not left her mind, despite his reassurances. "Did all of this *really* happen?"

Albern cocked his head. "I told you already that stories are—"

"—Are meant to be learned from, yes," said Sun. "I understand, but . . . how can you expect me to take it to heart, to learn from it, if I do not know for certain that it even took place as you say it did?"

Albern looked at her askance. "Do you think *I* am certain of how it happened?"

"I . . . what?" said Sun, frowning up at him. "Of course you are. You lived it."

"Hm," said Albern. "I see the lesson still has not taken root. Let me ask you this, then. Tonight you told me your name, but you left out your family name. Do you know if that answer was true or not?"

"Of course I do," said Sun. "I knew what the truth was, though I did not speak it."

"Mayhap. Or mayhap, in crafting a lie, you struck upon a deeper truth."

She frowned. "I do not understand."

"Do you really think you are still the noble daughter who first entered that tavern?" Albern chuckled. "I doubt she would have gone scarpering off with a decrepit, one-armed man. Those sound like the actions of a girl with no family, the actions of Sun of No Name."

This was almost too much. Sun's thoughts spun, and her feelings gave her no peace. She had often wished she was not a daughter of the family Valgun, but she *was.* Was she not?

Her parents' guards must have reported that she had gone missing by now. She knew there would be consequences, and that they would be worse the longer she remained away. Yet she was not returning to her family, but traipsing off with an old man, simply because he was telling her a good story.

That did *not* seem very like something Sun of the family Valgun would do.

Her mind whirled, and she felt that strange, unmoored feeling again.

"Why are you telling me all this, about Northwood and the rest of it?" she asked. "Why will you not tell me what happened to your arm, or what happened to Mag?"

"Because you *want* to hear one story, Sun, but you *need* to hear another," said Albern. "Any talespinner must seek a balance. He must tell the listener what they *need* to hear, but tell it well enough that the audience is willing to stay and listen, no matter what they demanded in the first place. Do you think, when your Dulmish king brings a skald into her court, that she merely searches out the one with the best voice? No, not if she is wise. She seeks the skald who will tell her the stories she most needs told, even—mayhap especially—when she does not want to hear them."

"So you think you know better than me what story I need to hear?" said Sun. "You are just like my parents, and that is no compliment."

"I think I do, yes," said Albern mildly. "But if I judge correctly, I am different from your parents in one important respect: if you do not wish to take my advice, I will not force it upon you. You are free to go at any time—or, if you wish, you can simply ask me to stop telling the tale, and we can talk of other things."

"You compare yourself to a skald," said Sun. "Yet if a king demands a tale, her skald will tell it if he is a true servant."

Albern's eyes flashed as he looked at her, and for the first time he appeared truly angry. "You vastly misjudge us both if you call me a servant and yourself my king."

Hot blood rushed into her cheeks. "I am sorry. I did not mean it like that."

He held her gaze for a long moment. But then the hostility in his expression faded somewhat. "No, I suppose you did not. It is clear to me—forgive me for saying so—but I would guess you have little opportunity to exercise your skill at argument. I would wager that people in your life have been of two kinds: those who obey you, and those who *you* must obey without question."

"Is it so obvious?"

"As obvious as the fact you come from Dulmun. You walk like you wear a crown, and those leathers of yours are hardly Dorsean, nor are they the garb of a poor commoner. I knew nothing about you when you stepped through the door of that tavern, but you told me much in the way you moved and spoke. And you are avoiding my point."

Sun still did not wish to look at him, for her cheeks still burned with shame at the way she had spoken to him before. "What point is that?"

He fixed her with a look. "I am trying to tell you the story you need, Sun of the family Valgun. Yes, I know your family name as well. I think I know what you need to hear, and I am certain I know how badly you need to hear it. But I am trying, also, to make it a tale worth your time. Have I done a good enough job so far? Do you want to hear more?"

Sun felt many things. She was frightened, uncertain, and more than a little apprehensive about the shadowed wilderness they now rode through.

But above all of that, when she looked deep into her own heart, she had to admit one thing: she *did* want to hear what happened next.

"Yes," she said quietly. Then, louder, "Yes. Tell me. Please."

FIFTEEN

I TOLD YOU OF MAG FETCHING HER SPEAR FROM THE Reeve. You should know something of that spear, before I continue the tale.

You had heard, before I told you, of Mag's prowess in battle. But whatever you have heard, and however well I myself describe it, all tales are inadequate. Never have I seen or heard of such a master when it comes to combat. Her mastery extended to any weapon—in the battle of Northwood, she fought with a sword, you remember—but she became truly terrifying when her spear was in her hands.

I was with her when she got that spear, as it happens. We were in the western reaches of Dulmun. I had persuaded her to join the Silver Stirrups for a time, and that company had been summoned there for . . . sky above, I cannot remember. We were there for months, yet I cannot remember the conflict that brought us. Yet I remember every detail of the moment Mag found her spear. It is often that way when we age, and our memory begins to fail us.

The two of us had been given a day's leave, and we were spending it in Vaksom, the city that sprang up around the warlight Arod. It was my first time visiting Dulmun, and I found myself uncomfortable—meaning no offense. To an outsider, your people appear quick not only to laugh, but also to anger, and they almost seem to enjoy settling disagreements with their fists. It left me feeling on edge.

But Mag seemed curiously at home in Vaksom. It was strange to see the way she looked at everything, as if she was trying to solve a mystery. Her head was cocked and her eyes were narrowed, and it seemed that half-hidden thoughts swirled around each other in her mind.

"What is it, Mag?" I asked her. "You look pleased to be here, and at the same time confused."

"I suppose both are true," she said. "There is something familiar about this place, though I have never been here that I recall."

"Mayhap you came here as a child?" I said.

"Mayhap," she murmured.

Suddenly she stopped dead in the street, staring at a shop. I looked it over. It seemed to be the shop of a bladesmith, but a far grander one than I had ever seen. Two stories tall it stood. Its front windows were open, and in them were displayed blades of the highest quality. I saw swords, daggers, and spears, but also many strange weapons that I had never seen the like of. Too, I had never seen a smithy with someone standing guard, but there was one here—a large brute of a man with horribly scarred hands.

"You have good taste," I told Mag. "But I think your eyes are larger than your purse. Sellswords such as us could not bring the custom a place like this demands."

Mag did not appear to hear me. She only stepped towards the shop's door. As she approached, the guard barred her way and held up a hand.

"Stay yourself," he said, his voice rumbling like an ocean wave. "What business do you have here?"

"What sort of business do you expect?" said Mag. "I wish to buy a weapon."

The guard eyed her up and down. "You are no customer of this place. Begone."

"You do not know how much coin I am carrying," countered Mag.

"You could not carry enough coin on your person, and since you do not have a pack horse behind you—"

"Friend," I said quickly. "You are a hired sword like us, are you not?"

The guard's mouth twisted. "Not like you."

I spread my hands wide, giving him a friendly smile. "Oh, not a mercenary, certainly. But we all have something in common: we are paid to fight. You have a greater appreciation for the art of battle than most people could imagine—as do we. And my friend here is special. I swear to you that you have never seen her like in combat."

The guard arched an eyebrow as he looked down at Mag, who stood a good two heads shorter than he. "If you mean to intimidate me, you are not doing a good job."

"Not at all," I said. "But when someone ascends to her lofty heights of skill, they gain a rarefied taste for weapons of war. You may be right: we may not have enough coin to afford your master's astonishing wares. But can you not understand a desire to simply see them? Let her at least have the dream of fighting with such tools of war, though they may be fit only for the nobility who pay our wages."

His expression did not change a whit, and I thought my words had been for nothing—and, too, I feared that Mag might escalate matters, for that was a bad habit of hers in those days. But after a moment the guard drew aside, waving an admonishing finger at both of us.

"Disturb nothing," he said. "Touch nothing. And do not approach my master if she does not speak to you first."

"You have our word," I said, nodding my thanks and ushering Mag into the shop.

"I could have taken him," Mag muttered once we were safely away from the man.

"I know you could have," I said. "But it might have put a damper on our experience here. Now you can peruse the weapons without worrying about constables showing up."

It is customary for shopkeepers to put their finest wares on display in the windows, using them to draw in customers. But I could hardly have said the weapons in the window were any better than the ones we found inside. Every new blade I saw seemed to be the finest I had ever beheld, until I saw the next one. I am and have always been an archer first and foremost, but I know my way around a sword, and I found myself transfixed by those on display. They were made in the Dulmun fashion—longer and heavier than those in Calentin—but that did not prevent me from appreciating their quality.

After a moment I looked up and realized that Mag and I had become separated. I sought her out quickly, as I still did not trust her not to make trouble if anyone should bother her. I found her standing before a display of spears. The weapons were arranged in racks that held half a dozen each. These were no long infantry spears, meant for fighting in formation, and which are usually much taller than the soldiers that wield them. These were Dulmish dueling spears. If you have never seen one, they can appear a bit strange. They are usually only a little taller than the shoulder—just long enough to serve as a walking stick, not so long that they are burdensome for long journeys. Their spearheads are larger than those of infantry spears, and they have long edges so that they can be used to slice and cut, not just to pierce. There are smaller, curved blades just behind the head, almost like a hilt, that you can use to entrap and entangle the weapon of your opponent.

I had never seen anyone wield such a weapon before—after all, most of the battles I had seen had been formation fighting. It struck me as curious that Mag was so transfixed by the weapons, for I had had no inkling that she knew how to use them.

"Mag?" I said, for she did not appear to have seen me. "What is it?"

"These spears," she muttered, and it sounded almost as if she was talking to herself. "I . . . I almost remember."

"Remember what?"

She only shook her head. And then came a voice from close by, startling both of us out of our thoughts.

"It is rare to have someone lavish so much attention on my spears."

Mag and I turned quickly. Before us stood the woman who I knew must be the master of this shop. She was of medium height, but as broad as a barn. Her arms, like any good blacksmith's, were thicker than my thighs, and her torso had several more layers of weight over thick muscles. The back of her hair was done up in a tail, but the front cascaded like the wings of a crow wrapped around her moon-shaped face. Over her shoulder, I saw the door guard surveying us, his face stern but impassive.

"Do we have the honor of addressing the owner of this fine establishment?" I said, speaking just loud enough that I hoped the guard could hear my courtesy.

"You do," said the smith. "Smedda of the family Stalhert is my name."

"I am Albern of the family Telfer," I told her, placing a hand over my heart. "And this is Mag."

Smedda cocked her head. "Sellswords, I suppose. What brings you to my shop?"

"Why, only the desire to gaze upon your incomparable wares," I said.

"Flattering," said Smedda. "I am not in the habit of entertaining those who wish to peruse and not to buy, but courteous words can go far in changing my mind. I imagine you did much the same to Bronhil at the door, or he would not have let you in."

"We impressed upon your noblest and most loyal servant," I said, projecting my voice in Bronhil's direction with all my might, "that our appreciation for your work was nearly limitless. Truly, your purse must overflow with wealth from grateful patrons."

"Only one patron, really," said Smedda. "King Lannolf, of the family Valgun. Once I secured his custom, it is rare to find anyone else who can match the coin my wares fetch."

I had two curious sensations at the same time: I felt as though the walls were pressing in upon me, and at the same time it was as if I had shrunk to the size of a mouse, and the shop had become incomprehensibly vast. I gasped suddenly, realizing that I had forgotten to breathe for the space of several long heartbeats.

"You are King Lannolf's armorer," I said, my voice a mouse's squeak. Mag had stopped paying attention to the conversation and was looking at the spears again. I smacked her hard between the shoulder blades, trying to get her to turn around. She ignored me.

"I am one of his smiths," said Smedda. "He has others. And I rarely attempt armor. It is not my passion, and therefore my work is not as good as it could be. But when it comes to weapons: yes, I arm the king, and all his kin, and anyone else who catches his favor or fancy. And I am well rewarded for it."

At once I dropped into a deep bow. I noticed that Mag still seemed to be paying no attention to what we were saying, and I smacked her again. "It is our deepest honor to be in your presence."

"I can tell," said Smedda, eyeing Mag, who had not stirred despite my actions. "May I ask why you are so—"

"What do you call them?" said Mag, turning suddenly and pointing at the spears. "I have never . . . that is, I do not recall ever seeing spears like this before."

"They are rare, even here in Dulmun, and I have

seen them nowhere else," said Smedda. She stepped past Mag and lifted one of the spears from its rack, lowering it and running her fingers along its length. "They are called spontoons. Meant for a single fighter, not for soldiers in formation, but then you can tell that. Nobles today rarely seek them out, for they are not considered 'fashionable'—which just goes to show you how useless fashion is. If two fighters of equal skill face each other, one with a sword and one with a spontoon, I would bet half my considerable fortune on the one with the spear, every time."

"They are a weapon of Dulmun?" said Mag, as though she had not heard anything Smedda had said after that.

"They are," said Smedda. "The skill of their making was passed to me by my master, whose family has dwelled here since the time of Roth. As I said, I have never seen them in any of the other kingdoms, and I have visited all of them." She cocked her head again and regarded Mag carefully. "Would you like to feel it in your hands?"

"Yes," said Mag at once.

"Mag," I said, "are you sure that is wise? If you were to damage it in any way—"

"Do not worry," said Smedda. "I will not hold you accountable. There is a light in your friend's eyes, and I wish to see what it might illuminate. I have a small yard in back of my shop. Choose whichever spear you wish, and meet me there."

She set off for the back of the building at once, leaving Mag alone to choose her spear in peace. But Mag hardly seemed to need the privacy—she scarcely glanced at the rack before selecting one of the spears. Its haft was somewhat thicker than the others, its head a bit broader and a bit shorter.

Mostly, I noticed that it looked to be the most expensive spear on the rack. Mag had that habit, too—walking into any shop and choosing among its wares at random, she would inevitably gravitate towards the priciest item in the place.

But that thought fled my mind as Mag handled the spear. She tossed it lightly from hand to hand, and then she spun it on either side of her like a staff. The movement was natural and fluid. That was hardly a surprise, for I had seen Mag with all sorts of weaponry, and she was always formidable. But I could tell at once that this was different. The spear had become part of her almost from the moment she laid her hand upon it. Thunder did not crash in the sky, but it felt like it should have. A shaft of sunlight did not pierce through a high window to illuminate her, but it felt less like something that had not happened, and more like something that *should* have happened, but which the sky had forgotten about.

Silently I followed her out the back door into the yard. Smedda waited there—and to my great shock, she had thrown on a set of light padded armor, and in her hands was a blunted training spear of the same kind as Mag's.

"That looks good in your hands," said Smedda, nodding towards Mag's weapon.

"It feels . . . familiar," said Mag.

"I thought you said you had never seen such a weapon before," said Smedda.

"Not that I remember," said Mag. "Yet holding this one feels like embracing an old friend."

Smedda nodded slowly. "I have seen such things before, though rarely. Come. Let us spar, and we shall see what you can do with it."

A pit formed in my stomach. "I am not sure that is wise," I said at once, stepping between the two of them. "Mayhap you should let me face off against Mag." Thoughts raced through my mind of the unimaginable wrath we would bring down on ourselves if Mag were to injure the king of Dulmun's personal bladesmith.

"Afraid she will hurt me, are you?" said Smedda, and she laughed. "Do not be a fool. You know your friend better than I do, but even I know that that blade will not kiss my skin unless she means it to—and she does not mean it to. Do you, girl?"

"I swear I will do you no harm," said Mag solemnly, gripping the spear in both hands and taking a wide stance. Then she smirked. "No lasting harm, that is."

"That is the spirit," said Smedda, grinning. "Now, let me see what you can—"

And then suddenly she was on her back, the tip of Mag's spear a fingersbreadth away from her throat.

"What—" gasped Smedda. Her face scrunched up, for all the world as though she was searching for a distant memory. "You tripped me."

"Yes," said Mag. She put up her spear and lowered a hand to help Smedda rise. "Your reaction almost saved you, but it was just a tad too slow."

"A tad?" said Smedda, frowning. "I did not even know what had happened until it was done."

"Is the spear all right?" I said, leaning forwards and peering at it.

"You stop that," said Smedda, glaring at me and holding up a finger, like a grandmother scolding her progeny. "No warrior can fight while worrying about the state of the blade in their hands. No matter a weapon's value, no matter its heritage, when you fight with it, it has only one purpose: to be a tool with which you enact your will." She turned back to Mag. "If you would indulge me: I would like to try attacking you and see how you defend yourself. One of the great strengths of a spontoon is its use for protection as well as for aggression."

"Of course," said Mag. "Whenever you wish."

"First," said Smedda, going to the side of the yard. From the wall she pulled a battered practice shield, tossing it to Mag. "Use that. It is imperfectly balanced, but it should serve for this purpose."

Mag began to slip her left arm through the straps—

and Smedda struck before she was finished. But even the moment's distraction did not matter. Mag's shield was like a wall guarding her from harm, and wherever it could not protect her, the haft of the spear came in to block Smedda's swipes and turn her jabs. Mag danced around Smedda's every blow, barely even stepping back to avoid them.

I felt then, as I would go on to feel many, many times, the sheer awe of seeing Mag with that spear in her hand. She had already been a peerless warrior in my estimation. But in that moment—though I did not quite know it—she was taking her first steps on the road that would turn her into a legend.

After a short while of sparring, Mag finally turned the tables. Rather than blocking Smedda's thrust, she caught the spear between her own and the shield, and then twisted to flip it out of Smedda's hands. Finally, almost as an afterthought, she flipped the spear around and jabbed the butt of it hard into Smedda's belly. All Smedda's breath left her in a rush, and she fell on her rear on the sandy yard.

"My apologies," said Mag. "Instinct took over. You understand, of course."

"Of course," said Smedda ruefully, holding up a hand for Mag to help her again. "Well, that settles it. You have to buy that spear."

"What?" I said. "She could not possibly afford it. You said your prices—"

"Are considerable," said Smedda. "And I cannot

give you the spear for free. I have a reputation to uphold, and no warrior values a weapon they did not pay for—in gold, or in blood."

"I would value this spear," said Mag fervently.

Smedda grinned. "I imagine that is true. It belongs with you, and you with it. Therefore I will let you buy it for two hundreds of weights."

Even as my guts turned a somersault, Mag said, "Done."

"Mag!" I said. "That is more than either of us will earn in a year. If you paid for nothing else, if you avoided all costs for—"

"I may be green, but hardly any more so than you. I know full well what I am doing." Mag sighed and removed her shield, then held the spear out to Smedda. "I will return when I can. Please, hold it for me."

"I will hold it, but not for long," said Smedda. "Before I can allow you to take it, it must be enchanted."

Behind Smedda's back, I threw my hands into the air and tried to mouth "No!" to Mag. Enchantment was a service provided only by wizards trained at the Academy, and it was fantastically expensive, beyond the reckoning of anyone but royalty. Mag did not even glance at me, but only nodded at Smedda.

"And how much will that be?" said Mag.

Smedda waved a hand. "The enchantments are simple. They will protect the blade from wear and keep the haft from breaking. The spear will not be wreathed in magical flame or anything so ridiculous. I have a shipment bound for the Academy next week already, and I will include the spear with the rest of them, for the same cost."

I froze, my hands in midair where I had been trying to gesture to Mag that she should abandon this foolish idea. Now I cocked my head. Two hundreds of weights was already a bargain, even if Mag could not afford it. But with enchantment at no extra charge . . . that changed the nature of the deal considerably. I doubted if I could have resisted such an offer, and I knew Mag would never be able to.

"Done and done," said Mag. "I imagine I can write you here, as I acquire the funds I will need before I can retrieve the spear?"

"I told you already, I will not hold the spear that long," said Smedda. "You two are with the Silver Stirrups, yes? They will be in Dulmun for at least another half-year. Before you leave the kingdom, come and retrieve the spear. You can send me your payment later, or even in parts, as you are paid."

Still behind Smedda's back, I grabbed great fistfuls of my own hair, my face filled with delight as I looked at Mag. For her part, she seemed utterly thunderstruck, and it was a moment before she spoke.

"That is generous," said Mag.

"I can afford to be generous," said Smedda. "I do not know if you have heard, but I serve King Lannolf.

I trust you to send the payment when you can; only a great fool would try to cheat the king's own blade-smith, and you are not a great fool."

"You still extend a great deal of trust," said Mag. Where a moment ago she had sounded so self-assured that it annoyed me, now she seemed full of doubt. I almost thought she would refuse the deal. "The spear could be lost, or I could die in—"

"Ha!" barked Smedda—a single shout of laughter that I suspected was meant more to shut Mag up than to express mirth. "Girl, I *just* fought you. You, dying before you are able to pay me? You jest, and poorly."

Mag seemed at last to be overwhelmed. She sank to one knee in the sand of the yard and bowed her head towards Smedda.

"Thank you," she said softly. "You do me a far greater honor than I deserve, and I will not forget it."

"I expect you shall not," said Smedda. "But you honor me as well. Any craftsman has only one wish: to see their creations used well. King Lannolf and his kin are fine warriors, but when was the last time they went to war? The blades I make for them languish in training yards, or in fine halls where they are used as decoration. Fah! When you take this spear from me, you will take it and use it the way it was meant to be used. I could ask for nothing more."

Mag knelt there for a moment, silent, looking at the spear in her hand. In her eyes was some trouble, or some deep thought, at which I could not begin to guess. But it seemed clear the spear was more than a weapon to her.

I almost remember, she had said before, when I first found her looking at it.

But remembered what?

We left the shop soon after, and two months later we returned for the spear. Mag carried it ever afterwards, and it became part of her legend.

She never told me what she had almost remembered—not for many, many long years, anyway.

SIXTEEN

After leaving Northwood, we rode into the Greatrocks together, traveling up the same path I had used to come down out of them. It had taken me six days when I rode with Loren. Now, we took the journey more slowly, for I was still tender from the battle. I slept long each night, setting camp as soon as night fell and often rising hours before the sun. It was ten days before Mag and I got very deep into the mountains.

It surprised me how easily we both fell into old routines. There are little tricks one learns after years spent on campaign trails—the best way to unfurl and repack a bedroll, the tricks of choosing a campsite, the skill of falling asleep quickly and waking up with speed. It came somewhat more easily to me, for I had ridden a long trail just a few weeks ago, guiding Loren through the mountains. But though Mag had not left Northwood in years, she picked up our routine just as quickly as I had.

Though we rode as fast as we could with my tender condition, we kept a wary eye out in case of attack. Yet we saw no sign of the Shades, nor of any other creature, save for an occasional rabbit or game bird fit for hunting. The satyrs and harpies, if any remained, avoided us entirely.

In the middle of the third day, we came to the Shade stronghold in the mountains. Then, for the first time, I ordered Mag to slow. We approached the fortress slowly and with stealth. If the Shades were to stop anywhere in the Greatrocks, it would be here.

Leaving the horses behind us, we crawled up a steep slope that brought us to a lesser peak overlooking the fortress. We crawled on our bellies for the last few paces, poking our heads over the edge of the land to peer down.

There it sat: the stronghold about which I now had so many evil memories. It crouched on a rock platform like a lurking, malicious spider. There was a chasm below its eastern wall, and a stone bridge reached across the gap. It was mayhap seven paces wide and had only low stone walls for railings. It was from that bridge that Jordel had fallen to his doom, though he brought a great foe into the darkness with him. Barely visible from where we lay in the grass, I could see the long stone ramp that led down from the stronghold's west wall, falling away to the valley far below.

The stronghold itself, however, looked empty. I saw no signs of motion within, nor was there any indication that anyone had been there recently. From what I could see, it looked as though the Shades had passed straight through the fortress without stopping.

"No one there," said Mag.

"Not that we can see," I said. "We must still be cautious."

"When have I ever been incautious?"

"Always. Every time, everywhere."

"They had too many soldiers for them all to be hiding within those walls," she said, ignoring my answer. "Not even if all of them were clustered together and standing as close as lovers."

"Yet they may have left behind a rearguard," I said. "I do not mean to say we have to inspect the whole fortress. But when we pass through it, let us be careful."

She crawled back down the slope and away from the ridge. I followed her back to the horses, and together we rode out across the narrow stone bridge towards the stronghold. I paused for a moment in the middle of the span, looking at the low stone wall that rimmed it. Xain had used fire to burn words into the stone there, a eulogy for Jordel. But Mag did not notice, and she pressed on without stopping. I hurried to catch up with her.

The eastern gate stood open, as did the western gate on the other side. The wide courtyard within the walls was just as empty as it had appeared from the outside. The only thing to be found was some hay scattered about the place, floating and scraping along the ground in the mountain wind. Mag stopped in the middle of the yard and dismounted. I did the same. She looked about, brows raised.

"A good fortress," she said. "The walls are strong."

"Yet not infallible," I said.

"Hm," she said. "No walls are infallible. No enemy beyond reach."

I grinned. "Do you speak of the Shades, or the weremage?"

Mag smirked. "There appears to be no one here. We should ride on. But hold a moment. You have a loose strap."

She stepped up, fiddling with my saddle. I stared at her. My straps were tight, and we both knew it. Once she drew close, she spoke in a low voice.

"There are satyrs watching us. On the rocky slopes above the walls. Fetch something from my saddlebags. It will give you an excuse to look."

I went to the other side of her horse and unbuckled one of the pouches hanging from the saddle. My eyes slid up the side of the mountain that towered over us. Tiny flashes of movement caught my gaze as satyrs ducked back out of sight. I took out a waterskin and brought it back to Mag.

"There are several of them," I said, handing her the water skin. "But they do not seem interested in troubling us. Likely they are only keeping watch. We are past the border of their homeland, after all."

Mag took a small swig of water and handed it to me. As I drank, she murmured, "They will have seen where the Shades went. We should ask them."

I pursed my lips and put the stopper back in the waterskin. "Agreed. But try not to kill them, will you?"

She arched an eyebrow. "I thought they gave you a great deal of trouble when last you came this way."

"They did, at the orders of their elders," I said. "And their elders are under the sway of another."

"The Shades?"

"Whoever leads the Shades," I said. "The satyrs spoke of a Lord."

"Satyrs have no lords."

"No, they do not. To hear them speak of one worried me more than anything else we found in these mountains."

"That is little concern of ours now. But let us get our hands on one of them, and we will have some answers about the weremage."

I finished pretending to dig through her saddlebags and returned to my horse. "And I will have them answer for other things as well."

We mounted again and rode through the western gate, down the long stone ramp into the valley. I found no good excuse to look back at the satyrs shadowing us, but every so often I would hear the soft clatter of hooves on the rocks high above. They were still there.

I knew we had to lure them into open lands, as far from any slopes as possible. Satyrs can nearly fly up a mountainside, and they could rain arrows down on us. But on open ground, they were no more nimble than a human. Only there would we have any chance of taking one of them alive.

To tell the truth, and despite my words to Mag, I found myself filled with anger that almost defied reason. Yes, the satyrs had only acted upon the directions of their leaders. But they had still nearly gotten me killed, along with all of my friends. That was not easy to forgive, though I was trying. After all, satyrs are not quite beasts, but neither are they quite human.

Not far from the bottom of the stone ramp was a small cluster of trees, a little wood that bent and huddled over the thin stream that ran through the middle of the valley. I led Mag towards it. The satyrs would think we were merely watering ourselves and the horses. But if they tried to approach us among the trees, we would be able to take them by surprise.

Though it was not very late in the day, the sun had already hidden itself behind the tips of the western mountains above. Dismounting, we ducked in among the shadows of the trunks, quickly losing ourselves among the trees. Once we were a good distance in, I stopped Mag and drew her against the side of an old beech tree. Together we looked back in the direction we had come.

There were the satyrs. They were making an attempt at stealth, but they were not used to it on such open terrain. They approached the trees warily, darting between brush and rocks with their awkward, loping gait. I counted six of them. Not an inconsiderable group, but against Mag and me they stood little chance.

"Let us tether the horses," I said. "We do not want them to run off during the fight." The beasts were already nickering nervously, for the satyrs had approached from upwind. My gelding eyed me as though trying to plan the right time to bolt.

We lashed the horses to a tree deeper in the wood and then returned to the beech tree. The satyrs were creeping between the trunks now, heads darting nervously back and forth in search of us. I had my bow in hand, and Mag had her spear and shield. We waited in total silence, listening as the creatures came closer.

Mag nudged me with her spear, and we sprang.

I fired two arrows in quick succession. One satyr went down with a shaft in its leg, another with fletching sticking out of its arm. Mag swung her spear in an arc, slamming the flat side of the spearhead into the temple of a third. It fell with a pathetic bleat. The other creatures screamed in fear, but they did not flee. They leaped towards us, flailing with clubs and short stone axes.

I got off one more shot, and another satyr fell with an arrow in its shoulder. Then they were too close, and I had to draw my sword. But there were only two left, and Mag and I made quick work of them. Mag blocked one blow with her shield before piercing her foe's thigh with her spear. I backed up step by step, warding off my foe's club with wide sweeps of my sword, until Mag came around behind her and slammed her shield into the back of the creature's head. It fell to the ground, senseless.

Looking up, I saw the other satyrs fleeing for their lives. The ones with leg wounds limped away, while the ones with maimed arms fled in great, bounding leaps. The first satyr Mag had downed had regained its senses, and it stumbled out of the woods, swaying as if drunk. That left only the creature on the ground before us now.

"Rope," said Mag. I nodded and went to my gelding, fetching a coil from one of the saddlebags.

SEVENTEEN

LONG BEFORE THE SATYR AWOKE, WE HAD HER bound to a tree a few paces from the river. We had set up a campsite for the night. When the sun fell, we started a small fire. I knew its light might be visible through the trees, but that worried me little. The satyrs were few in this part of the mountains, and they seemed to be even fewer since the Shades had passed through.

After a while our captive stirred, her head lolling back and forth before snapping up. One of her horns had a large chip near the top of its curve. She bleated angrily at us, but she winced with pain even as she did it.

"Hello," I said. "We have some questions."

"Die, human," hissed the satyr.

"No, I am afraid that is not the answer we are looking for," I said. "A weremage passed through these mountains, leading the humans who fled west from Northwood. What do you know of her?"

The satyr looked away. "I know nothing of what you speak."

"Come now," I said. "You speak the human tongue well. That tells me you are wise. Surely you have heard which way she and her friends went."

"I know better than to speak to you." The satyr tried to spit at me, but the gobbet fell short, landing on the ground by my feet.

"Let us start with something simpler," I said. "What is your name?"

She glared at me and said nothing.

"I shall tell you ours, if you wish," I said. "This is Mag. And I am Albern, of the family Telfer."

She only scowled harder. "I know your name, human. You tricked Tiglak. You made him betray us."

"I did no such thing," I replied. "I spared Tiglak's life in exchange for safe passage."

"He had no right," said the satyr. "The elders punished him for his cowardice."

That made me angry. I had known Tiglak for a long time. Humans and satyrs will never be friends,

I fear, but I respected him, and I like to think he respected me.

"He was both brave and honorable," I said. "Yet he knew I could kill him if I wished, and he hoped his elders might be more merciful. He could have fled into the mountains in shame, but he returned, courageously, and faced their judgement. It is not my fault, nor his, that they were cruel in that judgement. I ask again: what is your name?"

She tossed her head, but some of the fury in her eyes had died. I guessed that she, too, thought better of Tiglak than she was trying to lead us to believe. "Greto," she said at last.

"Greto," I said. "Do you see? That was not so hard."

"Now, Greto," said Mag. "As we have said, we require more answers. What can you tell us about the weremage?"

Greto's eyes burned with fury. "Your ugly human words are meaningless."

"Ah, I forgot," I said. "A weremage is a shape-changer. A human wizard who can take other forms."

"Pah," said Greto. "Your wizards are nothing to us. I know nothing of any skin-shifter."

"What of the Shades?" said Mag. "Which way did they go?"

Greto's dumbfounded look was too perfect to be false. "The what?"

"The humans who wear blue and grey," I said.

"They are called Shades, and they passed through the mountains. Where did they go?"

A hunted look came over Greto's face, and she dropped her gaze to the ground. "I do not know."

"You are an awful liar," observed Mag. She lifted her spear and placed the tip gently on Greto's shoulder. "I thought we were past the point where you would try to deceive us."

Another snarl broke out on Greto's face, but she relented. "They went north through the mountains. We did not follow them past the next bend in the valley floor. But a small party of them left the others."

"And went where?" I said.

"West, towards our home," said Greto.

Mag and I tensed in the same instant. "Are they still there?" said Mag. "Are they there *now?*"

"I have been away for several days," said Greto, sounding like nothing so much as a plaintive child. "I do not know."

"Was there a woman with them?" said Mag. "Skin the color of a satyr horn, and black braided hair?"

Greto sneered. "All humans look like humans to—"

Faster than blinking, Mag turned the spear so that the edge of it was pressed to Greto's throat.

"Yes!" cried Greto. "Yes, the woman went west, into our lands!"

"Why would she go there?" I asked. "I know from experience that you are not kind to trespassers."

"Sometimes they—the Shades—they visit our elders. They speak with them, delivering messages and directions from the Lord."

"Is that where the weremage is going?"

"I do not know." Greto's eyes widened as Mag pushed the spearpoint forwards, just a hair. "I do not know! I swear it! She may be!" she bleated.

Mag dropped the spearpoint to the ground. Greto relaxed for a moment.

"My apologies," said Mag.

Greto looked confused until Mag brought the butt of the spear spinning around and slammed it into the satyr's face. Her head crashed back against the tree with a *thud* and then lolled forwards.

"West," I said.

"Yes," said Mag.

"The western mountains are deep in satyr territory—in the very heart of their home."

Mag shrugged. "We have already said we will march into the middle of the Shades' forces if need be. The satyrs cannot be worse."

"They are not more fearsome," I said with a sigh. "But neither do they bear as much blame as the Shades for what has befallen us. I hope you will bear that in mind."

Her expression softened. "Of course I will. And I do not think they bear any great love for our enemies. If we remove the Shades from their homeland, they may even be grateful."

I gave a short, barking laugh. "You have much to learn about satyrs. If the weremage aims to speak with them, she will seek out their elders. Humans are forbidden from even seeing elders, on pain of death."

"Yet it seems the Shades visit them on occasion."

"Traditions may change," I said with a shrug. "Yet I doubt we will be afforded the same courtesy. We should be ready for a fight."

She grinned. "Have you ever known me to be otherwise? We should rest now and set off early tomorrow. I will take the first watch."

She went to the edge of the camp and sat on a low, moss-covered rock there. I went to unfurl my bedroll, trepidation in my heart. Mag was a peerless warrior, but we meant to march straight into the homes of creatures who had little love for us. I feared that if things went horribly wrong, even Mag's considerable skills might not be enough to keep her alive. And if the Uncut Lady could not escape her doom, what hope did I have to save her?

EIGHTEEN

The next day, Kaita rode west out of the Greatrocks with her party of six Shades. In the mountains' western foothills, she stopped her horse and turned to the soldiers accompanying her.

"And now we part," she said. "Once you have finished with the satyrs, return to the Watcher. You should find Tagata there, for Rogan will be in Dorsea by now."

"Very well," said Ertu, his beard twitching as he frowned. "And can you make the journey to Lan Shui unaided?"

"You need not worry for me," said Kaita.

"Yet I may if I wish," said Ertu. "That demon woman from Northwood is chasing you, not us."

"I can care for myself," said Kaita.

"I hope that is true," said Ertu. He extended a hand. Kaita grasped his wrist firmly, and they shook. "Fare well, until we meet again. Until life ends."

"Until life ends."

He turned and rode away, and the rest of the Shades accompanied him. Kaita did not ride on, but sat watching them for a moment. She had joined the Shades many years ago. She loved Rogan, as he loved her. But Rogan's affection extended to all who wore the deathly livery, and in that he was different from Kaita. The Shadeborn, like Tagata— and Trisken, death keep him—were one thing. But Kaita could never muster any great love for the rank and file soldiers like the ones riding away now, half of whom served for love of coin and not from belief.

Yet Ertu believed. Yet Kaita disdained him, and she did not know why.

She sighed as the last blue cloak vanished around a fold in the land. Turning her horse, she struck out for Lan Shui. She had to reach it before nightfall, or she would lose her horse.

Lan Shui is no great burg. A mere pinpoint on a map compared to Bertram farther west, and not even so big as Northwood used to be. It sits near the place where the Blackwind River comes tumbling out of the

Greatrocks. There are many beautiful falls in that area, and it gives Lan Shui a chilled and often-misted air—which is excellent for tales and for atmosphere, but horrible for wooden buildings, which often warp and rot. "Rich as a carpenter in Lan Shui" was once a saying in those parts, and it might still be.

Despite its proximity to Bertram, which is the second-largest city in Dorsea and was once that kingdom's capital, Lan Shui is a quiet, uneventful place, for it is bordered on the west by a sharp and insurmountable spur in the land, as though the Greatrocks were kicking up one last time before letting the earth lie flat. That spur cannot be traveled across, but must be ridden around, and that adds half a week to any journey between Lan Shui and the King's road.

In other words, it is the perfect sort of town for one to go to when they wish to avoid being found.

Kaita approached in the afternoon, careful to wait out of sight in a small wood just visible from the town. Soon a young man, hardly more than a boy, came to her amid the trees. He had a sallow face and bulging eyes.

"You are she?"

"If by 'she' you mean a servant of our father, then yes," said Kaita. "Are you not supposed to ask me for a password?"

He avoided her gaze. "I . . . forgot it."

"Fool," spat Kaita. "What if I were one of our enemies? You still do not know that I am not. We do not play at some child's game."

"Of course," mumbled the boy. "I am sorry."

Her nostrils flared. "Sorry" would not save them from the King's law if it sniffed them out in this town. "I care little for your apologies. Can you get me within the walls?"

The boy ducked his head. "I can. No one will see you. My name is Pantu, by the way."

"I do not remember asking for your name. Get moving."

He took the reins of her horse and set off, and Kaita followed. First he took her to a part of the eastern wall that was out of sight of any gate, and then he led her along it until they reached the south entrance. No guards stood there to watch them enter.

"That was simple," said Kaita. "I could have done it myself."

"The constables and guards are much preoccupied during the day," said Pantu. His voice grew hushed as he continued. "And besides, only the night is dangerous now."

Kaita gave a grim smile.

They moved wordlessly after that, passing through the streets until they reached an old, abandoned-looking building near the center of the town. A woman came to take their horses without having to be called. After they made sure no one was nearby to see, Kaita followed Pantu into the home, where they both threw back their hoods.

The front room was wide and low. In the back wall was set a stone hearth with no fire, and around it sat three people in thick wooden chairs. They turned as one to see Kaita and her companion standing in the doorway, and all three of them shot to their feet at once. One of them, a brawny woman with her grey hair in a braid, took a step forwards and looked at Kaita in bewilderment.

"Kaita," she said. "At last."

"Happy to see me, Dellek?" said Kaita, giving her a wry smile.

"Always." Dellek came and embraced her. "Ever since we received word you were coming, I have eagerly awaited your arrival. Some of us—including myself—wanted very much to join the rest of you in Northwood."

"There were more than enough of us to do what needed to be done," said Kaita. "Now, let me see how you have progressed in your work for our father."

Dellek nodded and led her deeper into the house. In the back room, she opened the secret door, revealing a dank stone staircase leading deep into the earth. After Dellek lit a torch, Kaita followed her down the steps. Dellek held the torch high as they descended, and Kaita kept a hand on the wall to steady herself. The stone beneath her feet was slippery.

A wide chamber opened up before them. The walls

had been formed by alchemists, and were lined with smooth ridges. High above, the wooden ceiling looked incredibly fragile compared to the thick rock walls, and between the boards, minute shafts of sunlight pierced the shadows, occasionally blocked as someone above walked across them.

But Kaita's gaze was drawn immediately to the massive cauldron in the center of the room. It was more than two paces across, and shallow, and a black liquid bubbled within it, hardly illuminated by the many torches on the walls. Three Shades stood in the room, tending the cauldron nervously, careful not to touch it. They looked briefly up at the newcomers, but when Dellek gave them a nod, they returned to their tasks.

Kaita could feel the power emanating from the room. The smell was heady, powerful, intoxicating—even a bit overwhelming. For an instant, she had the mad desire to cup her hands and drink of the liquid. The magic within her bristled, sensing the energy that saturated the air. It filled her with exhilaration, anxiety, and anger in equal measure.

She knelt to look beneath the cauldron. The flames were well tended and did not quite reach the iron bottom of the cauldron. She could feel the vicious heat of them, though they were small and she was well over a pace away. Standing, she turned to Dellek.

"You are being wary not to stoke the flames too high?"

"Of course," said Dellek.

"And it is having the desired effect?"

Dellek gave a grim smile and tossed her grey braid back over her shoulder. "Indeed, it is far more effective than we had dreamed it would be."

"Very well," said Kaita. "Let us return upstairs. I must speak with you privately."

Dellek took her back up into the house, and then she climbed another staircase to take her to the second floor. The largest bedroom had a small antechamber, and within it were two chairs and a small table with some wine. Dellek poured them both a cup and gestured for Kaita to sit.

"Well?" she said. "Ever since I knew you were coming, I have wondered what this was all about."

"I am being pursued," said Kaita. "By a woman from Northwood named Mag and her companion, whose name is Albern."

"Pursued?" said Dellek, arching an eyebrow. "I imagine you must not want them dead, then, or you would have used your magic."

I want them dead more than you can believe, thought Kaita. But she nodded, as though Dellek had the right of it. "I am leading them home."

Dellek went very still, and her eyes widened. "Really?"

"Yes," said Kaita. "And I need them to know that that is where I am running to. But Dellek—they must *not* learn about anything else the Shades are doing here. Albern is a master tracker, and I came through the mountains with a party of six horse. He will have a trail leading him to Lan Shui. But I need one of your people to give them the next part of the trail."

Dellek pursed her lips, running a finger along the edge of her wine cup. "Interesting. There are a few here who I can trust to—"

Kaita stopped her by putting a hand on her arm. "That might not be wise. This woman . . . Mag . . ." She almost winced as she remembered the pain of Mag's strikes. "She is a killer. Whoever gives her this information could very well die."

Dellek's mouth twisted. "Say no more, then. I will send that boy Pantu, the one who brought you into the city today. He knows nothing of the underground chamber, and he is little more than a nuisance, anyway. Completely useless."

That drew a small smile from Kaita. This was one reason she and Dellek got along so well. Dellek understood that, whatever Rogan might say, not *everyone* was worthy. Not everyone was useful. Rogan would not approve of such a course of action, but he would never know.

"Excellent," said Kaita. "I will remain here to ensure everything goes well."

Dellek drained the rest of her wine and stood. "It will. And now, let me get you arranged in a chamber. I imagine you could use a long sleep."

As if the words were a spell, exhaustion came crashing down on Kaita. She had been on the road for a week, and had not had a proper rest since the battle of Northwood. "I could," said Kaita, getting to her feet. "Thank you, Dellek."

All is well, she thought, as Dellek led her to a small bedchamber and she began to undress herself. *Come to me, my prey. Find me in Lan Shui.*

NINETEEN

The next morning, we released Greto. Before we loosened the rope that held her to the tree, I fixed her with a hard look.

"We will release you now," I told her. "You are free to go your own way, as long as you leave us alone. We will not trouble you again, and I hope we can expect the same courtesy."

She merely spat in response. At least she did not seem to be aiming for me, this time.

"I thought you might say something like that," I told her. "But before you decide to run home and tell your clan what transpired here today, I would bid you to remember Tiglak. He, too, thought he could rely on the mercy of your elders."

Her eyes filled with fear at that, and I was satisfied. I untied her, and she bounded away south, in the same direction her fellows had run after our fight the day before.

"Do you really think she will leave us be?" said Mag.

"I know no reason why she should not," I replied. "She may stalk us as she did before, but she will only see us heading west, and she knows we are chasing the weremage. She would never guess that we mean to find the satyr elders and threaten them, because, of course, that is an incredibly idiotic course of action."

Mag gave an easy smile and began to fetch food to break our fast. "Then we will have the element of surprise."

I laughed and helped her prepare the meal. As we ate, I began to form a plan. I had some vague idea of where the satyrs were—many treks through the mountains had brought me to their borders, so I knew the edges of the lands, at least. Most of their homes were in the western end of the mountain range. They had dwellings in the caves there, which they had connected with a series of tunnels so that they could travel through the mountains with relative ease. But satyrs did not naturally dwell within the earth except when they denned to birth and raise their children. More often, they were to be found in the open air, leaping from slope to slope and across all the flatlands along the valley.

Therefore I guided Mag west, across the valley floor and into the mountains on the other side. There were no roads or paths in this part of the mountains, but we did not need them. The trail of the Shades was plain before us. Hundreds of feet had trampled the ground, so that it was churned and muddy, like a farmer's field laid open and ready for fresh planting. Sometimes groups of bootprints would break off from the rest, turning north or south and away from the main march.

And then, on the second day, the army's tracks turned and headed north, deep into the mountains. But the tracks of a smaller party carried on west from the spot. They were few—mayhap a half dozen, no more. We stopped on the spot and ate our midday meal, enjoying the warm sun above, and then pressed on as soon as we had finished.

I continued to lead Mag west, until we came to the end of the valley and the beginning of the mountains again. There we found a wide road leading up into the peaks. It was bordered by perilous drops in places, but wide and firm enough to provide no great danger. I had never traveled this road before, but in past years I had espied it from afar. I guessed that it was no construct of some long-gone king, as the Shade stronghold had been. This track was not paved at all, but had been worn into the ground by many feet—or, more likely, many hooves. It looked like an animal track that had been adopted by the satyrs, who would not have cared how steep it was or how high the drops on the side. It branched often, but I always led Mag on the most well-worn routes. Those, I hoped, would take us to the heart of the satyrs' domain. The side tracks would likely lead to smaller camps and settlements throughout the mountains, or mayhap even into the heart of the cave system the satyrs had built.

The horses did not seem to enjoy the journey much. They had some difficulty on the steeper parts of the road, and on occasion I had to find another way around, a gentler slope that would allow us to circle back to the main path.

I should have been reassured by the absence of any satyrs watching us, but I found myself growing more and more perturbed as we pressed on. We had passed the borders of their lands already. All my experience told me they should have attacked us long ago. But there was no sign of them. I could not fathom it, though I spent much thought on it during the day when we rode and during the night when I stood watch. I could understand if the bulk of them had retreated farther into their caves and mountains when the Shades had passed this way. But their patrols should have increased. Instead they had vanished entirely.

It was the third day after we had left the valley floor that I finally spotted signs of the satyrs again. We came around a bend in the path to find ourselves suddenly standing in plain view of one of their villages. It was little more than a glorified camp, with a few huts built of wood and mud, along with caves in the mountainside where I guessed most of them dwelled. Several campfires could be seen on the ground outside the dwellings, but none of them were lit. The place had been abandoned.

"Where did they go?" said Mag.

"I wish I knew," I said. "Let us hope they are only hiding from the Shades."

We looked through the huts and poked our heads into the caves. The satyrs were not hiding—they had abandoned their homes. All their supplies and tools were gone. Though that seemed an ominous sign, it actually eased my mind somewhat. It meant they had had time to plan their departure, and had not been driven to flee in terror. I had harbored half-formed fears of some great force sweeping through the mountains, driving these creatures before it. But whatever had prompted them to go, they had had some forewarning.

Still, I did not feel comfortable making camp in their village, so we found a flat shelf not much farther along on which to stay the night. I was especially dour as we laid out our bedrolls that evening, and Mag could not help but notice.

"Your frown will freeze on your face soon," she remarked.

"I like the look of things less and less the farther we go," I said.

"Yet our way has been easy so far."

"Easy, yet troubling. Do you not wonder what drove all the satyrs out of this region?"

She shrugged. "You are the guide, not I."

"I *am* the guide," I grumbled, "and a wise woman listens to her guide when he says something is wrong."

Mag chuckled at that. Then she pointed over her head at the horses. "What are you going to name your gelding, by the by? Bad luck cannot be far off if you continue to ride him nameless."

"You think I am not already overwhelmed with bad luck? I am by your side, am I not?"

A rock came flying, landing right between my legs. I gasped and rolled on my side, clutching myself as I fought a wave of nausea.

"You have not chosen a name, then?" she said innocently. "Come, Albern, you know you tempt fate."

"Dorsean superstition," I wheezed.

"If you have not noticed, we are in Dorsea, or near enough to it," she retorted. "Some guide you are, forgetting which kingdom you are in."

I blinked away the last of my tears. "Very well," I said grumpily. "I shall call him Foolhoof, if it pleases you."

She raised her brows. "I cannot say that it does."

"And your mare? You have not named her, either."

"Oh, but I did," said Mag. "She is called Mist."

I snorted. "Mist. You are like Loren, naming her black horse Midnight. No imagination at all."

"Midnight *is* a foolish name," said Mag, smirking.

"She is a child with dreams of being a legend," I said, waving a hand. "What do you expect? Sky above, she calls herself the Nightblade."

Mag laughed. "Still, you wound me. Mist is a better name by far."

"I think you made it up on the spot," I retorted. "If you named her before this very moment, I will eat my bow."

"You have caught me," said Mag, bowing her head.

"You see? And you had the gall to say I tempted fate. What tragedy will your destiny heap upon you for such a transgression?"

The smile on her face died at once. "I think it has given me quite enough already," she said, in a horribly forced attempt at nonchalance.

I cursed myself for my foolish words. Yes, we had remembered many of our old habits from our mercenary days. But I had forgotten that campfire talk was supposed to steer away from bad fortune, and especially the grief of the near past.

The rest of our conversation that night was stilted and awkward, and I was grateful when I finally rolled myself in blankets to sleep.

Far, far away, in the woods northwest of Lan Shui, a creature stalked through the woods.

Through the trees, it could see the soft glow of firelight shining through the windows of a human home. And even through the walls, it could smell its prey inside. There were several of them—enough to feed on for days.

The creature knew that would not sate its deeper, stronger hunger. But it was enough for now.

It came out of the woods and stalked forwards, approaching the house's front door. Each motion was virtually silent. The smell of the humans in the house was nearly overwhelming. It ran a black tongue along its browning teeth.

Suddenly there came the sound of padded feet inside the house, and a snuffling. Then a low, rumbling growl.

A surge of hate and hunger ripped through the creature. A dog. It had been so focused on its emptiness and the smell of the humans, it had missed the scent of the dog.

Careless.

It tried to step back, away from the house. But its broken claw caught on the ground, and it stumbled.

Inside the house, the dog's growls turned to full-throated barking. Chairs scraped against a wooden floor as the humans stirred.

"Oku?" said one of the prey. "What is it?"

The creature screeched with impatience and lunged, bursting through the front door into the house. Inside, the prey shot to their feet. They had weapons close at hand, and they seized them. Standing before them was the dog: a large wolfhound almost a pace in height, brown with black spots in its fur.

The creature screamed in hatred and hunger.

Snarling furiously, the dog launched itself at the creature. But a wild swipe staved the beast off, and it slunk back, favoring a light gash in its left flank. The prey drew closer to each other and took a step forwards.

"Liu!" cried one of them. "Run into the woods! Take Oku!"

"Mama!"

The creature's eyes shifted. Behind the three larger prey, one of their offspring stood at the back of the room, cowering in terror. Its eyes were wide, and palpable fear radiated from it.

"Go!" cried another of the prey—young, but nowhere near as young as the child. "Oku, tiss!"

The wolfhound bounded towards the child, taking his tunic in its teeth and tugging. Reluctantly, the child rose to its feet and scurried for the house's back door, vanishing into the night. The creature dismissed it at once. It had been a tiny thing, and there were three full-sized prey still in the house—not enough to completely satisfy the hunger, but enough to stave it off for days.

Roaring in fury, it leaped and sank its claws into its first victim.

TWENTY

The day after we camped near the empty satyr town, we reached the crest of the western Greatrocks. Then, for the first time, I took us off the most well-worn path and up one of the side routes that climbed south, riding even higher into the peaks. South, because that was the direction of the heart of satyr territory, at least as far as I was aware. If we meant to find the elders, I was confident we would find them there.

It was not long before we started to come upon more satyr encampments and villages. These were less populated than I had imagined they would be, but they were not entirely abandoned. I spent almost half an hour scouting the first one we came upon. Many satyrs moved from building to building, but from what I could tell, there were no fighters in the village, only children and those caring for them. The warriors were elsewhere. I guessed we would find them with the elders. That was not an entirely comforting prospect.

When I had inspected the village to my satisfaction, I returned to Mag. "We must hide the horses somewhere and leave them," I said. "If we bring them any farther, they will certainly alert the satyrs to our presence."

"There are no woods this high up to hide them from view," said Mag.

"We need a cave," I said. "The satyrs do not dwell in all of them, nor are all of them connected. We should be able to find an empty one without too much trouble."

And that proved to be true; in less than an hour of searching, we found just what we needed. The cave was too shallow for the satyrs to have bothered with, but more than deep enough to conceal our horses. We hobbled them and tethered them to a rock that thrust up out of the ground. Foolhoof tossed his head as I wrapped his reins around the stone, and I gave him a reproachful look.

"Do not even think of chewing your way free," I told him. "I will find you if you do."

"Mist would never think of doing such a thing," said Mag haughtily.

I shook my head and led her from the cave.

Without the horses, it was easy to slip past the first satyr village, and the second. We passed them every few spans now, clusters of crude buildings built onto whatever flat ground was available on those high slopes. Occasionally the villages had a sentry posted nearby, but they were easy to bypass. They appeared to be weaker members of their kind, satyrs with missing or twisted limbs, and they leaned heavily on their weapons.

Always we found our way back to the main path, and now I began to notice markings upon it. They were not the prints of cloven hooves, but of heavy boots. Other humans.

"Look," I told Mag, pointing at the tracks. "It seems we are not too late. We might find our foe at the end of this road."

"I am right more often than you give me credit for," said Mag. "Let us hurry. The weremage could be dead before the day's end."

We were neither of us wont to bloodthirst, but hunting a foe will quicken anyone's pulse. We pressed on faster. Yet despite our speed, it was early evening before we found what we sought. To our right, the sun was setting in a display that was as beautiful as it was fiery. It painted the ground in hues of red and gold, and the scant clouds in the sky blazed like the fires of war. But the light had not yet faded when we came upon a great gathering of satyrs, and I had to be quick to rush Mag behind cover before we were spotted. Together we crouched behind a boulder shaped like a black, broken tooth.

On what looked like the top of the highest mountain for many leagues, a great circular space had been trodden flat by what looked like centuries' worth of satyr hooves. Upon that space were now gathered mayhap two scores of satyr warriors, wearing wooden shields on their arms and hefting axes and clubs. They stood in a half-ring two rows deep, all their attention fixed on the center of the circle. There sat ten carved stone chairs, though only eight of them were occupied. The satyrs upon those chairs were old, wizened, and grey of fur, and I knew we had found the elders of the clan.

But almost immediately, my attention went from the elders to the humans who stood before them. They numbered six, and they wore clothing of blue and grey. The Shades were here, just as Greto had said they would be.

"Can you see the weremage?" whispered Mag.

"I cannot," I said. "Not from here."

"She may have taken another form."

"I cannot hear anything. We must get closer. I want to be certain before we attack."

"Very well." Now that we were here, I found myself quite reluctant to draw any closer to the satyrs. But my desire to find the weremage overpowered my caution, as did my curiosity. I wanted to know what the Shades were saying that put such fear in the faces of the satyr elders.

We left the cover of the rock and crept along a slope that fell away from the platform. We were careful to keep ourselves concealed, but it hardly seemed necessary. No one, neither the Shades nor the satyrs, looked away from what was going on. At last, when we were only a score of paces away, I bade Mag to hide again, for now we could clearly make out the Shades' words. Again we ducked out of sight, each of us poking one eye into view to see what was going on.

"—after you killed the messenger?" one of the Shades—a burly man with a thick, bristling beard—was saying. At first I dismissed him, searching only for the weremage. Then my better sense caught up with me, and I realized the weremage might very well have changed her appearance. Though why would she do so, when she had no idea we were watching her?

The elder in the center of the row shifted in her stone chair and bleated an answer in the satyrs' tongue. I spoke but a little of their language and did not understand her, but there was a clear defensive tone in her voice, like a child who had been caught in wrongdoing and was inventing an outlandish tale to excuse it.

An elder at the end of the row spoke in the common tongue. "Elder Seko says: Tiglak's debt was paid. Then we drove the humans towards you. We have told you this already."

"But what you have *not* told us," growled the Shade, "is why you did not tell us of these interlopers."

More bleating from Seko, and then the translator spoke again. "Elder Seko says: the Lord never said to tell you. He said not to let any humans pass through the valley and live."

The Shade thrust a finger towards the center elder. "Which is exactly what you did!"

The translator quivered at the anger in his voice, but now one of the other elders spoke. He was not quite so hoary as the first, and there was a clear current of anger in his words. The translator looked uncomfortable, but after a sharp reproach from the elder, she spoke. "Elder Hagan says: we allowed nothing," she said, her voice shaking. "We brought them to you. You allowed them to escape, not us."

I looked at Mag behind our rock. "We were right on that count, it seems."

"Never mind that," said Mag. "I cannot see the Shades clearly enough to tell if the weremage is among their number."

"What of the leader?" I said. "Satyrs respect only strength and size. She would have better luck speaking to them as a large warrior than in her natural form. You saw how slight she was."

Mag frowned. "So it could be her, but how can we know?"

Before I could answer, something happened in the

circle. The Shades seemed to have had enough of the satyrs' arguments. Their leader raised his hand, palm pointing towards the elders, and the circle fell quiet.

"Enough," said the Shade. "The Lord is tired of your excuses. There will be payment in blood. Two of you may present yourselves, or we can make the choice for you."

My stomach turned. The elders cowered in their seats, and as they did so, I glanced at the two empty stone chairs. Did I see bloodstains on the rock, or was it my imagination? Had this Lord already demanded such a sacrifice once in the past?

Elder Seko looked at the others. They chattered back and forth in their own tongue for a moment, with Seko sounding increasingly desperate. Finally, Elder Hagan shot to standing and barked a series of short, loud words. The rest of them fell silent.

Slowly, Elder Seko stood from her chair. Beside her, another elder, almost as grey and wizened, stood as well. Together the two of them stepped towards the Shades.

"The two oldest," I muttered.

The Shade leader stepped forwards. He held up a hand—and then his eyes began to glow. My heart did a somersault, thinking of the weremage—but then just as quickly, it sank into my stomach. Elder Seko gasped and clutched at her throat. Slowly, a finger's width at a time, she rose into the air.

"You are servants of the Lord," intoned the Shade. "As are we. And he does not brook failure."

"He is a mindmage," I said. "He is not who we seek."

"He will kill them," said Mag. Her voice had taken on the lifeless monotone of her battle-trance.

"I am not certain that it would be wise to—oh, sky save us," I said, for Mag had leaped out over the top of the slope. She sprang forwards, shield raised and spear held high.

Mag was among the Shades before they knew what was happening. From five paces away she threw her spear. It impaled the Shade mindmage through the chest. He froze, staring at her weapon as the glow died in his eyes. His magic fell away, and Elder Seko fell gasping to the ground.

Before the Shade had started to fall, Mag seized her spear and kicked him away, ripping the weapon from his torso. She had killed another of the Shades before the rest could react. I loosed two arrows, each taking a Shade in the head. They fell like puppets with cut strings. Two stood, but not once Mag reached them. One managed to get his sword out—Mag batted it aside with her spearhead before it sliced around in a wide arc and laid his throat open. The other leaped towards Mag with raised blade, but I fired another arrow. It took the Shade in the chest, and she fell to one knee, wheezing. She looked up just in time to take

Mag's spear in the neck. Her body fell to the floor, her hands jerking as they tried to reach for her throat. She died before managing it.

It was over almost before the half-ring of satyr warriors realized what was happening. But once they saw the corpses on the floor, they raised their weapons with angry brays, smashing the weapons against their shields in a violent cacophony. Mag fell into a fighting crouch, her shield up and her spear ready to strike. I nocked another arrow, but did not draw.

"Enough!" I cried. "It is over."

Elder Seko had risen by now, helped to her feet by the other satyr who had offered himself in sacrifice. She spoke in anger and fright using the satyrs' language. I frowned at her and then looked over at the translator. The translator shook worse than ever, but she tried to compose herself as she spoke.

"Elder Seko says: it is not over," she whimpered. "Who are you? Why have you done this?"

I arched an eyebrow. "We have saved the lives of two of your elders. You do not sound particularly grateful."

The elders might not have deigned to speak the human tongue, but they seemed to understand it well enough, for the oldest one screamed a reply without waiting for my words to be translated. The translator swallowed hard. "Elder Seko says: you are no servants of the Lord. This was not his will. His retribution will fall upon all of us now, and it will be swift and merciless."

"Then I suggest you stop obeying this Lord, whoever he may be," said Mag. Elder Seko drew up straight and raised a hand. The half-ring of satyrs edged forwards, but Mag stood firm. "I would not do that, if I were you. It will only result in a pile of satyr corpses to go along with these human ones."

I gritted my teeth. Mag did not know the nuances of speaking to these creatures. Threats rarely worked unless one had a satyr utterly at their mercy. The satyrs might have been in such a position, in truth, but they could not know that—they only saw a normal human woman, and would know nothing of Mag's skill.

"We saved your elders," I said loudly, trying to draw attention to myself and away from Mag. "Two of your most venerable and wisest leaders would have died if we had not intervened. That ought to earn us at least a moment's clemency."

Elder Hagan, who had interjected before, brayed a response. The translator spoke quickly. "Yet now all our lives are in danger. What are two lives compared to the whole clan?"

"Do you think the Lord would have stopped there?" I pointed to the elders' stone chairs. "Two of your seats are already empty. What would have stopped the Lord from killing the rest of you, if it pleased him?"

There was a long moment of dead silence. The satyr

warriors were looking between each other and the elders now. Hagan looked furious, but Seko studied us, frowning but not quite hostile. At last she spoke in a slow voice, and the translator hastened to relay her words.

"Elder Seko says: who are you?"

"I am Albern of the family Telfer," I said. "This is Mag, the Uncut Lady, the greatest warrior in the nine kingdoms."

Mag gave me a wry look. But as the translator spoke my words in the satyr tongue, a low, angry rumble ripped through the satyr warriors. Quickly I realized my mistake.

"The greatest *human* warrior," I corrected. "We would never presume to question the might of your own brave fighters."

"Elder Seko says: your name is known to us, Albern," said the translator. "You turned the mind of Tiglak, our warrior. We punished him for his leniency towards you."

Anger blossomed in my heart at those words. I had met Tiglak more than once in my travels through the mountains, and more than once he had taken up arms against me. But he had not been bloodthirsty, and he had been an honorable warrior, in his way.

"I knew Tiglak," I said. "And I never tried to turn him, nor would he have let me. He was a faithful servant of Skal, the holy mother between the moons, and I know she honors him in the sky."

Elder Hagan erupted in a series of furious screams,

but Seko silenced him with a raised and gnarled hand. She looked at me with an expression I could not read. Understanding? Curiosity? From what I knew of the satyrs, I was certain she had never been in the presence of a human who spoke of Skal with true understanding. That is a deep secret of the satyrs, and one no outsider could learn of easily.

After a moment's pause, she spoke again. "Elder Seko says: I am Elder Seko," said the translator. "What do you seek here, Albern?"

"We are looking for a wizard," said Mag. "A skin-shifter. In her human form, she is short and slim, with horn-colored skin and black, braided hair. Have you seen her here?"

Seko looked displeased as she shifted her focus to Mag. "Elder Seko says: we have seen many humans who serve the Lord," said the translator.

Before Mag could answer, I stepped in. She would care little for the Lord, but his agents had already tried to kill me, and I had had questions ever since. Besides, I thought, I still might find Loren one day, and she would want to know. "Who is this Lord? What is he? Some have said he is not human, and I believe it, for I know the wise elders would never serve a human."

The elders raised their chins with pride at that, and one or two of them bleated quietly. Seko spoke through the translator. "Elder Seko says: he has appeared only to us who sit in the stone seats. His form is unknown."

"But when he appeared, how did he look?" I pressed.

"Elder Seko says: he was a form all in white, cloaked in mist and light—as terrible as an Elf, but speaking words we could hear."

I shuddered at that. Even a fleeting thought that the Lord might be an Elf was enough to make me want to run and hide in the deepest hole I could find, never to emerge.

"Enough of the Lord," said Mag. "The weremage. Have you seen her?"

Seko stamped a hoof and bleated. Soon the translator said, "Elder Seko says: how are we to know? You are humans. Humans look like humans."

Mag had enough sense not to point her spear at Seko, but it seemed a near thing. She slammed the butt of it on the rocky ground, and the satyr warriors shifted uneasily around us. "I have told you what she looks like. Surely some of you have seen her."

The elders seemed displeased. Mag's insistence was not far away from calling them liars. I stepped close to her and spoke in a voice I hoped was too low to be overheard.

"If she never performed magic in front of them, they may not know who she is."

Mag gave a frustrated growl. "I had not thought of that. Then what should we do?"

Before I could answer, Seko suddenly spoke more loudly and rapidly than before. My pulse skipped, and

I looked to the translator. But she said nothing. Then, behind us, the warriors began muttering to each other. It took me a moment to realize the truth: Seko had not been speaking to us at all, but had been addressing her clan directly.

After some hurried conversation, one of the satyr warriors stepped forwards. He was large for a satyr, almost as big as Tiglak had been, and he rolled his shoulders as he answered whatever question Seko had put to him. Now Seko turned to the translator and spoke. The translator nodded and relayed the words.

"Our scouts have seen the woman you seek," she said. "She left the mountains heading west, and went to a village there. It stands near the place where the southern river of the Great Spearhead leaves the mountains."

"Thank you," said Mag, nodding to Seko. The elder inclined her head.

"Elder Seko," I said. "I have only one more question. How did the Lord first come to you? How long ago was it?"

Seko snorted, her nostrils flaring. "Elder Seko says: we have no more answers for you."

My breath had grown quick, and I tried to calm myself. "The Lord has caused great suffering in the human kingdoms," I pressed. "In this, we share your—"

Seko cut me off without waiting for the translator, and the translator relayed her words as soon as they were spoken. "Human worries are nothing to us. You have saved two lives, and we have answered more than two questions already. Leave now, and remember our generosity and kindness."

Though my nerves felt grated almost to the root, I knew better than to try to press her any further. Instead I took a step back and bowed low.

"Of course," I said. "Thank you, Elder Seko. We will never forget your mercy or your lenience."

Mercifully, Mag managed not to laugh, though she had to cough to hide it. I tossed my head at her, and we walked away from the circle of satyrs. I did not look back until we were well out of sight, though I imagined I could feel the satyrs' eyes boring into my back long afterwards.

TWENTY-ONE

MAG AND I CAME RIDING DOWN OUT OF THE MOUNTAINS some days later.

Elder Seko had said the weremage went to a village near the southern river of the Great Spearhead. I thought long on those words, and soon I thought I had an answer to them. I remembered Dorsea well enough, for I had often campaigned there, and I remembered how the Blackwind River came down out of the Greatrocks to join the Bluewater, forming a sort of spearhead in the land. I knew there was a town there, though I did not recall the name of it. And so it was in that direction that I guided Mag, and soon brought her to the outskirts of Lan Shui.

It looked a sizable town to us. Not a large city, certainly, but big enough to lose people in. It was built around the river, and I guessed that they used it for trade and for travel. Farmlands were laid out beyond the town proper for leagues in every direction. But as we drew closer, I began to notice that some farms seemed abandoned. About half the fields had no one working in them, and the crops, though mature, were untended.

But I did not remark upon it at first, for Mag seemed to be in a poor mood. As we drew closer to the town, I thought I understood why. Though the homes were clearly of Dorsean make, and the people here wore Dorsean clothing, it was impossible not to see the similarities between this town and Northwood. And when thinking of Northwood, it was impossible not to think of Sten.

"Do you know why the river is called the Blackwind?" I asked her, trying to pull her from such thoughts.

Her head jerked around, as if she had forgotten I was there and was surprised to hear me speak. "What? No."

"It is the twin river of the Bluewater farther north, and they join at the city of Bertram to form the Fanrong," I said. "In the days of the Sunmane, one of her generals—a man named Torben—came through what would be called the Moonslight Pass into Dorsea's western reaches. His army was low on rations and water after the pass, where they had been attacked many times by satyrs, who were in those days more plentiful. They followed the Greatrocks south until they reached the river and the fertile lands that surrounded it. Torben named the river then, for as he said: 'It shone in midday's light like the purest sapphire, though I valued it more highly than gemstones, for instead of wealth, it brought my soldiers life.'

"His army camped around the river for one week, resting. At last they continued their journey south, seeking for the end of the Greatrocks and what might lay beyond them. Soon they arrived here and found this second river, and Torben called it the Blackwind."

My words cut off suddenly, more suddenly than I had intended, for in the middle of the tale, I had remembered its ending. Torben had called it the Blackwind because when his army came to it, they were attacked by a greater host of satyrs than they had yet faced, and there was a great swarm of imps as well. In the fighting, Torben's son had been killed, and so he had named the river as a curse. That was not the sort of story I thought it would be best for Mag to hear just then.

She did not seem to notice the strange way I had cut the tale short, for her eyes were on the town's gates ahead. I followed her gaze and saw why. The gates were almost fully closed, and in front of them stood three constables with less than friendly expressions.

"Trouble, do you think?" said Mag.

"I doubt it. It is not unusual for a town to be wary of strangers, especially this close to the mountains, where there are many perils." But we both knew that was not entirely true. There was no war near here, and so there was no reason for this town to be wary of anything except satyrs and harpies, neither of which would be hampered a whit by a closed gate.

We spoke no further word as we approached the constables, and for their part, they made no move and said nothing as we pulled to a stop before them.

"Hail, friends," I said in a cheery voice. "We beg your leave to enter this town—and, too, we ask its name, for we have never been here before."

One of the constables stood a pace ahead of the others, and the white stripe on her red leather armor marked her as a sergeant. Beneath her red helmet was a shock of bristling yellow hair. I guessed she stood a head taller than me, and half a head over Mag, and she had muscled limbs as impressive as her height. Now she stepped forwards, crossing her arms, and spoke.

"You stand at the gate of Lan Shui. Who are you, and where did you come from?"

"I am Mag, and my friend is Albern of the family Telfer," said Mag. "And we have little business here. We need a place to rest and refresh ourselves before making our way to the road that will take us to the Western Sea."

"Then why are you not on the King's road?" said the constable.

Her words made me frown. It was a reasonable enough question, but the tone behind it was strange—almost desperate. Something was wrong here. I thought again of the untended farms we had just passed.

"There is no great urgency to our journey," I put in. "The King's road would have taken us to Bertram more quickly, it is true, but that would have put many more days between us and a bed to sleep in. You have nothing to fear from us. We are merely weary travelers who have just passed west through the Greatrocks."

That did not have quite the desired effect. The constable sagged, passing a hand over her eyes. "You are from Selvan."

I glanced at Mag, confused. Dorsea and Selvan were fighting in Wellmont, but we were so far north that it should not have mattered. "Yet we are all citizens of Underrealm. I am a man of Calentin, and Mag here is Dorsean."

I pointed at Mag, who tensed. It was true that she had come from Dorsea before I met her, but at the same time, I was not telling the whole truth. Despite her sudden despondency, the constable seemed to notice Mag's reaction, and her frown deepened.

Before she could ask another probing question, I spoke again. "My apologies, but this conversation is rather hard to keep up when you have not told us who you are. We gave you our own names freely enough—may we know yours, as a matter of courtesy?"

The constable's mouth twisted. "I am Constable Yue of the family Baolan," she said at last. "You have told me your destination, but not your business. Why are you traveling west?"

"Why, to visit Mag's family," I said. "And I thank you for your courtesy, Constable Baolan."

"Family, is it?" said Yue, who seemed to have ignored my second statement. "The two of you are wed, then?"

"Not at all," I said. "We are merely friends traveling together."

"Well-armed travelers," Yue pointed out.

"And would you go riding through the Greatrocks without a weapon?" said Mag. It was not exactly what you would call a polite question, but I was relieved that she did not let any anger show in her voice. And to my delight, Yue smiled at the question, though she quickly hid it.

"I suppose I would not," said Yue. She pulled off her helmet and swiped a hand through her bristling yellow hair. "Enter, then, travelers. Keep to yourselves while you are here, and stay indoors after nightfall. And before you leave Lan Shui, come and speak with me."

"Are we not free to—" I began.

"You are free to do whatever you wish," said Yue,

scowling at me. "But if you have a lick of sense, you will come and speak with me before you leave my town. Is that understood?"

"Of course," I said quickly, raising a hand to pacify her.

"One question before we go," said Mag. "A traveler may have arrived here ahead of us—a woman with nut-brown skin and—"

"No travelers have arrived here," said Yue. "Not for many days."

"Constable, if I may," I said. "It sounds as though there is some trouble here. Is it anything we can help with?"

Yue's scowl deepened. "That is my business. Keep to your own. And heed my words."

"Of course," I said at once, nodding. "Can you recommend an inn for us?"

"If you have coin to spend, find the Sunspear," said Yue. "If you do not, the Stag's Sty will be easier on your purse, and they do not have too many fleas."

"A stellar recommendation," I said. "Fare well, constable."

She turned and nodded to the others, who heaved the gate open for us to ride through.

TWENTY-TWO

I WAS MORE ALERT NOW THAN EVER, AND AS I RODE through Lan Shui, I tried to take stock of the town. Though the wall was poorly kept up, it was manned, with several archers pacing its length. But though the guards looked alert and wary, they were few. It would have been easy to slip past them unnoticed, if that was the aim. It gave the air that this town was wary and watchful, but was unused to being either.

Armored soldiers walked the town's streets as well, but they wore neither the king's livery nor the red armor of constables. I guessed they were locals, pressed into service to guard the town. But against what? Had the Shades passed this way? Or had some rumor of their coming reached these people? I could think of no other threat that would have put them so on edge. But I saw some people weeping in doorways and in alleys, clearly in mourning.

"What has happened here?" I said, hardly meaning to speak the words aloud.

"In many places across Dorsea may be found the consequences of war," said Mag.

"Yet Dorsea makes war on no one but Selvan these days," I said. "And this town is far from those battles."

"It must have something to do with the Shades, then."

I shook my head. "If that were the case, and the town had been attacked, Yue would never have let us in."

"Then guess at the answer yourself, if you are so wise," grumbled Mag. "One thing we told Yue was the truth: I want a bed to sleep in, and quickly."

We had a fair bit of coin on us—with the excellence of Mag's ale, she had never wanted for money—and so we asked after the Sunspear and found it before long. Its sign hung over the door, a spear thrusting up with a red-rayed sun in the background. I glanced at the spear on Mag's saddle and bit my tongue. A girl at the stables took our horses, and we purchased dinner in the common room for a handful of pennies. The food and ale were fine enough, but I found myself longing for Sten's cooking and Mag's brew.

Before we had finished eating, an old man walked into the common room. There were only a handful of people there aside from the two of us, but they all looked up eagerly. The man's eyes were grey and blind with age, and he picked his way through the room with a walking stick. One patron quickly moved a chair from his path to ensure he would not strike it as he walked. Though the top of his head was entirely bald, he had thick, bushy grey brows and a long grey beard down to his waist. He wore deep blue clothes in a common Dorsean style, with a shirt that tied at the side and loose trousers collected at the ankle. Despite his stooped figure and slow walk, his lips curved in a smile that seemed nearly permanent.

The old man sat on a small platform near the unlit hearth, sitting with his legs folded and his walking stick across his knees. A barman appeared beside him with a bowl of broth and a cup that looked to be filled with wine. The old man took a few sips of the broth and a deep swig of the wine, and then settled himself on the platform. I noticed that he had not paid for the meal.

And then he leaned back, lifted his head, and began to sing.

From the very first notes, I knew I was in the presence of a master. Here was a man who had been singing—and, unless I missed my guess, telling tales—for decades before I was even born. Though his frame was diminutive, his voice was thick and powerful, and I could feel it thrumming in the wooden chair upon which I sat.

He sang some songs I knew by heart, and others I had never heard before. He sang some songs I knew, but to strange tunes, and some songs with new words, but set to tunes that were as old as the hills. I had to keep reminding myself to eat, for I kept staring at him, spellbound by the sound of his voice and his effortless command of melody. I was not the only one. All conversation in the common room ceased as everyone listened to the old man. Mag, who had far less appreciation for song and story than I, was yet as entranced as I was. Though the man sang alone and without any instrument, it seemed to me that I could almost hear a troupe behind him: a pipe and a lute and one steady, thudding bodhran.

After mayhap a quarter hour, the man subsided into silence and reached again for his broth and wine. I shook myself as if waking from a dream and turned back to my stew. It had very nearly gone cold.

"That was astounding," I said, surprised at the reverence in my own voice.

Mag smiled at me. "Sky above, you look jealous. I always said you would have made a better bard than a mercenary."

I pointed my spoon at her. "That was not a compliment when you first said it, and it is not a compliment now. Where would you be if I *had* pursued a life in a king's court, and had not been there to look after you?"

Her eyebrows shot for the ceiling. "Oh, I would surely have perished long ago," she said, straining mightily to hide the joke in her voice.

"And do not forget it." I glanced over my shoulder at the old man, who was still resting before he resumed singing. "Besides, it is hard to say that I should have been a great and renowned bard when in the presence of one who deserves the honor so much more."

"If you are so enchanted with the man, go and speak to him," said Mag, chuckling.

"In fact, I think I shall," I told her. "And not just for my own entertainment. We want information, and who better to give it to us than a man who tells tales for his supper?"

So saying, I stood and went across the room to sit beside the old man. He heard me coming, and his head tilted up as he listened to my footsteps approach. His milky eyes looked just over my left shoulder, and I smiled, entirely forgetting he could not see the expression.

"Greetings, friend," I said. "I wished to give you my praise for your songs, and your voice. I have rarely heard a singer so fine."

"Rarely?" said the old man. His grin revealed a few missing teeth in the back. "I am losing my touch, then. I must work harder until it becomes 'never.' But I thank you for your kind words."

I chuckled and pulled up a chair to sit beside him. "That would be a tall order. I have traveled to many lands and been in many fine courts of nobility."

The old man's bushy brows rose. "Courtly bards," he scoffed. "If you ask me, they are limited in skill to the moment when some foolish noble hires them. They think they were hired for the songs and stories they already know, and so they never bother to learn any more."

"That is an interesting thought, and I am somewhat glad to hear it," I said, smiling still wider. "I sometimes think I should have become a bard, but if it would have stunted my skill, I am glad I never did."

He laughed at that, and then he held out his hand. I grasped his wrist and shook firmly.

"They call me Dryleaf here in this town," he said.

"And what do they call you elsewhere?" He smiled and did not answer. "I am Albern of the family Telfer."

"Telfer?" he said, cocking his head. "From Calentin then, are you?"

That made my heart skip a beat. Of the many people I had met across the nine kingdoms, only a handful had ever recognized the name Telfer. Even when they did, it was rare they could place the kingdom it came from.

I tried to speak easily, passing off the moment of

hesitation. “I am indeed,” I told him. “But you do not look like a man from my homeland.”

“Nor am I,” he said. “I am from everywhere, as they say. In my day I was a wandering peddler who roamed all over the nine kingdoms. But one day my eyes went”—he pointed to the milky white orbs—“and once they started going bad, it happened fast. I was on my way north, but I was injured crossing the Blackwind just outside this town—I had an uppity horse, and it threw me, and my leg broke. It was not such a bad injury, but old bones are slower to heal. By the time I was ready to ride again, my traveling days were over. Since then, I have waited for anyone traveling to Selvan, hoping I could beg to come along, but the opportunity has never presented itself. It must be . . . three years now? Lan Shui does not lie on any of the great roads that cross Underrealm. We rarely see travelers at all—and even more rarely, lately.”

His mention of Selvan dampened my mood. Even now, the Shades would be pursuing Loren through the Birchwood, and I doubted anyone who lived there was safe. I thought to myself that it was a good thing Dryleaf had never reached his destination. Sometimes fate is kind in cruel ways.

But the last thing he had said caught my attention. “I thought something seemed amiss when I came here. Why is everyone so afraid? We were questioned quite closely by the constable when we arrived.”

“Yue, you mean?” said Dryleaf. “She is a good sort,

if a bit stern. But if she let you in, you will have seen that for yourself."

I noticed that he had deftly avoided answering my question. "A good sort indeed. But why did she suspect us so?"

Dryleaf pursed his lips and nodded a few times, as though bobbing his head in time to some beat I could not hear. His bushy brows had drawn close together. "I am not so sure I should speak of it," he said. "After all, you are a stranger, if an exceedingly polite one. Some strangers are folk of pure intent, but others are less so."

"And have you met any of the latter sort?" I asked. "Anyone in the town who seems not to have the best interest of the people at heart?"

He shook his head, but he did it with a little smile. "I am sorry, but I will not say more. Not yet. If you remain here for a while, we might discuss matters in more detail. But for now I think it is best if you look to yourself, and I do the same." He shifted where he sat and reached for his meal. "And now, if you will forgive me, I must have a few bites before I get back to what earns my meal. I wish you well, and I hope we speak again."

Despite his courtesy, the end of the conversation came so abruptly that I felt myself at a loss for a moment. Yet it seemed clear that I would glean nothing more from him just now, so I politely excused myself and returned to Mag.

TWENTY-THREE

"WHAT A STRANGE OLD MAN," SAID SUN.

Albern laughed. "He was."

"He has died, then?"

"Oh yes," Albern said quietly. "He was old even then, and as I said, this was decades ago."

Sun frowned. "I do not understand. Why was he so polite, and yet unwilling to help? He said strangers could not always be trusted, but if that was the case, why would he speak with you at all?"

Albern's somber mood vanished. "You must learn to allow the elderly their peculiarities," he said. "Oftentimes we do things only to make your life difficult, as revenge for the toll time has wreaked upon us."

"But the town was in danger!"

"And how did he know it was not in danger from me?" said Albern. "That is pulling a little ahead of the story. But you should remember not to be too trusting of strangers, even if you still manage to be courteous to them."

"I should not have trusted you, if I took that advice," muttered Sun.

"True enough," said Albern. "But as Dryleaf himself would discover, I am no one of ill intent."

He remained silent for a good long while, staring down at the reins he held in his hand. He did not look as mournful as when he had recounted Sten's death, but Sun thought she could still sense a deep sadness in him.

"What is wrong?" she asked.

"Nothing exactly," he said. "It is only that I have not recalled Dryleaf in a very long time. The old man and I rode many long miles together. When you get older, you will find that all your stories are laced with grief, for they always concern at least one person who is no longer with you. It is a curse that grows worse the older you get—that fewer and fewer people are left who attended the most important parts of your life. But enough somber talk. In truth, I was only thinking that our expedition tonight is rather like those adventures then, though of course I am much younger now than Dryleaf was, and you are much younger than I was."

Sun blinked. "You mean that Dryleaf is a part of the story?" she said.

Albern smiled. "Oh yes, very much a part of it," he said.

"He did not seem very important when you met him," said Sun. "I thought he would be just another name in a tavern, heard briefly and then never seen again. Like Elsie, who you left in Northwood. I have never heard of him in any other tale of you and the Wanderer."

"But you had never heard of Sten either, and yet you can see how important he was," said Albern. "None of this would have happened without Sten. Indeed, I was just some man in a tavern when first you laid eyes upon me. Yet now here we are, riding off together."

Sun raised her eyebrows. "We are not riding anywhere together. You are riding, and I am walking."

That made Albern laugh aloud, his voice ringing through the night to be swallowed by the trees on either side of the road. "A privilege of age. And you will not have to walk for much longer."

"I am pleased to hear it."

Albern smiled and shook his head. "In any case, you should never discount strangers met by chance—if, indeed, you believe in chance at all. My own thoughts on that matter are far from settled, and my opinions have changed much over the years. But the more I see in my life, the more I begin to believe that there is indeed some great pattern that binds everything together, drawing certain people closer to each other before pulling them away.

"I do not think it was chance, for instance, that brought Mag and Sten together. The moment those two met, it was as though they had been together all their lives. Sten was a simple farmer in northeastern Selvan, and Mag and I were passing through in one of those years when we served no mercenary company in particular. We only intended to stay in the town for a day or two, but then, there was Sten. We had been there almost a week before I even realized we had remained longer than we planned. And that was strange, for I spent most of those days alone, while Mag and Sten would go walking together. I usually only shared their company in the evenings, when we would sit and talk and drink in the way that only young people can drink, with no fear of the pain morning will bring. Yet it all seemed . . . right. Natural. I was traveling with Mag, and Mag belonged in that town, at that time, by Sten's side. And so nothing seemed untoward, as far as I was concerned.

"We left the town after three weeks, and we joined another mercenary company soon afterwards. We campaigned for some months, and then we returned to northeastern Selvan—and we went back to Sten's town while we waited for the company to get hired again. We only stayed a week that time—but the next time we returned, we were there for two. Every time the company came home, Mag and I found ourselves in that town, and Mag found herself by Sten's side.

"Now, as I have told you already, Mag was not the sort to seek out bedfellows. She had had one or two whirlwind romances while I had known her, but they never went past a certain point. But in those early days with Sten, it never even went that far. It was as though she and Sten did not even think of each other as lovers. Rather, Mag seemed to have adopted the attitude that time spent away from Sten was simply foolish. If she had to, for our duty to the company, of course she would part from him. But given the option, she would always be with him, and that was simply the way it went.

"Not long afterwards, the company went out on one of the longest campaigns I have ever seen. Almost a year we were on the road, and Mag's mood grew more and more dour. About six months into the campaign, Mag approached the captain and requested a leave of absence. 'To visit family,' she told him, but I knew full well that Mag had no living family. Of course, she told me where she was really going—she was returning to northeastern Selvan for a month, to see Sten, because she was worried how he was getting on.

"The captain was loath to let her leave, but he did it anyways. Mag was gone for three weeks, and then she returned. In some ways, it seemed as though a great weight had lifted from her shoulders, and she joked more often and laughed more readily. But I could tell she was troubled, and when she thought no one was looking, I caught her staring into the distance, her expression one of deep thought.

"At last I approached her. 'Mag,' I said. 'Something happened while you were gone. Would you spit it out and tell me, so that I can stop worrying about you?'

"She looked entirely confused. 'What do you mean?' she asked. 'I am the same as I have always been.'

"'May the dark take me if that is true,' I said. 'You seem relieved ever since you visited Sten, but it also seems as if something else troubles you. Why are you upset?'

"'I am not upset,' she assured me. 'Though I suppose you are right that something has bothered me. But it is not my own sadness that bothers me—it is Sten's. He was happy to see me, of course. But something weighed on him, and no matter how I asked, he would not tell me what was wrong. There was a great sadness in his eyes when I left him, and I have not been able to stop thinking about it since.'

"Then I laughed at her, laughed long and loud. 'Mag, you are the greatest warrior I have ever known,' I told her. 'And you are also the greatest idiot. Sten is troubled because he loves you with all of his heart. And judging by the fact that you took leave to go visit him—when you have never taken leave in all the years I have known you—I would guess that you love him, too, and are too stupid to realize it.'

"Mag dismissed my words as preposterous, and the conversation ended soon after. But deep down, she knew I was right, and it did not take her long to realize the truth. Over the next year, something changed within her. Battle and warfare, which she had always loved, suddenly became distasteful to her. She no longer loved to throw herself into a fight, nor to spar with me and the other sellswords. Before, she had loved to practice, no matter how easy it was for her to beat us every time. Now she could hardly be mustered to the practice yard even for mandatory drilling.

"A year later, she officially tendered her resignation, and I did the same. Our captain begged and pleaded with us to stay—Mag more than me, of course—but she would not be dissuaded. We left together, and we returned to Sten, and soon they married and moved to Northwood.

"Sten was nothing special—and I say that as one of his dearest friends. He was a farmer's son like many others across the nine lands. But he was exactly what Mag needed, in that place, and in that time. The life of a mercenary had nothing new to offer her, but she could not see that. So she met one who would teach her the lesson, instead. The timing was too perfect to be mere luck.

"The same has always proven true, at least in my experience. Mayhap it was chance that put Dryleaf and me in that tavern together at the same time, all that long while later. But I have had my doubts, and those doubts have not slept in the many years since."

"What else would it be, if not chance?" said Sun.

Albern leaned low in his saddle, and his voice grew somewhat hushed. "Can you look at everything that has happened across Underrealm—everything that is still happening now—and tell me you do not think there is some greater power at work? Some great force we cannot understand, pulling our strings like puppets?"

Sun frowned up at him. "I . . . what power? What force?"

He straightened and shrugged. "If I had the answer, I would surely sell it to a king for a wagon full of gold. But I will advise you not to be too ready to believe in chance. The smallest actions can have the most profound effects, and we can hardly guess at them. For even the most mundane of occurrences, there may be reasons we can but guess at."

That was not an entirely pleasant thought, and it lingered in Sun's mind. If even the ordinary choices in her life could contain some great and hidden purpose, then what of the more consequential ones? She had thought her adventure with Albern tonight was little more than a lark. She did not like to imagine what else it could be.

These thoughts troubled her more and more as they went on, and as Albern resumed his story.

TWENTY-FOUR

I WAS SOMEWHAT DISGRUNTLED AFTER MY CONVERSATION with Dryleaf, but there was little I could do about it. Mag and I slept well that night, happy to have a mattress beneath us instead of a bedroll on the hard ground. The next morning, we broke our fast quickly and then returned to our room to discuss what we should do.

"I think it is clear what danger threatens the town," she said. "The people here are frightened of the Shades. They must be terrorizing the countryside."

"But then why would Yue let us in?" I asked.

"Mayhap they know the Shades, or know what they look like," said Mag. "You and I are no friends of theirs, certainly. Mayhap Yue knew it when she permitted us to enter."

I shook my head. "That seems quite a guess."

She spread her hands. "Do you have a better one?"

"No," I admitted.

"Then let us carry on as if I am right until proven otherwise, unless you would rather sit in this inn and wait for the weremage to come to us. Any plan of action, carried out with certainty, is better than no plan at all."

I had to laugh at that. "Do not throw Victon's words at me after all these years."

"You obeyed him easily enough when we fought for him," she said with a grin.

"And that has not been for many long years."

Despite my protests, I knew she was right. We had no better ideas, and even if a thorough search did not reveal the Shades themselves, it might lead us to another answer. Still, I was nervous we might draw attention to ourselves. Constable Yue had made it clear that we were not to cause trouble in her town, and we were planning to do exactly that.

For caution's sake, we set out into the streets with our cloaks on and our hoods up, despite the heat of the day. Soon we were both drenched with sweat. I did my best to ignore it, but Mag complained mightily. We worked our way through shops, ostensibly to pick up supplies so that we could continue on our journey.

"If the Shades are indeed terrorizing this town, the people will know where they are," said Mag. "Keep an eye out for places that the townsfolk avoid—even if they only avoid looking at them."

We did so, but we soon realized we had a problem. The town was much the same as it had been yesterday; the people were afraid and despondent no matter where we went. It was hard to find a place they were avoiding when they seemed to be avoiding going outside at all. Few townsfolk would look at us, and in every shop we visited, the owner would conduct business as quickly as possible without speaking. When we tried to make conversation, they gave short, clipped answers or simply asked us to leave. And most curiously, when we told them we were looking for supplies to leave Lan Shui and continue our journey, they looked at us with terror in their eyes.

Probably out of frustration, Mag's course became increasingly erratic, crossing back and forth through the town on a dizzying path with no pattern that I could discern. At last, just past midday, she stopped in the middle of the street and balled her hands into fists.

"Let us get ourselves a meal and something to drink."

"That would be a welcome relief," I said. By now my shirt was clinging to me with sweat.

"Mm-hm," said Mag with a nod.

Something in her manner was strange, and I grew alert at once. She seemed distracted.

"Mag?" I said in a low voice. "What is it?"

"Mayhap nothing," she said. "I might say more when we find a place out of the sun."

Though I was intensely curious, I followed her without further questions. She stepped into the first tavern she found and paid for a light meal of bread and cheese and ale. Leading me to a corner table, she sat facing the door with her back against the wall. I sat beside her, facing out into the rest of the room.

"Well?" I said.

"I thought I saw someone following us," she told me. "They were being careful not to be seen, but stealth did not seem to be their strong suit. There! Look at me and pretend we are talking."

We turned our heads towards each other. "We *are* talking," I pointed out.

"Yes, good," said Mag. "Just like that, as though we are really having a conversation."

I laughed at the joke, but also to help the ruse. The laugh gave me an excuse to turn my head back towards the rest of the room, and I saw the person Mag must have been talking about. He was a young man with bulging eyes and short black hair, his light brown cloak thrown back over his shoulders in the heat. As soon as he had entered the room, he had gone straight to the proprietor, and was speaking with him now. Their words were inaudible from where we sat.

"The boy?" I said, turning back to Mag.

"Yes," she said. "I kept seeing him on whichever street we were on, no matter how wildly I turned our path."

"So that is why you took such a strange route through the streets," I said. "I was wondering about that."

"He is leaving," said Mag, glancing out of the corner of her eye.

"We should go after him."

"Do you think so?" said Mag with a smirk. "Be careful, though. Capturing him will be useless, and of course we cannot kill him. He looks young. I think he will be easily frightened. Let us spring an attack that fails. He might lead us straight back to his masters."

"Unless he is the weremage in disguise," I said.

Mag sighed and shook her head. "Albern, you know I love you, like one loves a helpless pet, but you can be intolerably foolish. We know the weremage can take a bird's form. If she knew we were here, and if she were following us, she would watch us from the sky."

She stood and made for the tavern's front door without waiting for my answer. I lifted one finger and opened my mouth to call out a retort, but could think of nothing. Lowering my hand, I stood to follow her, grumbling many ominous things about *pets* and *helpless* and what I would show her about intolerable foolishness. I was careful Mag heard none of my words, of course.

We left the tavern and headed down the street, back the way we had come. As we did, a figure detached itself from a nearby wall and followed us, trying to stick to the sparse shadows cast by buildings. Mag had been right about one thing: the boy was about as stealthy as a troll with an arrow in each eye and a spear in its backside.

"Now," whispered Mag, and ducked suddenly down an alley.

I dashed after her. We ran to the end of the alley and split up on the other side, each of us hiding behind a corner and waiting for the boy to follow. We heard his hurried footsteps drawing nearer. Mag gripped her spear and nodded to me from across the alley mouth.

The boy cried out in terror as we leaped upon him. Mag brought the butt of her spear around and struck him in the ribs with it. It was a light tap, but he squealed like a shot squirrel. I had already drawn back my fist to swing at him, but when he doubled over, my fist sailed over his head and into Mag's jaw. She stumbled back, apparently stunned for a moment, and then attacked again. But she seemed to overestimate the swing of her spear this time, and the butt crashed into my shoulder instead of the boy's face. I fell against the building beside me, grunting in pain.

The boy, who had all the wit of a bit of over-cured leather, stared at us in confusion. I growled at Mag through gritted teeth.

"Stop just standing there, or he will *get away.*"

As though the idea had never occurred to him before, the boy screamed and ran back through the alley the way he had come. Mag seized my shoulder and pulled me after her.

"You swung a bit harder than you needed to," Mag remarked.

"My deepest apologies. I am only a helpless pet, and cannot always control my own strength."

Mag snorted and redoubled her pace, for the boy had vanished around the side of the buildings up ahead. Mag and I followed him just as he had been following us, but with one important difference: we knew what we were doing. We hung back at each corner, only peeking around to make sure we saw which way the boy had gone.

It seemed to me, however, that we hardly needed to take such precautions. The boy did not glance back even once, and he did not seem to complicate his route at all, but led us straight to the heart of Lan Shui. At last he threw open the door of a ramshackle house and then slammed it shut behind him. Mag and I skidded to a halt just outside the door, looking up at the building.

"Is there any reason not to follow him straightaway?" said Mag.

"This is a large building that could contain a dozen enemies or more," I said.

"Any *good* reason, I mean?"

I drew my sword. "None."

Mag grinned as she hefted her spear. Together we launched ourselves forwards, slamming our shoulders into the front door.

It burst open, and I took in the room at a blink. Just before us stood the boy, his eyes bulging more than ever with terror at the sight of us. He stood with two others, a thin Heddish man and a fat Dorsean woman—Shades, I guessed, though they did not wear blue and grey. A fourth Shade stood in a doorway at the other end of the room. She was older, but hale, and wore her grey hair in a braid.

"Well met," I said. "Did we meet in Northwood? I have such a terrible memory for faces."

"Pantu, you fool," hissed the woman with the grey braid. Then, to the others, she cried, "Kill them!" But she did not heed her own advice, instead turning and fleeing deeper into the house.

The thin man shoved the boy out of the way and rushed us, unsheathing a sword. The woman picked up a warhammer before doing the same. I braced myself to receive the man's first lunge, but that turned out to be unnecessary. Mag gave a savage thrust, and his sword arm was dangling useless at his side, while his blade clattered to the floor. The fat woman swung her warhammer twice, driving us both back one step, but then Mag pounced. Her spearhead pierced the woman's gut, making her gasp, before withdrawing and striking again, this time straight into her heart.

I almost relaxed, before I saw the thin man trying to retrieve his sword with his left hand. My own sword came sweeping down, and the Shade fell to the floor.

The boy cowered in the corner of the room, his hands raised helplessly before him, terrified. Mag advanced on him, but I darted forwards and took her arm. She whirled on me, and I flinched before her dead-eyed gaze.

"Mag," I said. "Look at him."

She hesitated and looked down at the boy. He looked back up at us, terrified. I felt the tension bleed from Mag's arm.

"Run for your life," I told the boy. "And if you know what is good for you, stop working with these Shades. They will come to ruin in the end."

I tossed my head, and the boy bolted through the open front door.

"There will be more of them," said Mag, her voice the emotionless monotone of her battle-trance. "Let us clear the house, and carefully."

She started for the door to the left, but I took her arm and stopped her. When she turned on me, I tried not to flinch at her dead eyes.

"Wait," I said. I pointed to the room's second door on the right. "If we chase the woman, she might be able to circle through the house and come out this way. One of us should stay here to guard the exit."

"There could be a back door, too," she said tonelessly.

"There could be, but we *know* about the front door," I said. "Go after her before we waste too much time."

She nodded and darted through the left-hand door. I felt a twinge of shame at how easily I had let her go off on her own. But both of us knew that, if one of us should go alone into the house, it should be her. I could be overwhelmed if more foes waited within. Mag could not.

I took a stance by the front door, sword ready in my hand. After the first few moments, the house was silent; not even Mag's footfalls could be heard. My pulse thudded loud in my ears, but it was thick and muddy. I shook my head, trying to clear it.

What was wrong with this place? The air was heavy with more than the midday heat. I could feel an evil energy seeping from the very walls. I had heard wizards talk of sensing magic at work. This felt like what they described, but of course I was no wizard. Even if there was magic here, I would never have been able to sense it. Yet I could sense . . . something.

Footsteps came pounding from behind the left-hand door. I tensed, raising my sword—and then I realized that it had to be Mag. No foe could have gotten past her to flee here.

The door opened to reveal the Shade woman with the grey braid.

She skidded to a halt at the sight of me, her well-lined eyes going wide. She, too, held a blade in her hand, but it dipped for a moment as she dragged a hand down her face.

"This was not supposed to happen," she muttered, almost as if talking to herself. "You were never supposed to come here."

I shifted my stance slightly, watching for a trick. "I am sorry to be such a disappointment, though you may be relieved to know I have always been such, according to those who know me best."

She spat on the wooden floor. "Shut your prattling lips. You were not meant to die here, but dark take me if I will let you kill me instead."

"Now, be calm," I said. "There is no reason anyone has to—"

She lunged before I could finish, and I barely blocked her overhead swing. But hardly had her blade rebounded before it came again, swinging from my left this time. I tried to twist out of the way, but I felt the tip of the blade slice a deep cut in my forearm. I grimaced in pain and tried to step away, but she followed.

"You people do not poison your weapons, do you?" I said, trying to keep my tone light.

"Do you think servants of the Lord have no honor?" she said. Then she smiled. "You will have to find out, I suppose."

She attacked again. I warded her blows, but each one forced me another step back. I could not risk a glance behind me, but I could *feel* the closed door at my back. The woman saw it, and she gave a grim smile. She was a better fighter than I was, and we both knew it. I took a wild swing that forced her a half-step back. But even as my sword came around, I could feel myself losing my balance. I stumbled, and she saw her opening.

"Die, wretch," she hissed, swinging for my side.

The only thing I could do was fall to the floor. My sword clattered out of reach. Her blade hissed harmlessly through the air where I had stood a moment before. But I had only prolonged the inevitable. I rolled desperately onto my back, hoping against hope that I could roll out of the way of her next swing.

But the woman was not standing over me with her blade held high. In fact, she was only standing at all because Mag's spear had pierced straight through her head and embedded itself in the wall. Now the woman hung feebly from the middle of the spear, bouncing up and down slightly with its spring. Her eyes were cold and empty.

I looked over. Mag stood in the right-hand doorway, blood spattered all across her clothing. She had arrived just in time to throw her spear across the room and through the head of my foe. Even as I watched, her battle-trance slipped away and warmth came back into her expression.

"Five, Albern," she said. "I took five of them, and still I had to help you against one."

"In a building like this, yes," I said. "Put me on an open field and put a bow in my hand—"

"—and stand your enemies in a line facing you like practice dummies, and do not give them any weapons to fight back, yes, yes," said Mag. She came to me and held out a hand to pull me up, forcing a slight smile. "We cannot always fight in perfect circumstances, you oaf."

"Oh, be silent," I grumbled. "And would you take back your spear? That is unnerving." I pointed at the grey-haired woman, still suspended where she stood by Mag's weapon.

Mag's little smile died, and she went about the messy business of retrieving her spear. Once she had extricated it from the woman and the door, she cleaned it on the woman's cloak. I went to where my sword had fallen and picked it up, keeping a suspicious eye on both doors leading out of the room. I did not want to be taken by surprise again.

Mag noticed my attitude and shook her head. "I got them all. The house feels empty."

"But still evil," I remarked. The air was still thick with the curious power I had felt earlier.

"Yes, still evil," said Mag.

"How did the woman get past you?" I said. "She emerged from the left-hand door—the same one you went through. Did she slip by somehow?"

Mag turned to look at the door, frowning. "She did not. I circled the whole house and came back around the other way, and I did not see her until I killed her. But I passed a staircase leading up. The woman must have run upstairs, and then come back down after I had passed. She, and three others—they found me in the back room, surprising me by attacking from behind."

My eyebrows shot for the ceiling. "However did you survive."

Mag put a hand over her heart. "It was a near thing."

I could not find it in me to laugh. A mercenary learns to lighten their mood, even in the midst of the grim business of killing, but I was never able to laugh in the presence of an enemy's corpse.

"I wish now that I had not killed all of them," said Mag. "I did not think to let any of them live, for I thought we could interrogate this one." She pointed at the corpse of the grey-braided woman.

"Interrogate . . ." I closed my eyes and sighed. The weremage. She was not here. In the fighting, I had almost forgotten about her. "Sky. I had not thought of that."

"Clearly not," said Mag. "In any case, we did not find what we sought, and I feel it would be unwise for us to remain here overlong. Let us be on our way."

"A sensible suggestion," I said.

I turned to the front door and threw it open, relieved, at least, that I would be able to escape the oppressive feeling that permeated the house. The open air outside felt like cool springwater on a midsummer day. I stopped just past the threshold and took several deep breaths. Mag was not so dramatic about it, but I could see the relief on her face as well. She planted the butt of her spear on the ground and leaned on it with a sigh.

"You!"

The voice—new, but still familiar—froze my blood. I looked up, the sinking feeling in my stomach growing worse, to see Yue marching towards us, her face red beneath her shock of bristling yellow hair.

"Dark take the both of you—you are under arrest, under the authority of the King's law."

TWENTY-FIVE

"Constable Baolan," I said, raising a hand to wave at her. "Well met, again."

She stalked up to us in a huff, hands balled to fists by her sides. Behind her were the same two constables we had seen at the gate the day before. They looked at each other warily, hands near the handles of their clubs.

"I told you not to make trouble while you were in my town," growled Yue. "And then, a short while ago, someone came and told me they saw you chasing a boy through the streets of the town."

"He was following us," said Mag easily. "We wanted to know why."

"He is from this town," said Yue. "You are not. And before—wait."

She stopped abruptly and pulled her club from its hook on her belt. Her companions did the same, though more slowly. Yue pointed at Mag and me, glaring.

"That is blood."

I winced as I looked down at myself. "It . . . is. We were attacked."

"Where?" snapped Yue.

I pointed into the house behind us. Yue glanced at it and then looked back to me.

"You go in first," she said.

There was nothing for it. I did as she asked, with Mag just behind me and the constables bringing up the rear. We filed into the front room, and Mag and I stepped to the side. The bodies of the first two Shades, along with the grey-haired woman, lay on the floor in clear view. Blood had already begun to pool around them.

Yue hissed and raised her club as if expecting us to attack. But I had already raised my hands in surrender, and Mag had made no threatening move, though she still held her spear.

"Drop your weapon," Yue ordered.

Mag sighed and did so, slowly raising her hands

just as I had. "Constable, as my friend has already told you, we were attacked. We only defended ourselves."

"After breaking down the front door, if I am not mistaken," said Yue. My spirits, already low, plummeted further. The front door *had* plainly been smashed open, a detail I had not recalled until Yue mentioned it.

"We did, it is true," I said. "But only in haste."

"Because of the boy, you claim," said Yue.

"Yes," I said. "He fled once his companions attacked us. He is young, between a child and an adult. He has short hair and wide, prominent eyes."

Yue's face went white. "Pantu? Did you—"

"We did not harm him," I said. "And he made no move to harm us—only these ones did so. He fled soon after the fighting started."

"If that is true, we shall soon find out," said Yue. "Sinshi, go and fetch him."

The constable hesitated a moment, looking uneasily between us and his master. But when Yue fixed him with a furious look, he hastened to obey, awkwardly trying (and failing) to close the front door behind him.

My stomach did another turn. We could hardly expect the boy to speak in our defense—though he had not seemed as bloodthirsty as his Shade companions, we had chased him and then murdered his fellows. We had to figure out a way to turn Yue to our side before the boy got here, or else we had to hope he had already hidden himself so well that the constable could not find him.

"May I explain our case further?" I asked Yue.

"I think I have heard your side," spat Yue. "Now I would hear from the boy you chased, for no good reason that I have heard yet."

"Is it so strange?" I said. "You know we are travelers, and you can likely tell that we are no strangers to battle and fighting. We are in a strange place, and then someone starts following us. Would you not be curious, if you were us?"

"Of course I would be," said Yue. "But I imagine that, were I in your shoes, my path would not have ended in murder."

"Not murder," said Mag. "We told you—"

"Yes, that you defended yourselves," said Yue. She looked at me. "You are right, Albern of the family Telfer, in that I can tell that you are no strangers to fighting. And given the chance, I would do much to avoid any sort of fight against your friend Mag, here. Tell me: if she is so great a warrior, could she not have defended you both without taking three lives?"

Beside me, Mag tensed and gave me a quick look. As I met her gaze, my mouth twisted as though I had bitten into a lemon.

"Albern—" began Mag.

"What?" snapped Yue. "What is it?"

Ignoring Mag's urgent look, I spoke softly to Yue. "These are not the only three," I told her. "There are three more in the back room."

Yue's face went as pale as the corpse of the Heddish

man on the floor. But to her credit, her voice seemed entirely calm when she spoke again. "I see. And they were killed in self-defense as well, I take it?"

"Albern, you fool," muttered Mag.

"Do you think she would not have found them?" I said. I met Yue's gaze without flinching. "We should not be afraid of telling the truth, for we have nothing to hide."

"That is a noble sentiment, though one I find hard to believe," said Yue. She turned to the constable beside her. "Ashta, collect their weapons." Ashta hastened to obey while Yue fixed us both with another hard look. "Indeed, the only reason I have not clapped you in irons already is that I can hardly believe two murderers as ruthless as you appear to be would behave so foolishly that they would let themselves be caught by constables and then freely admit to their own killings."

"That is one point in our favor, then," I said, taking off my sword belt and handing it to Ashta. Mag grimaced as the constable picked up her spear.

"Do not be flip with me," said Yue.

"Why do the deaths of these people bother you so?" said Mag suddenly.

The rest of us froze—even Ashta, who had been halfway back to Yue with our weapons. Slowly, all three of us turned to stare at Mag.

"Are you . . . are you joking?" said Yue. "You have murdered six people in my—"

"Six people, yes, but not six people from this

town," said Mag. "None of these people are from Lan Shui, are they? I think the boy is local—Pantu, you called him?—but none of the others look Dorsean, or even half-Dorsean, like you. And they all seemed to be living here, in a house that looks to have suffered many long years of disrepair. I would guess that no one from Lan Shui has lived here in mayhap half a decade, and that you did not know the house was occupied at all. That means they were living here for some secret purpose, under your nose. And they are fighters, just as we are. What noble purpose could such warriors have for dwelling here, out of sight of the King's law?"

Yue said nothing for a long moment. Ashta frowned as she drew near her sergeant again—but it was a frown of deep thought, not of anger or denial. Mag had struck upon something I had not even considered, and from the looks on the constables' faces, I could tell her guess was at least close to the truth.

"Regardless of any of that," Yue pressed, "the King's law still applies, whether these people were born in Lan Shui or not."

"Yet the King's law provides for defending oneself against unprovoked attack," I said.

"You keep saying that," said Yue. "How far do you think such an excuse will stretch? There are *six* corpses in this house. Why did you not simply flee after the first two attacked you?"

My mouth opened, but no words came for a long moment. "Well . . . it all happened very quickly," I said at last, well aware of how weak the excuse sounded.

I was spared further embarrassment as the front door opened and Sinshi returned with the boy, Pantu, in tow. Pantu did not look to have come entirely of his own free will. I was afraid his bulging eyes would nearly fall from his skull, and he was covered with a sheen of sweat that I guessed was not entirely from the heat outside. When he saw Yue looming over him, he flinched.

"I found him, Sergeant," said Sinshi.

"Hello, Pantu," growled Yue. "I thought we had moved past the point where I would find you involved in some sort of trouble every other week, and yet here we are."

Pantu looked resentfully at her from under his hooded lids. "I did not do anything wrong," he mumbled.

Yue thrust a finger at Mag and me. "These strangers say you did. Did they attack you and your friends here first, or was it the other way around?"

The boy stared at us for a long moment. The room went utterly quiet, and it felt as if time itself had stood still. The only sensation in my body was the same oppressive weight of power that had pressed upon me since the moment we first entered the house.

"These ones attacked first," said the boy, pointing at the corpses on the floor. "The strangers only defended themselves."

Yue's shoulders sagged. She looked utterly flabbergasted as she thrust a finger at the corpses. "You are saying you were *with* them, boy," she said. "If they committed a crime, you are complicit. And you are telling me they attacked Mag and Albern for no reason?"

"I did nothing," whined Pantu. "These ones shoved me out of the way before the fight began. I wanted to escape, but they were blocking the door."

"That is true," said Mag quickly. "He did not join these others in the attack, and only—"

"Enough from you," said Yue, her face flushing. She spoke derisively to Pantu. "Your friends are dead, and you will not even speak in their defense. Why did you even truck with them, boy?"

Rather than cowering further, Pantu straightened and pointed at his own face. An angry bruise shone on his cheek, a few fingers beneath one bulging eye. "They were not my friends. They paid me, and I ran errands for them, but they were never grateful for my work. They were a bad lot, and I thank the sky that these strangers rid the town of them. We did not need them here any more than we need the vampire."

"Hist!" cried Yue, knuckles going white as they gripped her club.

"Vampire?" I said. "What vampire?"

"Nothing," said Yue. "Ignore him. He is a foolish boy." She seized Pantu's shoulder and pulled him to her side, as though protecting him from Mag. "With the only living testimony on your side, I cannot hold you. But I am warning you now: you are no longer welcome here. Fetch what supplies you need, and then ride from Lan Shui with all haste. Trouble follows the two of you like a heavy storm, and I will not tolerate it. Now get out."

"We still want to know why he was following us," I said to Yue.

"I suggest you accustom yourselves to disappointment," she replied.

"What was that talk of a vampire?" said Mag. "If this town is in danger—"

"I said it was none of your concern," said Yue. "Fetch what you need, and go."

"Yesterday you told us you did not want us to leave without speaking with you first," I pointed out.

"Consider those orders changed," said Yue. "If you are gone before the day's end, it will not be too soon."

We collected our weapons from Ashta and left the house. I did not glance back over my shoulder until we were several streets away. Finally I stepped to the side of the street, Mag beside me.

"Well, that was a near thing," I said.

"Near indeed," said Mag. "Not that I was in any great danger. I could have trounced those constables with my eyes closed. Though I can understand why *you* would be frightened."

I glared at her for a long moment, and she met my gaze without flinching. But both of us could only last a few moments before our faces broke into grins, and we chuckled together.

"Sky above, I thought we were doomed when that boy stepped into the room," I said. "I wonder what made him speak in our defense?"

"I would like to ask him," said Mag. "And we should ask after the weremage, too, since he is the last person we know who might know anything about her."

"Yet he is with Yue," I said. "And I think we would be pressing our luck if we tried to seek him out again, after all the trouble we have raised today."

"Agreed," said Mag. "Home, then, or what passes for it."

We turned our steps towards the Sunspear.

TWENTY-SIX

As we ambled away from the Shade hideout, Kaita watched us go, rage and grief burning in her heart.

She wanted to swoop down on us. She wanted to claw our eyes out in her raven form, and then she wanted to take her cat form and rip us limb from limb, feasting on our steaming flesh. No, that would be too quick. She would drag us off into the wilderness and play knives across our skin, and then leave us bleeding in the night to be a vampire's feast.

None of the Shades were supposed to die. Dellek, especially, was not supposed to die. It was only supposed to be Pantu. Instead, he alone had survived. What an evil joke of the darkness below.

She had thought of intervening when she saw us enter the house. But she still feared the cold fury in Mag's eye, and the brilliant flash of her spear. And in the end, she had hesitated too long. She had seen us emerge from the house, bloodstained but still alive, and she knew that all the Shades inside had been murdered.

Now she would have to find another way to lure us along the trail. But first she would kill the boy. With his own blood, he would atone for the far, far more valuable lives that had already been lost.

She watched the constables emerge from the house, Pantu in tow. Sinshi still had him by the scruff of the neck, dragging him like a wayward pup. Yue seized his shirt and pulled him away from her constable, shoving a finger in his face to give him a final admonishment. When she had finished with him, she shoved him away, and Pantu went scuttling down the street.

Kaita took wing, flapping to catch up with Pantu and watch him from above.

He ducked around the first corner he could, then poked an eye around it to watch Yue and the other constables. They stood in conference for a moment before Yue bade them all leave. From so high in the air, Kaita could not hear what she said to them, and she did not care. The constables vanished into the streets of the town.

And then, to her great surprise, Pantu snuck from cover and made his way back towards the Shade hideout.

Kaita swooped lower, watching him, her mind whirling. What was the boy doing? Did he have something stashed away in the hideout? Or did he have no other home in Lan Shui to which he could return? Suddenly she regretted not having learned more about the boy from Dellek. He had seemed so insignificant.

She watched as Pantu opened the hideout's front door. He paused there for a moment, recoiling with a hand over his mouth. If she had had lips, Kaita would have sneered. *Weak. Weak, and a fool.* But after a moment he mastered himself. He slipped inside the door, shutting it behind him.

Kaita felt a thrill race through her. She had him now.

With a flap of her ebony wings, she landed in the alley beside the hideout. Her eyes glowed, and in a moment she had resumed her human form, complete with the form-fitting clothes she was able to bring with her during transformations. After listening and watching to make sure there were no witnesses, she crept to the front door of the hideout and slipped inside.

The house was utterly silent. She felt the pulse of the evil magic within, seeping up through the floor from the chamber below, where the Shades had performed their rituals. It pulsed through her body, far more powerful thanks to her magic. She breathed deeply, relishing the feeling of the power.

For a moment she considered: should she seize the strength of the cauldron? Could she even do so? No one knew what it would do to a wizard.

Best not to risk it. Not yet.

Silent as a cat, she crept from room to room, ready to reach for her magic in an instant. But the house seemed empty. Frowning, Kaita sped to the stairs leading up. She climbed them, impatience making her incautious—her footfalls were now audible. But if the boy was upstairs, he would not be able to escape her anyway, even if he did hear her.

He was not upstairs. She searched every room, even under the beds, as though this were a child's game of catch the imp. After searching under the last bed, Kaita straightened. She looked towards the stairs leading down, her eyes narrowing.

There seemed no possibility the boy knew of the basement. Dellek would never have permitted him to learn of it. Yet it was the only place left.

She returned downstairs and opened the secret door. Ignoring the torch, she leaped down the steps two at a time, soon reaching the underground chamber. There she paused for a long moment, letting her eyes adjust to the thin shafts of light that came through the floorboards above.

The chamber was empty.

Kaita gave a low, outraged cry. He had heard her. She did not know how, but he must have, and he slipped out of the house when she was searching for him. Or mayhap he had climbed out a window. Either way, he was not here.

She tried to calm herself with long, slow, shaking breaths. The boy did not matter. He was insignificant. Less than nothing. Revenge would have been sweet, but it was nothing compared to her mission. She would let it go. Mag and I were all that mattered, in the end.

Whirling, she climbed the stairs and left the house.

Pantu waited a very, very long time, likely longer than he needed to, until he was sure she was gone.

When her footsteps had long since faded away, and the creak of the house's front door was a near memory, he emerged. He pushed open the door of the cabinet and uncurled himself from the cramped space within.

He stood now in the underground chamber. The massive cauldron sat before him, and sunlight glinted through the floorboards high above.

Still shaking with fear and drenched with sweat, he nevertheless looked behind him at the cabinet with a little smile. He might not be a fast runner, and certainly he was no fighter. And as he had learned just that morning, he was awful at trailing a mark without being spotted. But hiding? Yes, Pantu was very good at hiding. It was, mayhap, the only thing he was good at. Certainly his father would have said it was the only thing he was good *for,* dark take the man.

Pantu still did not know how the day had gone so

wrong. But now the Shades were dead, and the only one left—Kaita—seemed to be hunting him.

I wonder, these many years later, if he thought of going into town and finding Mag and me and telling us what had transpired. We would have helped him, of course, the poor fool. But whether he wanted to or not, he did not do it.

Instead, he went to one of the other cabinets—one of the high, locked ones on the other side of the room. From a nook in the wall he pulled a key.

The Shades had not known that Pantu knew about the key. Indeed, they did not know he knew about this chamber. Pantu was a poor one for stealth, but he was an expert at being ignored. He had discovered long ago that he could go almost anywhere, so long as he did not try to hide it, and everyone around him would simply ignore his presence. In truth, it was what he had tried that morning with Mag and me. Only Mag's heightened sense of danger had discovered him and led to all the rest of the day's madness.

And so, lurking in the background and keeping to the shadows, Pantu had learned much of the Shades' doings. He had seen the ritual they performed with the cauldron of black liquid. And he thought he knew what they were doing.

The key turned easily in the cabinet's lock. He opened it to reveal a small pile of black, almost translucent crystals. These were magestones. Simply owning them was one of the highest crimes listed by the King's law. Using them was even worse. Eaten by a wizard, they granted a terrible power—but, too, they ate away at the mind, creating a hunger that overpowered all reason.

Magestones had given Xain the power to save my life in the Greatrocks. Magestones had driven him mad to the point that he almost killed me.

But Pantu knew none of this. He knew only that the Shades burned the magestones in a fire under the cauldron—and he thought he knew why. The Shades had been secretive about their motives, of course, but Pantu had made several guesses, helped by the papers the Shades left strewn about their shelves and desks. Pantu had never learned to read, but the papers also bore many sketches of vampires.

A vampire plagued Lan Shui. The Shades were performing a ritual that had something to do with it. It stood to reason, in his mind, that they were trying to drive it off, using some magic that was beyond the King's law.

Therefore, Pantu now drew five magestones from the cabinet. The Shades had only ever used two at a time, added to the fire once every two days. But Pantu was tired of that. He was tired of hearing about attack after attack, townsfolk and those beyond the walls slaughtered in the night. Entire families devoured by a beast that no one had lived to speak of.

Five stones. Five stones would drive it away for certain.

Taking the stones in his hand, he crept beneath the cauldron. The fire still burned there, black as night, its flames somehow draining light from the room, rather than bestowing it. Pantu cast the stones into the fire. It swelled, licking at the bottom of the cauldron.

The evil energy in the house swelled. Pantu clutched at his chest, feeling for a moment that he could not breathe. The feeling passed, and he backed away from the cauldron on hands and knees, shaking.

There. That sensation would spread, now. The vampire, frightening as it was, could not withstand such a ward.

Or so Pantu thought. But then, he had never seen what the Shades had put into the cauldron that they heated with their darkfire.

His work done, Pantu left the underground chamber as fast as he could.

TWENTY-SEVEN

In a dejected frame of mind, Mag and I returned to our inn and went to our room. With Mag's help, I bandaged the cut on my arm. It was not so deep as I had feared, though it still stung when we put a healing poultice on it. Once we were finished, we changed out of our bloody clothes and into fresh ones. Mag threw herself on her back atop her bed, while I sat in our one chair, in the corner of the room.

"A vampire," I said. "Now I understand the fear in the eyes of these people."

"And Yue's words make sense," said Mag. "Do you

remember? When we first arrived, she told us to inform her before we left. I imagine no one has been able to leave or reach Lan Shui since the vampire arrived. We only managed it because we came from the Greatrocks, into which the creature will not tread."

"And why would it?" I said. "It has plenty of food here."

"We must help these people," said Mag. "Though I have never fought a vampire before."

I cocked my head as I regarded her. "I am glad to hear you say so. I feared you might wish to pursue the weremage."

Mag scoffed. "The weremage is well beyond our reach, and we have little hope of finding out where until we can get our hands on that boy. But even if I knew she was just over the next horizon, I would not abandon these people to the slaughter. Do you think me heartless?"

"I do not, and I am glad to be proven right," I said. "Very well. Like you, I have never hunted a vampire before. But we may have to pursue it regardless, even without information. Time is not on our side. Yue has made it clear that she wants us gone."

"Have you heard tales of them?"

I snapped my fingers, for her words had given me an idea. "I have not. Yet there is one here who knows far more tales than I do. That old singer, Dryleaf. He said we should poke around the town and tell him what we found. I have a feeling this is what he meant."

Mag's mouth twisted. "I wish he had spoken plainly to us, rather than leading us on with such games. But mayhap he had his reasons. Let us find him, then, and ask."

Together we went down to the common room and found the barman. I feared he might not wish to tell us where Dryleaf's room was, but he offered no resistance whatsoever. It seemed it was not uncommon for the townsfolk to seek the old man's wisdom.

Dryleaf had a room on the first floor, towards the back of the inn and just next to the door leading to the privy. The smell was rather awful, but mayhap he did not mind. Or mayhap he appreciated the ability to relieve himself at a moment's notice—often a requirement for older folk, as I can now tell you from long experience.

He appeared soon after our two brief knocks, and when he opened the door he stood there for a moment blinking over our shoulders, pulling his blue robes closer about himself.

"Yes?" he said at last. His voice was bright, but weary, and I wondered if we had woken him. "Who is it, and how can I help you?"

"Good day, Dryleaf," I said. "It is Albern. We spoke yesterday. My friend and I are the visitors from the Greatrocks?"

"Ah, yes, of course," he said, wrinkles deepening in a wide smile. "How can I help you both?"

"That is rather a long conversation," said Mag.

"Mayhap we could take you to the common room and buy you a meal?"

"I do not pay for my food here, but of course I will accompany you," said Dryleaf. "A moment."

He turned back to his room, but I held the door open. "Can I help at all?"

"Oh, sky no," he said. "I have it all arranged, you see. Can find everything by touch. But bless your path for offering. No, go sit, and I will see you shortly. Or at least, we will speak shortly." He gave a little chuckle at his own joke.

Mag and I went to the common room and sat. Neither of us was hungry, but we both ordered ale, and Mag even managed not to turn her nose up at it when the barman was looking. Soon Dryleaf emerged from the back of the inn. I called to him, and he used his stick to poke his way over to us. I helped him into a seat.

"How has your morning been?" he said, once he had settled himself.

"I will not say 'good,' but certainly eventful," said Mag. "We found some in this town who were up to evil deeds."

"Ah," said Dryleaf carefully, folding one hand over the other. "I may have heard something of them. And what did you do when you found them?"

"We fought," I said. "They lost. They will do no more harm."

Dryleaf's face went somewhat paler. "I . . . please tell me, friends. There was a boy—"

"Pantu," said Mag, cutting him off gently. "He is fine. Frightened, I am sure, but unharmed."

Dryleaf gave a deep sigh of relief. "Thank the sky. He is not a bad child at heart, but he has often landed himself in trouble. He is a poor judge when it comes to choosing companions."

I leaned in closer. "We learned something else today, Dryleaf. When you and I spoke yesterday, why did you not speak of the vampire? Why has *no one* spoken about the vampire?"

Dryleaf shrugged. "I told you as much yesterday: you two are strangers here, and these are uncertain times. I said nothing, for I thought you might be one of those ruffians, aiming to see how much I knew about your doings here in town. I did not *think* so, for you did not sound the sort—but I could not be sure. As for the rest of the townsfolk, can you blame them? You are strangers from beyond the walls. Seeing a town weak and afraid, some might try to take advantage of the situation. You would not be the first highway robbers to think they could leave Lan Shui with more gold than they brought."

"Well, that is not our aim," I said. "We seek a weremage who attacked our home in Northwood."

Mag cocked her head at me, and I frowned at her. Only after a moment did I notice what she had: I had called Northwood *our* home without thinking of it. A flush crept into my cheeks, and I turned back to Dryleaf.

"She attacked Northwood and killed many who are dear to us," Mag said, covering for my sudden, awkward silence. "We followed her trail here. We have not found her, but we think those we fought today were her companions."

"Hm," said Dryleaf. "That may be. They have not been here long. Indeed, many in Lan Shui did not notice their arrival at all. I always keep a sharp ear out for the town's news, and I only heard vague rumors of their presence—most of those through Pantu. But the town has been very different since they arrived."

"Different?" I said. "Different how?"

"Well, for one thing, the trouble with the vampire only began after they arrived," said Dryleaf, pursing his lips. "I have tried to point this out to some in the town, including Yue, but they ascribed it to coincidence."

I frowned, suddenly doubtful. "I . . . cannot say that I blame them. I have never fought a vampire, and I know little about them. But they cannot be controlled by any human, that much is certain."

"That is as may be," said Dryleaf. "But still it makes me uneasy."

"I am not overly interested in the vampire's arrival in Lan Shui," said Mag. "I am more interested in how we can kill it."

Dryleaf was taken aback. "Kill it?"

"Yes," I said. "We are pursuing the weremage, as we said, but we cannot with clear hearts leave Lan Shui in danger. We will help get rid of the vampire before we leave."

The old man sighed, his shoulders drooping. I was surprised—I thought he would be happy to hear that we were going to help. But he seemed to have been overcome by some old sadness, something he had been able to forget but had suddenly been reminded of again. He overcame it quickly, though, seeming to marshal himself even as we watched.

"Well, I am grateful for your help, as I am sure many in the town are—or would be, if they knew of your aim. As for the vampire, I will tell you what I know. It has struck near the village, but so far it has not come within the walls. They prefer to attack victims who are alone and unaided."

"Well, your words explain the abandoned farms we saw outside the town," I said.

"Just so," said Dryleaf. "The vampire seems to be watching Lan Shui. It was after the second attack—three weeks ago now—that we became certain of what we were facing. When we did, Yue sent a messenger to the Mystics in Bertram to request their help. But that messenger was discovered a few days later in the wilderness. Her body had been torn apart and drained of blood. We sent another, but he met the same fate. No one would go a third time—or rather, Yue would not send them."

"But that seems almost intelligent," said Mag. "I thought that vampires were like animals."

Dryleaf shook his head. "In some ways, yes, but not entirely. They have no society or culture, the way that satyrs do, and they never work together. They are solitary hunters. No one is sure where they come from, since they do not seem to breed, or at least there have been no sightings of vampire young. But in any case, they are possessed of incredible cunning, and they will study the actions of their prey with a single-minded obsession. The vampire could easily have seen the messenger and known they were going to get help."

Mag frowned. "That is ill news. I wonder how it keeps watch. It would be difficult to watch all the roads leading away from Lan Shui to other, larger towns and cities nearby."

"To us, it does seem incredible," said Dryleaf. "But vampires are possessed of astounding speed and agility, and they can see in the dark. Sunlight, on the other hand, is poisonous to them, and they hide from it. But the messengers stood no chance when the vampire stalked them in the night."

"Well, it will not find me such easy prey," said Mag. Then, glancing at me, she smiled. "And I shall ensure it does not eat Albern, either. Now, how do we find it, and how do we kill it?"

"The second question is more easily answered," said Dryleaf. "Wood is poisonous to a vampire. Stab it with a steel blade, and it will only become enraged and kill you faster. But pierce it through with wood, and it will die as if it had drunk pure nightshade oil. A stab in the heart is best, for that will kill it instantly. You can also cut off the head, or burn them, though that is much harder to accomplish."

"Easy enough," said Mag.

"The much harder prospect is how to find them," said Dryleaf. "The best advice I can give is what I have already told you: they avoid civilization, and sunlight burns them. Therefore they are forced to lurk near lairs where they can ensure no sunlight will reach them. That usually means caves, and Lan Shui lies at the very feet of the Greatrocks. Though I think you are more likely to find this beast somewhere in the western spur that lies between us and Bertram."

"That was my thought," I put in. "If this creature has found and stopped two messengers, we will not find it to the east."

"You will find a home northwest of Lan Shui, on the lower slopes of the spur," said Dryleaf. "It was attacked six days ago, and everyone who dwelled there was killed. The barman should be able to point it out to you upon a map."

"Then our path is clear," said Mag. "We head west, search the spur, find the vampire, and kill it." She clapped her hands and stood.

"I only hope it is as easy as you make it sound," said Dryleaf, a cloud of doubt passing across his expression.

"We will set out at once," I said, rising to my feet.

"If we hurry, we should be able to get there in plenty of time to stalk it to its lair and set a trap."

"One more ale for the dusty road," said Mag, turning and making for the bar. Dryleaf chuckled as her footsteps retreated.

"She is a fighter, that one," he said.

"Indeed. Sometimes I think she is too much of one." I sighed.

"You sound troubled," said Dryleaf, frowning.

"We were both fighters, once. We served in a few mercenary companies, spending many years with the Ruby Crowns in particular. But we left that life behind a long time ago. Now I have been unable to rid myself of the feeling that I dragged Mag back into a world that she was much happier to have left behind."

"Yet you seem to be more reluctant, at least when it comes to this hunt," said Dryleaf.

"True," I said quietly. "I suppose I have less to avenge."

"Vengeance is a shadowed road with a mournful end, whether you are victor or victim," intoned Dryleaf.

"I have not heard that wisdom. I cannot say that I like it, but it has the ring of truth."

Dryleaf gave a grim smile. Then he cocked his head. "You say you served with the Ruby Crowns. I used to travel, as I told you, and I heard many tales of that company. Would I have heard of your exploits?"

"Mine?" I said. "I doubt it. But Mag is another matter. Did anyone ever tell you of the Uncut Lady?"

The effect was immediate. Dryleaf straightened at once and gave a little gasp. "The Uncut Lady? You cannot mean that she is your friend, just across the room right this very minute."

"I do," I said, grinning.

"To think that I have been speaking with her, and never realized," said Dryleaf. "Her voice is far more beautiful than I had imagined it would be."

"Do not tell her that, I beg you. She thinks highly enough of herself as it is."

Dryleaf giggled. "If half the tales of her are true, she deserves to think so. I must shake her hand."

I shook my head and laughed. "Sky above. The last thing Mag's ego needs is an admirer like you."

Dryleaf smiled in reply. The deep lines around his eyes crinkled when he did it, and his bushy beard jumped. But the smile faded almost as quickly as it had come.

"The two of you will take care of yourselves out there, yes?"

"We will," I told him. "As much as I can 'take care' of her."

"Do not undervalue yourself too much," said Dryleaf. "I am a fair judge of people, and that is just as easy to do when you cannot see them. I would say that the love and the companionship you give to Mag are worth more than a thousand swords at her side. From what I know of her, in any case, she has never needed help when it comes to fighting."

I studied him a long moment. "I will try to remember it. Thank you."

Mag returned with a mug of ale. It was half-empty already. "We should be off. I have told the barman to ready the horses for us. Dryleaf, you have our eternal thanks for your counsel. It is a pleasure to encounter such a wise and helpful mind this far from home."

Dryleaf's mouth opened, and a thin squeak came out. Mag frowned. I seized her arm and hurried her away from the table.

"Sky above, let us get on the road before he musters the strength to speak."

TWENTY-EIGHT

The horses were being led out of the stable when we walked outside, and we rode out at once. The main road led north out of the town and continued that way for some leagues before turning west in the direction of Bertram. But we abandoned that direction quickly, turning upon a smaller side road that led to the farms and homesteads across the land that led up to the western spur.

Just as Dryleaf had said, the barman had been able to tell us where to find what we were looking for. There were many homesteads and farms this way, but they became fewer and farther between as one drew away from Lan Shui. At first we rode through farmlands just like the ones we had seen when we first came to the town, and just as then, many of the farms looked abandoned. But soon the land was all wild, open countryside, with no one around. Trees began to grow thicker about us, until soon we were riding through a small wood, through which we could occasionally still glimpse the rising spur of land ahead.

Finally the ground began to climb, and the trees thinned again. We crested a slope and, as if it had sprung out of the ground to meet us, we came upon the homestead we had been searching for.

At the center of it was a house, and a little farther off, a barn stood at the bottom of a steep slope. Some crops had been grown on the lands surrounding the house, but weeds had begun to spring up among them unchecked.

Mayhap thirty paces from the house were the blackened remains of a funeral pyre.

We burned them, of course, the barman had told us. *It was the only . . . well, the only proper thing to do. But their child was—well, they had two, and we found the elder with his parents. The younger son . . . well, we never found his body.*

We paused at the sight, surveying the cleared land for a moment. Mag studied the pyre with a dour look on her face, and I wondered if she was thinking of Sten. After a time, she nudged her horse again.

"Come," she said. "The day is young, and there is hunting yet to do."

She led me to the house, and we took a brief look inside. If the cold pyre had cast a shadow over our mood, the house plunged our souls into darkness. Though the people of Lan Shui had removed and burned the bodies, they had done nothing further to clean the place. Pieces of smashed furniture lay strewn about, and blood stained the floors and even some of the walls.

"They had a back door," I said, pointing to it. "I wonder why they did not try to escape."

"It must have attacked too quickly," said Mag.

We left the place. It was clear that there was nothing inside to help us in our hunt, and I had no desire to remain there a moment longer than I had to. In the clearing outside, we spent a moment gathering ourselves. Mag's expression had soured still further, and I worried that she might do something rash. Not that I knew what that might be—we had no idea where the vampire had gone, nor, indeed, where to start looking.

"Let us explore the wilderness," I told her. "If I had to guess, I would say it came from the west. That is where the land rises again, and where there are most likely to be caves."

"As you say," said Mag.

She swung into her saddle at once, and I followed her a moment after. We guided our horses towards the wilderness out in back of the house. But as we drew within ten paces of the trees, I heard a sharp rustling in the underbrush.

"Hist!" I whispered.

We leaped down from our saddles again. Quick as blinking, I had my bow up and an arrow nocked, and Mag held her spear ready to strike. We approached the woods one step at a time. Behind us, the horses nickered nervously.

"Remember, they said it was fast," whispered Mag.

"It is not the vampire," I said. "The sun is up."

Mag frowned. "What, then?"

I said nothing, for I had no answer.

And then, from the shadows between the trees, a creature leaped forwards. I almost loosed my arrow but stopped myself just in time. My mind had seen a wolf, but in the space of a heartbeat I saw that it was only a dog. Granted, it was a large beast—a wolfhound of a kind common in Dorsea. Its fur was mottled brown with black spots. The hound growled at us, hackles rising.

"Mayhap it belonged to the family," said Mag.

"That was my thought," I said.

I could not help a small measure of disapproval as I looked at the beast. It must have run off into the woods when the vampire came. I knew it was only a beast, but in my homeland, we trained hounds to be loyal to their masters.

And then I caught another movement in the woods.

"Wait . . ."

A small, pallid figure peeked out from behind a trunk. As soon as it saw me looking, it vanished again.

My eyes widened.

"The child," I breathed.

I loosened my draw and stowed my arrow. Mag quickly put up her spear and knelt, extending a hand. The hound calmed down at once, its growls ceasing. But it did not relax its stance, nor move from its position between us and the boy.

"Hello," called out Mag. "We are here to help. We came from Lan Shui."

The boy poked his head out from behind the tree again. My heart ached to see the stark terror in his wide eyes. His hair was disheveled and matted with days' worth of dirt and grime from the woods, and his clothes, though sturdy-looking, were almost black with filth.

"Hello," Mag said again. "Will you come out? We will not hurt you. I swear it."

Slowly, achingly slowly, the boy took a step out from behind the tree. The hound at last relaxed its stance, straightening and turning to trot by the boy's side. He seemed to draw strength from its presence, for he walked forwards a bit more confidently, though he still kept a good distance away from us.

"You are from town?" he said. His words cracked, the sound of a voice that had not been used for days. "I do not know you."

"We are travelers," said Mag. "When we passed

through Lan Shui, they told us what had happened here."

His pale face whitened further. The dog whined.

"But we do not have to speak of it," said Mag quickly. "We only want to help you. Can we take you back to town?"

"I do not know you," the boy repeated.

"As she said, we are not from Lan Shui," I told him. "But Mag speaks the truth. We mean you no harm."

The boy said nothing, but only tightened his grip on the hound's fur. Mag went from kneeling to sitting, and drew back her hand.

"What is your name?" she said.

The boy's nose twitched. "I am Liu," he said softly.

"Liu," said Mag. "Some others came before us. Did you not see them?"

"When?" said Liu.

Mag looked up at me, and I answered. "Mayhap three days ago."

"I was in the woods," said Liu. "Oku and I hid there. We hid as far away as we could. I was afraid to come back until yesterday."

"His name is Oku?" said Mag, pointing to the hound. Its tail wagged once and then stopped. The hound tossed its head, as if it had realized what it had done and was slightly embarrassed.

"Yes," said Liu. "He went with me when I . . . when I ran."

Tears welled up in his eyes, and his lip trembled. I felt my chest grow tight.

"That was very smart and brave of you," said Mag, her voice thick.

"Mama told me to," whispered Liu.

"And you were very wise to listen to her," said Mag.

"She died," said Liu, his tears beginning to leak down his cheeks. "And Papa, and Qinsha. Did they not?"

Qinsha must have been his older brother. I looked at Mag helplessly, but she never took her eyes off Liu.

"Oku went with you," she said. "He seems like a very good dog."

Liu did not notice that she had avoided his question. Oku's tail wagged again, twice this time, and he padded slowly towards Mag. He sniffed tentatively at her feet before submitting to a gentle pat between the ears.

"He likes you," said Liu.

"I am glad," said Mag.

Liu took his first step forwards since emerging from the forest. Another long pause. Another small step.

"Are those your horses?" he said at last.

"Yes," said Mag. "But the brown one is an idiot. He is so stupid, my friend named him Foolhoof."

Liu giggled. It sounded as if the noise had been pulled from him against his will. "What about the grey one?"

"Her name is Mist. She is much smarter, and she loves children. Would you like to meet her?"

Liu gave a tentative nod, and Mag rose at last to her feet. I feared Oku would be startled by her movement, but the hound accepted it easily enough. It trotted behind her as she went to Liu and reached out. The boy took her hand and let her lead him to the horses, who had begun to drift off. I noticed that Oku seemed to be limping a bit as he walked by Mag's side.

"Here, boy," I said, walking over to him. Oku paused and looked up at me, his wide eyes glistening. I knelt by his side and extended a hand, slowly, towards his left rear leg. Oku tensed, but I kept my movements slow, and he let me take the leg. Part of the fur was matted, and probing it gently with my fingers, I felt a light cut.

"He has been hurt," I said, looking up at Liu.

"The monster did that," said the boy. "Oku tried to fight it, but it hurt him."

"I have some things in my saddlebag for that," I said, rising and going to Foolhoof. The gelding looked at me suspiciously, but he stood still as I opened a saddlebag. From it I drew some dried yarrow, crushing it in my fist and mixing it with some water from my skin. I returned to Oku and spread it on the cut. The wolfhound submitted to my ministrations, though he whined about it.

"Do not hurt him," said Liu, frowning.

"It stings a bit, but it will help the wound heal," I said.

"Liu," said Mag. "Did you see anything after you ran into the woods? We want to make sure no one else gets hurt."

The boy went silent for a long moment and avoided our gazes. But finally he nodded. "I saw the monster afterwards. It came from that direction, and it left the same way." He pointed towards the trees in a northwesterly direction.

I went that way, leaving Foolhoof behind me. Sure enough, right where Liu had pointed, there were tracks on the ground. They were not human, that I knew. Each step had torn deep gouges in the dirt, and I thought of the clawed limbs that vampires were said to have. It also seemed to run on all fours.

"I have it," I told Mag. "It will be an easy trail to follow."

"Thank the sky," she said. "Let us get them back to town quickly. We should be able to return with plenty of time to follow it before night comes."

Mag hoisted Liu up into the saddle before her. The boy seemed delighted to be riding atop a horse. I would have wagered that he had never been on one before. Oku ran by our side, and despite the wound in his leg, he kept pace with our horses' trotting easily enough.

We rode away from the homestead, careful to keep

Liu on the northern side of the clearing, where he would not see the pyre upon which his parents' and brother's corpses had been burned.

TWENTY-NINE

ALBERN DREW HIS HORSE TO A HALT. SUN WALKED another few paces before she realized the old man had stopped, and she hastily returned to him.

"What?" said Sun. "What is wrong?"

"Nothing at all," said Albern. "We have arrived."

Sun, who had become lost in the story again, blinked hard and looked around. They stood in a clearing in the woods, a good distance southwest of the town. She had a vague memory of Albern leading her off the main road and down the side path that took them here, but she had hardly noticed at the time. Above them was a rise in the land, and not far away was a cave with a deep, black mouth. It seemed somehow to loom over them in the night. Moonslight let her see only a few paces within the entrance.

"Would you help me start a fire?" said Albern amiably after dismounting. "I can manage it, but it is somewhat harder."

"Of course," said Sun. "Do you have flint?"

"Naturally," said Albern, pulling it from a pouch at his belt. As Sun collected dry leaves and twigs for kindling, Albern went to the trees and pulled down a few small branches to get the fire going. But when he had returned with those, he went to a small hollow nearby and retrieved some larger logs that looked to have been cut with an axe.

"Those were here already," said Sun. "You have been here before."

"I have," said Albern. "Just today. I told you I planned to come here tonight."

With Sun's help, he laid the logs in a crossing pattern. When it was done, Sun took a knife from her boot and struck flint to it, sending sparks across the leaves. They caught easily, and in no time a merry fire burned before them.

"How did the boy survive?" said Sun as Albern worked.

"It was only a few days."

"A few days without food is long enough to be perilous for one so young," she said. "A few days without water will kill anyone."

"There was a stream in the woods that his family would drink from, and he went there on occasion," said Albern. "I think it is likely he collected some roots and berries, too, for his parents would have told him if any were safe to eat. But more than that, do not underestimate the will to live. Even in a child, it can be strong enough to pull us through times of great peril. You would not enjoy a few days without food or water, but I imagine you would survive them."

Sun found a nearby branch to use as a poker, and then she settled herself on the ground next to Albern, staring into the flames. It was a little while before the old man looked at her, his eyes alight with interest.

"You seem to be deep in thought," he said. "If it is no imposition, may I ask what you are thinking about?"

Sun looked at him like one just waking up. "Hm? Oh, it is no great matter. Only, I do not quite understand what a vampire is. I have heard the name, but never a proper tale of them."

"Ah," said Albern. "A fair question indeed. Vampires were rare in those days, and they are more so now. But there is not much to tell beyond what I have already said. They subsist on blood. Though they will gnaw on corpseflesh, they seem to do so only to drain as much blood as possible. No hair grows upon their bodies. Their ears are pointed like an Elf's—though of course they are in all other ways entirely different from those terrible beings—and they walk sometimes hunched on two legs, sometimes on all four. They can leap several paces from a standstill, and their claws are sharp enough to sink into wood and most stone, meaning that walls are no proof against them."

Sun shuddered. "How horrible."

Albern nodded. "Yes. They are quite terrifying, especially if one does not know how to defeat them—which I did not, before Dryleaf told me."

"A good thing that he was there," said Sun. "You were most fortunate."

"Was I?" said Albern, and his eyes crinkled as he smiled. "I have already told you my views on fortune and luck. But if I may, as an aside—would you hold my bow?"

The question was so unexpected that Sun stared at him for a moment, blinking. "I . . . yes," she said at last. "But why?"

"Because we are in the woods at night, of course," said Albern. "I doubt anything like a wolf will approach our fire, but just in case it should—well, let us say that I am not quite the shot I used to be."

He lifted the stump of his right arm, and Sun could not help but laugh. Albern's smile deepened, and he reached for his bow, which he had placed on the ground at his feet. Sun took it with reverent hands.

She had heard enough tales of Albern to know how much he had accomplished with this bow, what deadly foes he had faced armed with nothing else. Seized by a sudden impulse, she drew the string. It pulled far more easily than she had thought it would, and yet she could feel the power contained in the wood. She felt that she could shoot farther, and with greater power, than any bow she had ever held in her life.

"It is a masterpiece," she breathed. "You made this yourself, did you not?"

"I did," said Albern. "And if I may be forgiven a moment of pride, I am glad you knew that."

"Whenever you are spoken of in tales, your skill with a bow is always listed first among your traits," said Sun.

Albern laughed at that, shaking his head. "If only those tales were true. I am a talespinner myself, and so I know something of how the truth of my stories must have been twisted through the years, becoming a count of accomplishments that I would scarcely recognize."

"Yet I have heard it said, on good authority," said Sun, "that tales are not meant to be believed."

"Then you have been well advised."

Sun smiled, but it died quickly upon her lips. "I must ask you another question, if I may be so bold."

"You have well earned at least one more honest answer."

"What under the sky are we doing here?" Sun gestured at the empty clearing around them, at the stars above and the black, looming mouth of the cave not far off.

Albern nodded, pursing his lips. "A fair enough question. Let me answer only that I am expecting someone. Do not trouble yourself overmuch; I expect them before long. After they have arrived, and then left again, we can be on our way. You can go back to . . . well, to whatever you were doing before you found me. Does that answer satisfy you?"

"Will you give me a better one?" said Sun, her brows rising.

"Not at present," said Albern with a grin.

"Then I suppose it will have to do."

"I thought it might. And now, would you like me to continue the tale?"

"Please," said Sun, settling herself upon the ground.

We rode into town with Liu and Oku. Guards must have spotted us approaching, for we found a small reception when we arrived. Several of the folk of Lan Shui were there, as well as Constable Baolan.

"What are you doing back here?" said Yue as we pulled to a stop before her. Her glare did not look promising.

"We found this boy near his homestead," said Mag. "We heard that it was attacked only a few days ago."

Yue looked at Liu again, and color rose in her cheeks. "Sky above. The Ton boy."

"Just so," I told her. "Is there anyone here who can care for him?"

"Give him to me," said Yue, rushing forwards. She extended her hands for Liu, but the boy recoiled, pressing back into Mag's body.

"Go with her, Liu," said Mag, urging the boy forwards with a gentle push. Though he still seemed reluctant, Liu let himself be pulled down from the saddle and into Yue's arms. She handed him off to a man from the town, who took off his coat to bundle Liu up in it.

"Now then," said Yue. "What are you doing back here?"

Mag and I both balked at that. "We returned a boy you thought was dead," I told her. "That should earn us at least some leniency."

"I do not deny our gratitude," said Yue. "But I thought you left this morning, for good, and I was not sad to see you go."

"We are staying for a little while at least, to help with the—" I shot a glance at Liu and cut my own words off. "With the creature that has been seen in the lands around here."

Yue scowled, and she, too, looked at Liu. "That is not a matter for you to concern yourself with. We are taking care of it."

"Are you?" I said, my blood rising. "Is that why we found this boy alone, abandoned in the woods? Despite your obvious desire to see us only as trouble-makers, we are not here to harm you, or anyone in this town."

Yue turned back to the boy, and then back to us. Her hands were twitching, as though she sought some-one she could feel justified in seizing and throttling. "Why did you go looking for the creature?" she said. "What is it to you?"

"A danger to the people of your town," I said. "And we think we can end that danger. As you have said be-fore, we are rather well-armed travelers."

"You turn my words on me like a jest," she said. "Forgive me for thinking this hardly matters to you."

"Because I do not always look like I am chewing on a lemon rind does not mean I am not serious."

Her scowl deepened, and she strode towards my horse. I jumped down from the saddle and planted my feet as she stalked up to me, looking down into my eyes. I did not realize until just that moment that she was almost a full head taller than I was. Mag tensed in her saddle, but she did not yet climb down to help.

"You think you can insult me in front of the people of my town?" growled Yue, too quiet for anyone but me to hear. Her breath washed over my face, and I was surprised to find it unexpectedly sweet.

"That is the first time I have done so," I said in an equally low voice. "Yet your words to us have been a never-ending stream of disrespect. I appreciate your position, constable. For once, try to see ours."

She looked over my shoulder at Mag. I felt some of the tension bleed from her, though she did not back away. "What position is that?"

I waited until she met my gaze again. "We want to help. We have other business that will carry us far away from Lan Shui, but we will not abandon your people while this monster threatens them. What do you have to lose? The worst that may happen is that the beast kills us. The best that may happen is the reverse."

She seemed to want to argue further. But the eyes of the townspeople were upon her, and they were pitiful. At last she stamped her foot in frustration.

"Fine," she said, loud enough for everyone to hear. "If you wish to go riding off after this beast, I suppose I cannot stop you. But do not expect me to go trooping off after you."

"We will not," I said. "Now, if you will excuse us, we mean to do more hunting before the sun wanes."

Yue's face went from dark to pale in an instant. "The sun is lowering. Night will be here soon."

"We mean to lure it out of its cave just after sundown," said Mag. "Better, we think, than following it into its lair, even during the day."

The constable shook her head. "I cannot say that is a wise course of action. But it seems clear you will do whatever you want."

"Take Oku!"

Liu's thin shout came from nowhere, and I looked up at him in surprise. The boy still clung to the man holding him, but he looked at us in earnest appeal.

"Take Oku," he said again. "He is a good hunter."

"Thank you, Liu," said Mag gently. "But we can look after ourselves."

"Oku is a good fighter. You will need him." The boy's eyes welled up, and before we could answer, he burst into tears. "He kept me safe," he gasped between sobs. "He will keep you safe, too."

My eyes stung, and I blinked hard before looking to Mag. She met my gaze and sighed. Oku sat near the villagers, his ears cocked as if he knew what we were saying.

"Oku," I said. "Tiss."

The hound's mouth parted in a smile, his tongue lolling to the side, and he trotted up beside Mag's horse. She gave a sigh and wheeled around, riding away from the wall. I remounted, looking down at Yue again—mayhap for the last time, I suddenly realized.

"We will return when we have killed the beast, or not at all," I said. "I wish you and your people good fortune."

I turned and rode after Mag, hoping I cut a suitably impressive figure as we trotted towards the lowering sun.

THIRTY

NOW THAT WE KNEW WHERE WE WERE GOING, WE pressed the horses harder, and we had returned to the homestead in what felt like no time at all. But looking up, I could no longer see the sun over the western spur ahead. Daylight would remain in the sky for a while yet, but we were running out of time. Oku kept up with us easily, apparently untroubled by the slight wound in his flank. As soon as we stopped in the clearing with the farmhouse, he trotted around the perimeter, sniffing at the ground.

I led Mag to the woods where I had seen the tracks

earlier. "We can follow them easily. But I am not sure whether we should bring the horses or not. They will make the journey faster, but I do not want them to panic if the vampire should attack us."

"Let us bring them, and if we sense we are nearing the end of the trail, we can leave them behind, or tether them to a tree," said Mag. "I want to find the creature's lair in time, or we may not catch it as it tries to slip out to hunt."

That seemed a sensible point, and so I did as she suggested. We nudged the horses into the woods, and I kept my eyes fixed on the ground, only lifting my gaze every so often to take stock of the land around us.

It was unsurprising that the vampire followed no trail I could see. Its path plunged straight through the trees and underbrush, paying no heed to any obstacle in the way. It was also unerringly straight—wherever the vampire had been heading, it knew the direction well.

The light was dim in the sky when we came to the end of the trail. It led into the mouth of a large cave, which came looming at us from the side of the slope ahead. We stopped half a span away. Oku began to whine immediately. I glanced down at him.

"I think we have found what we are looking for," I said.

"So it seems," agreed Mag. "But we do not have much time." Daylight was vanishing quickly.

"Let us tether the horses a little farther away and make ready."

We did so in short order, leaving them back down the trail we had followed to get here, their reins tied to the springy branches of a willow tree. Oku stuck close beside us now, and he began to whine the moment we approached the cave again.

"If we take care not to get injured, it should not be too difficult of a fight," I said. "You have your spear, and I have my arrows. If we pierce it through, the wood should do the rest of the work for us."

"Simple," said Mag.

We took up position near two trees that stood close to each other. I pulled some dried meat from a pouch on my belt and ate it, suddenly realizing I had not had a meal since the morning. I hoped I would not regret that in the coming fight. As the light faded further and the blue edge of night bled into the sky, the moons showed themselves in the east.

"I think I should lure it forwards," said Mag. "It will see me with my spear and, I think, approach me first. You can lurk in the trees, and when you have a clear shot, you can take it. Hopefully that will end it quickly."

"A good plan," I said. "As long as you do not let it spring upon you."

"It will be your fault if it does," said Mag with a wry look. "Do not wait too long to shoot."

I snorted. "As you say."

"And take the dog with you," she said. "It might distract the beast if it remains by my side."

"Careful," I said, glancing at Oku, who was watching Mag with his tongue lolling. "He is a clever hound. You would not want to insult him."

"Would I not?" said Mag indifferently.

I chuckled despite myself. "Tiss, Oku."

The dog leaped up and trotted to my side. Mag looked at me and frowned. "You said that earlier. What is it?"

"Tiss," I said. "A common command for trained hounds."

"How do I tell it to go away? I suspect I shall want to."

"Now you are just being cruel," I said, reaching down to scratch Oku behind the ears. His tail wagged with delight. "Do not listen to her, friend. She is nowhere near as fierce as she sounds."

Mag snorted and rose at last to her feet. The sunlight was nearly gone. I took Oku off into the trees, finding a place to stand that gave me a clear view of the cave mouth but did not put Mag in my line of fire. To the left of the cave mouth was a sort of natural wall in the side of the slope. The top of it was almost flat, and it climbed like a jagged stair up the side of the mountain and winding away out of sight in the woods. I guessed it would carry one closer to the peak of the spur, though I would have been hesitant to try the ascent with any speed. But I took position near it, one arrow held loose in my hand near the string.

Night advanced, and the stars twinkled above us. Still we saw nothing, heard nothing. When would the vampire rise? Did they ever have nights where they did not rise at all, but slept through to the next day, like a soldier just returned home from campaign? I wished I knew more about them, or that someone else in Lan Shui had been able to explain more—but then, if they had, they would likely have dealt with the creature themselves.

And then Oku growled.

I grew alert at once. The hound bristled, his nose pointed straight towards the cave, his paws spread. But his growl would not carry to Mag's ears. I hissed, and she glanced over. I pointed to Oku and then at the cave, hoping she could see the gesture in the moonslight. She nodded and hefted her spear and shield, planting her feet wide.

A few moments later, we heard a scraping sound. And then the vampire emerged into the night. It walked on two legs like a man, but it was grotesquely hunched, bent almost double so that its hands nearly scraped the ground. If it had straightened, I know it would have stood at least three heads taller than me. Its skin was mottled, pocked, and pallid. It reminded me of the skin of those who have been badly burned and then healed, covered with a mass of scar tissue. Its hands and feet ended in curved claws each as long as a human hand, and it clicked and clacked them against each other as it moved. Its eyes were black, black as a wizard's who had eaten magestones, and its pointed ears, which jutted backwards, flitted and twitched, straining to hear any sound. But once I saw its mouth, I forgot every other detail. It was round and wide, almost a circle, and the teeth were bared in a constant grimace. Those teeth were long and pointed and sharp, and stained so badly that in the moonslight they looked to be covered with fresh blood.

All this I took in with a moment's glance, and I felt my limbs seize with fear. My right hand, holding the arrow, was slack, and my bow arm lowered towards the ground. Oku gave a tiny whimper and slunk back behind my legs.

But Mag, of course, felt no fear at all—or if she did, she hid it perfectly. Without hesitation she took one step towards the creature, taking no care to soften her footfalls.

The vampire, which had seemed to be snuffling at the ground, snapped its head up towards her. Its sharp teeth pointed, and it let out a long, hateful hiss.

"Sky above, you are ugly," said Mag. "Come, let me wipe that hideous grimace from your face."

If the creature understood her, it gave no sign, but it did begin to slink towards her. I wondered for a moment why it moved with such caution—it knew something of humans, clearly, and had already killed many of them. Why would it not think that Mag could be hunted as easily as anyone else? Mayhap it was uncertain because Mag was so brazen in her defiance, because she did not show the slightest hesitation or dread.

And then I recalled that I was not just a spectator, and that I had remained inactive for too long. The vampire was a few scant paces away from Mag now, and soon I would lose my shot.

The arrow was already nocked. I lifted my bow, drew, and fired straight towards the creature's heart.

It moved.

When people of other kingdoms see the archers of Calentin, they are astounded at our skill. Most who met me thought my bowcraft was something of legend, that I must surely be the greatest bowman who ever lived in the nine kingdoms. Indeed, I am a skilled archer even by Calentin standards—or I was, in those days when I had both arms. And yet, for all my ability, I have met many masters who far surpassed me at the height of my skill. I was trained by a woman who could fire arrows faster than heartbeats, faster than blinking, and send them all with enough strength to pierce chainmail. If an enemy shot at *her,* she could shoot their darts from the air with her own. I know because I saw her do it. Her eyes were unerring and sharper than an eagle's, and her limbs were a blur.

And yet the vampire moved faster than her. It saw the arrow from the corner of its eye, turned, darted aside, and snatched the arrow from midair before

I realized what was happening. Then it flipped the dart around and threw it *back* at me—not with the strength of a bow, but still fast enough to pierce skin. I was saved more by luck than reflexes—I tried to duck, almost too late, and slipped on a patch of loose leaves. I struck the ground hard, the wind driven out of my lungs.

Sky save me, I thought. *How is it so fast?*

I heard an inhuman screech and looked up just in time to see it charge me. All four limbs ripped and tore at the earth to propel it forwards, sending clods of dirt in all directions.

But as fast as it was, Mag was able to catch it. She ran and leaped in between me and the vampire, and it skidded to a halt before her. But hardly had it paused before it struck with one clawed limb. Mag blocked the swipe, and I heard the deep rending of claws on wood. She stabbed in retaliation, but the vampire spun out of the way. It tried to turn the movement into another attack, but Mag's shield was there again to stop it.

It was not until that moment that I realized something about Mag. I had only ever seen her fight another human. When she did so, it was a slaughter. I had never seen her face another opponent who had stood a chance. But now, facing a foe that was so much stronger than a human could ever hope to be, Mag's skill was displayed in full. My eyes, sharp as they were, could not follow the speed of her swings and thrusts.

My mind could not comprehend how she knew where the vampire would strike next, nor how she could twist in *just* such a way to avoid it, place her shield in *just* the right way to block its swiping claws. Once or twice the vampire struck her mail instead of the shield, and I winced. But after the first time, I realized that even that was part of Mag's plan. She only let it strike her when the blow would glance from her armor, and when it gave her the opportunity to attack with her spear. Her armor was part of her, just like her shield and spear, and she fought now with her whole body instead of only her weapons.

Unfortunately for me, the vampire still outmatched her in strength. That meant she had to be more nimble than it was—and after a few heartbeats of frantic battle, that meant she had to leap out of the way of a swipe, landing on the vampire's other side.

It turned on me in an instant and pounced.

I shrieked—and not a noble battle-cry, either—and barely managed to leap to my left as its slashing claws sailed past. But now it had me backed up against the steep slope, with nowhere to run.

From the corner of my eye, I saw the natural wall that climbed up like a stair.

Nowhere to go but up.

I jumped atop the stone surface just as the vampire lunged, and it slammed bodily into the slope. Oku came flying from nowhere, snarling and yapping, and the vampire recoiled from the hound. Then Mag attacked, and the vampire screamed hatred at her as it retreated. But it, too, had nowhere to run other than the top of the wall.

It hopped up, still facing back down towards Mag. Suddenly my perch was far more dangerous than the ground had been. I edged towards the lip of the stone, readying myself to jump down. But the vampire spotted the movement out of the corner of its eye. It must have thought I was attacking, for it swiped at me again, forcing me a step back.

Three more steps up we fought that way, and now I was too high up the slope to jump down to the ground without risking a broken leg. Oku stood in front of Mag, trying to help but only, in fact, blocking her spear. And the vampire turned back and forth as it tried to pin one of us down, unable for the moment to do so.

My bow was useless with the vampire so close, and I drew my sword. But that proved to be even more futile. I swung, and for an instant I thought my strike would be true, for the vampire did not try to duck it. But that was only because it caught the sword in its hand instead. I felt the steel bite into flesh, but I did not lop the hand in half the way I would have a human's. It only hissed at me through its pointed teeth, dragged the sword from my grasp, and tossed it over the ledge.

"Blast!" I cried, my hand outstretched futilely towards the sword as it fell to the ground some ten paces below.

And then I saw something.

The vampire swiped at Oku, who leaped back only to become tangled in Mag's legs. She cursed as she spun, flipping over the dog, her green cloak flying about her.

But the moment's distraction had given the vampire an opening. It stalked towards me, black eyes glinting in the moonslight.

"A fair hunt," I said. "But I do not wish to grant you an easy meal."

I leaped over the ledge.

"Albern!" screamed Mag.

The vampire roared and leaped after me. A fall from this height would likely kill me—but the vampire would survive, and it would have a meal waiting for it at the bottom.

But then I grabbed the thick, outthrust branch of the pine tree that I had spied from the ledge.

The vampire's roar grew much louder, and then faded as it fell scrabbling past me.

I swung up and landed kneeling on the branch, slinging my bow off my shoulder and drawing an arrow in the same motion. I lined up the shot at the vampire, which was still falling through the air, and loosed.

The vampire landed. I heard nothing break, but the impact obviously winded it. Still, it looked up at the sound of the flying arrow, catching it in midair. It hissed up at me as it snapped the arrow between its dirty claws.

Then Mag's spear struck it in the neck, flying straight through it and into the ground. The vampire's eyes went wide with shock, even as a black corruption spread from the spear's wooden shaft through its skin. It looked like rotting meat, but it spread as quickly as flame.

Around us, the woods settled to silence except for Oku's throaty growling. I looked across the gap between the tree and the slope, and Mag looked back at me, panting.

"Sky above," she said. "That was a fight."

"It was," I said. "What do you think of your helpless pet now?"

"Much the same," she said. "After all, I still had to kill the thing."

My lips formed a thin line. "Only because I distracted it."

Mag chuckled. "That does seem to be what you are best at. Oh, do not look so offended, Albern. After all, we have a true pet now." She pointed at Oku.

I sighed. "Just get back to the ground. It will take me a little longer to climb down."

It did take me longer to reach the clearing than it took Mag, but not by much. When I joined her, she had already extracted her spear from the vampire's corpse and was cleaning it.

"We should take the head," I said. "Just to put Yue's mind at ease about the truth of our words."

"A good idea," said Mag. "And mayhap now she will not look upon us with such disdain."

"Mayhap," I said. "Where did my sword land?"

Mag pointed. Then, as I went to fetch the blade, she took the vampire's head off with one sweep of her spear.

We found the horses, who shifted nervously at the stench of the vampire's corpse, and rode back through the woods towards the road that would take us to Lan Shui. As we emerged from the woods into the clearing with the farmhouse, I took one last look at the darkness beneath the trees.

Something within me was still uneasy. The forest held no answers, only menace—and now a vampire's corpse. So why did I think I would not rest this night?

"It is irritating when you do that," said Sun. "When you ask a question like that, and then the story turns in another direction. You already know the answer. Why are you asking me? You could tell me if you wanted to. You choose not to."

"Hush," said Albern. "Let me have my fun."

THIRTY-ONE

PANTU PACED IN ONE OF THE UPPER BEDROOMS OF THE Shade hideout. He strained to hear any sound of fighting, of struggle, in the town outside.

That was a ridiculous urge, and he knew it. Even if the vampire *did* strike tonight, it would do so in the fields, the farms, a long ways away from Lan Shui itself. He would never hear it.

If it *did* strike tonight. But mayhap it would not.

Tonight was the night. Tonight was the test. Come morning, he would know whether or not his mad scheme had worked—whether he had finally driven the vampire away from Lan Shui for good. He had been trying to sleep, hoping to wake to a bright and happy morning, but he could barely lie down, much less close his eyes.

A floorboard creaked on the first floor.

Pantu froze. As he stopped pacing, the floorboards beneath his feet gave another, louder creak.

Had he imagined the sound?

But no. Now he heard something else. Someone coming up the stairs.

Someone? Or something? He heard claws scrabbling on the wooden steps.

Claws. No. Not possible. Not here.

He burst out the door of the bedroom onto the second story landing. At the top of the stairs crouched a figure. But it was not the vampire that Pantu so feared. It was a cat, dark of fur with a white tail, like one would find in the mountains. Pantu knew the sight of it well—every child of the foothills knew of mountain lions.

Even as disbelief struggled to work its way through his mind, even as he tried to reason out how the beast got this far into the town, the lion pounced. It gave two great swipes of its claws. Pantu felt them slice into his flesh like daggers. He gasped, his chest laid open, and felt the alien, terrifying sensation of cool air on his insides.

He fell on his back, the mountain lion perched on his chest. Its amber eyes, pupils wide as coins, stared into his own.

And then the lion said, “You were the one who was supposed to die.”

Pantu blinked through the pain, through the darkness creeping in at the edge of his vision. This had to be a dream. A nightmare. He would wake. But then he realized the truth: the lion’s eyes were glowing. It was already partway through a transformation—it had already formed a human mouth with which to speak. As he watched, the transformation finished, and Kaita knelt over him, one hand on his throat.

“Dellek should be alive,” she said. “All the others should be. Why are you the only one who survived? You are the weak one. The worthless one.”

Despite the terror, despite the knowledge of his own death, Pantu gasped out a laugh. Blood came with it. “Not so worthless. I have saved Lan Shui.”

Kaita hissed and narrowed her eyes. “You have saved nothing.”

“I completed the ritual,” said Pantu, wheezing. “Five magestones. It is finished now. The magic will drive the vampire away forever.”

He had expected Kaita to grow enraged, to storm at him, mayhap even to finish him off quickly. Instead, she only stared at him in amazement. And then she began to laugh. The laugh grew louder, ringing on and on, even as Pantu felt himself slipping into darkness.

Mag and I rode back to Lan Shui.

Though it was the middle of the night, we found many people awake and there to greet us. Yue stood among them, watching from the wall atop the south gate. Sinshi, one of the other constables, was there with her. The gate was closed, but as we rode up, Yue ordered it open before descending the stairs to meet us on the street.

"What happened?" she demanded, before we could even pull our horses to a stop.

"We fought the vampire," said Mag simply. "We won."

She cut the leather thong with which she had tied its head to her saddle and threw it into the street. The crowd recoiled and gasped. Yue's hard features were pale. "I . . . how did you—"

Most of the faces in the crowd had turned worshipfully to us, and I quailed under their gazes. "I played but a small part. I merely distracted it so that Mag could strike the killing blow."

"He almost killed it twice," said Mag. "Indeed, he might have had more clear shots if I had not gotten in his way."

I could see that Yue was growing frustrated with our modesty, and in the moment I agreed with her—at least when it came to Mag. I knew without a doubt that Mag could have defeated the creature alone, and that the same could not be said for me.

The small crowd now pushed in close around us, wanting to know more about the battle. Oku was nearly crushed against my legs by the press of people. He slipped through their legs and stepped away from the crowd, looking somewhat miffed.

As Mag, suddenly uncomfortable, tried to answer their questions, I looked over the heads of the crowd. There, near the back of the group, I saw the boy Pantu. He wore plain, grubby clothing, his face smeared with dirt. It looked as though he had been working all day. I hoped that meant he had at last found a more honest line of work. Beside him stood Dryleaf, one hand holding his walking stick and the other hand on the boy's shoulder. The old man beamed a pleasant smile, his eyeline a bit to my right. But Pantu's expression seemed strange—eager, but not as joyous as most of the other townsfolk.

I pushed past the crowd, which seemed preoccupied with Mag, and went to speak with the two of them. As he heard my footsteps approach, Dryleaf turned towards me.

"Is that Albern?" he said. "I imagine it could not be Mag, for it seems she has quite a following."

"It is," I said. "Greetings, Dryleaf. And to you, Pantu."

Pantu gave a start, as though he was surprised to have been noticed, and ducked his head. Dryleaf chuckled and patted the boy's shoulder.

"Do not mind him. He is only a bit shy. We heard what you did. This town will never be able to properly express its gratitude."

"As I tried to tell them, Mag did most of the work, and all the hardest part of it," I told him.

"I suspect you are underestimating yourself again, though I am sure the Uncut Lady fought admirably," said Dryleaf. "But no matter. I am here for quite another reason. Pantu came to me. He said he had something urgent to tell you, and so I brought him here so that we could both wait for you to return from your hunt."

I looked at Pantu in surprise. He ducked his head again. "Is that right? What is it, boy?"

His bulging eyes glinted up at me, though he hardly raised his head. "I think you should both hear it at once." He hardly stuttered, as he had last time, and he did not whine.

"A moment, then," I told him, and turned back towards the crowd surrounding Mag. Pushing my way through them, I put a hand on Mag's arm and spoke quietly. "If you are done playing the grand hero, I think we should return to the inn. I could use a meal and a bath. And that boy Pantu wishes to speak with us."

"Sky above, yes," muttered Mag.

We excused ourselves from the crowd. They did not wish to see us go, but Mag got rather insistent, and then at last, Yue commanded them all to be off to their homes before she started making arrests. I gave her a final grateful nod before we left, but she stepped close for a final word.

"I will not deny my gratitude for your actions, nor your right to a warm meal and rest," she said. "But I would speak with you again before you leave Lan Shui."

"Why, constable," I said, feigning surprise. "We would be honored. I thought you could not wait to be rid of us."

Her familiar scowl returned. "We shall see if I end up changing my mind on that count."

I laughed, and she stalked off. Mag and I went to Dryleaf and Pantu, who now stood alone on the torch-lit street.

"Well?" I said. "Here we are. What do you have to say for yourself, boy?"

"And why have you said nothing before now?" said Mag sternly.

Pantu avoided our eyes again at that. "I . . . I am sorry for what happened before. I was too ashamed to come speak with you right away. But I realized you needed to know something. About the weremage."

I tensed, stepping closer to him. "The one working with the Shades?"

He nodded. "Yes, that one. I know little about her—but I do know where she is going. She told all of us. She said her next destination was the town of Opara, in Calentin. They—the Shades—they are up to something there. She never said what it was, but it sounded important."

The boy's words struck me like a hammer blow between the eyes. Mag, too, suddenly wore a grim expression, though hers was mostly out of concern for me. My heart must have shown on my face, for Pantu looked at me curiously.

"What is wrong?"

"Nothing," I said. "Thank you very much for telling us this, Pantu. You did the right thing."

He nodded and turned, heading off into the town. It was as if he had forgotten Dryleaf was there. But the old man did not seem to notice, much less mind, for he only kept beaming at the two of us.

"Do you see what I meant?" he said. "A good boy, if sometimes misguided." He swallowed hard and put out a searching hand to shake. "Now then, ah . . . I understand I have the honor of addressing the Uncut Lady. Is that correct?"

Mag suddenly looked just as confused as she had seemed grim a moment ago. Without thinking, she took Dryleaf's wrist and shook, frowning down at him.

"I . . . have been called that, yes. But please, call me Mag."

"It would be my highest honor," said Dryleaf. "Sky above, to think I should have lived to see you in person. Or, to meet you, I should say." He gave a hearty laugh, and Mag gave a weak one as she tried to join him. "You are even better than in the stories."

"You are very much too kind," I told him. "Truly, I mean that. But come. Let us walk you back to the inn. It is late, and surely you are tired."

Dryleaf frowned at me—not out of anger, but with a sudden, strong interest. "It is late, but I am hardly weary. You are trying to cut our conversation short. Why?"

I opened my mouth, trying to summon a lie. But above us, a raven called, and I looked up at it. The bird perched on the edge of a nearby building, staring at me unblinking. My nerves tingled, a sensation that crept up and down my limbs, leaving me anxious and wishing to move. Whatever lie I had been dreaming up fled my mind.

"Pantu's words trouble me," I told him truthfully. "If the Shades are truly in Calentin, and if they are plotting something there . . . well, I wish to find out what they are doing, and why, and then I wish to stop them as quickly as I can."

"We should search their hideout," said Mag. "We hardly had any time to investigate it, the last time we were there. And I do not think Yue will begrudge us a little look about the place now."

"I would be surprised to find anything there," I told her. "But for lack of any better ideas . . . yes, let us go. In any case, I wish to ride for Opara in the morning."

"Agreed," she said. Together we turned and set off down the street, but we had not gone two steps before Dryleaf, who I had entirely forgotten, piped up behind us.

"Wait!" he said. "Wait for me!"

I clapped a hand to my forehead. "Sky save me, I am sorry. Of course I will walk you back to the inn."

"The inn?" said Dryleaf, stepping briskly up beside me. "Do not be silly. I will come with you. I would not wish to delay you for an instant, and it would be my great pleasure to accompany the Uncut Lady on one of her adventures, even such a small and uneventful part of the tale as this."

I looked over my shoulder at Mag. She shrugged. "What harm could it do?"

"I will try not to take that as an insult," said Dryleaf, his bushy eyebrows shooting skywards.

"Very well," I told him. "It will be our pleasure to have your company."

"Of course it will," he said, beaming. As we set off together, Oku fell into step next to the old man, his tongue lolling to the side.

THIRTY-TWO

Dawn was still a ways off, and the streets were mostly empty. We saw only a few people about, early risers pulling carts or hefting sacks in preparation for the day's toil. But despite the hour, they seemed almost cheery compared to when we had first arrived in the town. One of them even gave a happy smile and a nod to Mag, which she returned after a moment's hesitation.

When we reached the building where we had fought the Shades, we saw that the front door had not been closed, but still hung open. I helped guide Dryleaf through it, helping him avoid the jagged edge of the shattered doorjamb. The Shades' corpses were gone, but the bloodstains remained. For an uncomfortable moment, I was reminded of the shattered homestead to the north where we had found Liu.

Dryleaf paused inside the doorway, cocking his head back and forth as though listening. "This place has an evil feeling to it."

"It does," I agreed. In fact, the feeling had grown worse. It was stronger, more penetrating, like a thrumming in the air—a monstrous heartbeat that seized my own pulse and forced it to match time.

"Let us have a look about, then," said Mag.

"You can go with her," said Dryleaf. He released my arm and leaned on his staff. "I have my stick, and you can return to me if you have questions."

"We will be quick," I said. "Come, Mag."

From room to room we went, circling all around the first floor. All we found were some discarded scraps of food and rubbish. No messages or any other signs of what the Shades had been up to. We went to the stairs and climbed to the second floor, but it was just as barren as the first—though, thankfully, it was free of the bloodstains that spattered the first floor. Indeed, the floors of the bedrooms upstairs looked fresh-scrubbed. There were no possessions to be found. Even the clothing had been taken. Mag and I poked at the mattresses in case something had been concealed within, but there seemed to be only feathers.

"Yue has been here already," said Mag, frustrated. "If there was any clue, she has taken it."

"Well, we can ask her tomorrow," I said. "She said she wanted another word with us before we left town."

"If she *has* found anything, I doubt she will tell us," grumbled Mag.

"I think we have earned at least a little trust from her," I said. "Come. Dryleaf will likely be wondering what has happened to us."

Constable Ashta settled into her chair at the constable station. She would get no sleep that night, she knew. But the next day, for the first time in a long while, she thought she would be able to rest, well and truly.

She leaned her chair back against the wall, tilting her head back to rest against the wooden planks, and kicked her boots off. They fell to the floor, dripping a bit of mud. Twisting her feet, she reveled in the cool air washing across them, and released a deep sigh.

And then a thought occurred to her. A small, nagging thought, and yet it gave her no peace—the curse of a constable who held her duty as a sacred trust.

Did she forget to order the gate closed?

With a heavy sigh, she tilted the chair up again and reached for her boots. She was a citizen of Lan Shui. She had been born and raised here. But she still felt entirely fed up with the townsfolk sometimes. They would not wipe their own rear ends if the constables did not remind them.

Pulling on her boots—hating the warm, sweaty feel of them—she stood and strode out into the night again, turning her steps towards the north end of town. The streets were empty, thankfully, and so she was able to make quick progress. And the north gate was not far from the constables' station. She would ensure the gate was closed, and then she would return to the station, and enjoy her night's duty. Mayhap she could even sneak a nap. The sergeant would be in a lenient mood tonight.

Finally she rounded the last corner and came into sight of the north gate. Sure enough, it stood wide open. Ashta shook her head and looked skyward. She could not recall who was on gate duty that night. Was it Shen? That seemed likely. The woman had a mind like a sieve, and more than once Ashta had caught her sleeping in the guardhouse, or neglecting her duties in favor of a game of Moons.

Well, Ashta would give her a scare. Hopefully Shen would remember it, at least for a time, and not shirk her duties in the future.

She strode straight up to the guardhouse door and threw it open hard. The heavy iron knob slammed into the wooden wall behind the door, sending a loud *crack* reverberating through the night air.

The constable stopped dead in her tracks, her

mouth open, a shout ready but already dying on her lips.

The guardhouse was empty.

Mag and I came downstairs to find Dryleaf had left the front room and gone to the sitting room on the building's western side. The chairs had a thin film of dust. Oku sat by the old man's side, huddling against his legs. It was clear the hound was put off by the evil energy that suffused the building.

"And?" said Dryleaf. "Was your hunt fruitful?"

"Sadly, no," I said. "I fear we have only wasted our time, and yours."

Dryleaf shook his head slowly, clucking his tongue. "Do not trouble yourself over me," he said, shuffling towards the back of the room and feeling out the floor with his staff. "I am only sorry I could not be of more—"

He stopped.

Slowly, he turned and walked back the way he had come.

He stopped again.

"Dryleaf?" I said tentatively. "What is—"

"Quiet," he said, so sudden and brusque that I found myself complying at once. It was like the order of a battlefield commander, and I realized rather suddenly that I knew almost nothing about the old man's past. Mag, too, had fallen completely silent.

Back and forth Dryleaf walked, and now it was as if he was sniffing. But I could smell nothing other than whatever terrible, nameless stench seemed to permeate the very air in this place. At last he stopped near the center of the room. Then he turned and strode right towards us.

"Move," he said, again speaking in a voice that brooked no disobedience. Mag and I stepped aside, watching the old man. As he passed us, Mag looked at me, raising her eyebrows. I shrugged.

Dryleaf stopped at a tapestry hanging on a wall. He reached out and felt it with his hands before pulling it aside. He probed the wall behind it with his fingers. Then, suddenly, his fingers sank into the wall—or rather, a piece of the wall moved, taking his fingers with it.

There came a sharp *click,* and a section of wall beside the tapestry swung open to reveal a dank staircase.

The old man turned to us, folding his arms over each other and around his staff. I eyed him for a long moment.

"When I was a child," I said slowly, "I heard stories of blind people whose other senses grew sharper than was natural. Their other senses became so good, in fact, that they almost replaced the missing sight. Some of them could perform incredible feats, like seeing through walls, or catching arrows in midair. But I never believed such stories."

Dryleaf snorted loudly. "You were wise not to," he

said, grinning. "Such tales are ridiculous, at least so far as I have experienced. I cannot hear a mouse fart from a span away, or some such nonsense. But without my eyes to distract me, I do pay a bit more attention to my ears. That is why, when I was walking about, I heard *this.*"

He walked to the middle of the room. There, he took his staff and struck the floor at his feet. Then he struck the floor again a pace away.

Thoom.

Thunk.

Mag stared at him, astonished. "They sound different."

"Indeed they do," said Dryleaf. "Because there is a hollow spot here, and a deep one. A chamber under the house."

"Well," I said. "I suppose that makes more sense than my first thought."

Dryleaf grinned. "Sometimes, what appears to be magic is simply a matter of paying attention."

Constable Yue stalked through the street, entirely irritated. Ashta had come and fetched her as soon as she had found the north gatehouse unoccupied. She would have gone to find Shen on her own, but she did not know where the woman lived—and so it fell to Yue, as so many things did.

Yue hardly thought it was worth it. Shen was probably in her home getting drunk, celebrating the vampire's death. That was what Yue had been in the middle of doing, before Ashta came pounding at her door.

Two lefts, and then . . . and then a right? Yue frowned, stopping in the street and looking around. It had been this way. She was almost certain of it. But in the middle of the night, and with two cups of wine in her belly, it was suddenly less clear.

Kaw

Yue looked up. A raven perched on the edge of a building above her, looking down. It seemed to be studying her. For a moment Yue had the nonsensical thought that it was waiting for her to do something.

"Shoo," she growled at it. "I have little patience for anything tonight, least of all you."

The raven did not understand her, of course, and so Yue surely imagined the vague expression of amusement in the way it tilted its head at her.

She had had just enough wine that she did not wonder what a raven was doing out at night.

"Ah, there," she said, recognizing Shen's home and happy for a reason to leave the bird behind her. Shen lived in a small, two-room house wedged between a smith on one side and a tavern on the other—a tavern where she and Yue had shared many drinks in the past. Sky as her witness, Yue was going to make Shen buy her plenty of drinks to make up for this cursed nighttime adventure.

The front door stood slightly open. Curse the

woman, she must be well and truly drunk. Yue threw it open unceremoniously.

"Shen!" she cried. "Where in the darkness below have you gotten off to?"

But the front room was empty. Yue gave an exasperated grunt and stalked towards the bedroom in the back. She threw it open, but the bedroom, too, was empty.

That gave her pause, and she looked back into the front room, frowning. Where under the sky had Shen gone?

And then she heard a scraping against one of the walls.

Of course. The alley between Shen's home and the tavern. There was a privy there. Shen was having herself a piss.

"Shen!" roared Yue, stalking towards the alley. She would likely wake up some of the neighbors, but she did not care. Let them take their frustration out on Shen, once morning came.

She rounded the corner. There was the privy.

And there was Shen. On the ground, slumped against the wall, her face deathly white, her tunic covered with blood—but not as much as Yue would have expected, judging from the gaping wound in her neck.

Yue froze.

No, she thought. *No, that is not right.*

The vampire did not come within the walls.

Yet there was Shen.

The vampire was dead.

Yet there was Shen.

Even as she watched, Shen's fingers scrabbled futilely against the cobblestones. She shuddered one last time and died.

Yue turned and sprinted for the constables' station.

Dryleaf took my arm, and together we followed Mag down the stairs into a wide chamber beneath the house. With every step down, the evil feeling in the air increased. Oku whined, trotting just behind me, his steps hesitant. I thought about sending him back to wait outside the house, but I wanted him close to protect Dryleaf, in case of danger.

Below, I felt the air open up into a large space. But everything was pitch black, with no faintest light reaching us from the stairway.

"Is there a torch?" I said. My voice vanished into the empty space.

I heard the sound of Mag fumbling along the wall. "Here is one," she said at last. "Give me a moment to light it."

Sparks glinted in the shadows as she worked. Finally a flame sprang to life, and Mag lifted the torch high.

The chamber was large—larger than the first floor of the house, which meant it extended under the buildings on either side. There were desks and tables around the sides of the room, some of them littered with papers. But in the center of the room was a massive cauldron filled with a liquid I thought was entirely black. It was only when we took a few steps forwards, and the light of Mag's torch fell upon the cauldron, that I saw a glint of red.

"Sky above," I breathed.

Mag walked up to the cauldron and took a closer look. Oku went with her, growling in his throat at the cauldron. Mag sniffed. When she turned back to me, her expression was grim.

"Blood," she said. "Old blood. It smells almost . . . rotten."

I knew instinctively that this must be the source of the evil feeling in the house. But how could that be? It was a great deal of blood, true, but it was not as though we could smell it through the floor.

"Let me get another torch," I said. I removed Dryleaf's hand from my arm and went to the wall, fetching another torch and lighting it with Mag's.

"What is it?" said Dryleaf. "Tell me."

"My apologies," I said. "There is a cauldron here, filled with blood. It is paces across."

"Sky," whispered Dryleaf. "How much? How many . . ."

He did not finish, but I heard the words as plainly as if he had spoken them. *How many people died to fill this cauldron?*

I went to Mag's side and knelt, thrusting my torch close to the ground. A pit had been dug beneath the great iron bowl. The stones within were blackened and twisted. I could see no fuel. Whatever had burned there had burned away . . . but it had melted a great deal of the surrounding stone.

"Darkfire," I whispered. "These stones have been melted by darkfire."

"Darkfire?" said Mag. "What is that?"

"An evil magic," said Dryleaf. "You have heard of magestones?"

Mag frowned. "I know that they are a dangerous substance."

"Forbidden by the King's law," said Dryleaf, nodding. "When a wizard eats them, they gain immeasurable power according to their branch. Firemages gain the power of darkfire. It is a black flame that consumes light instead of giving it, and it will melt almost anything."

"But there is another way to create darkfire," I said. "Setting fire to magestones will do it."

"I have never heard that," said Dryleaf.

"Neither had I," I said. "I learned it only recently." It had been in the Greatrocks, with Loren.

"So these Shades you were hunting," said Dryleaf. "They used darkfire to heat the cauldron. To . . . to boil the blood."

"But for what purpose?" I said.

"The vampire," said Dryleaf. "It must have been. The feeling in this place . . . the *smell.* Mayhap that is what summoned the vampire. I was right all along, though I wish I had not been. The Shades *did* bring the creature. But why? What did they hope to gain?"

"Some sort of weapon," said Mag.

I looked up in surprise. She was across the room, standing by one of the desks that lined the walls, and she had a stack of papers in her hand through which she was riffling. "These mention the vampire. The cauldron appears to be part of some ritual to summon it—to unleash it on the Shades' enemies. Using a magestone fire infuses the blood with the stones' essence. It increases the strength of it, gives it some sort of . . . magical property. I am not certain. There are many things written here I do not understand. But that is what brought the vampire out of the mountains, if indeed that is where it came from."

That was a thought so dark, I was stunned to silence for a moment, and Dryleaf seemed to feel the same way. Only Mag still moved or made a noise, flipping through more and more of the papers.

"I do not understand," I said in a hushed voice. "A vampire cannot be controlled. But even if you could set it loose in a town and unleash it, it is . . . well, it is still just a creature. If we had not arrived to kill it, the people of Lan Shui would have done so in time. They would have gotten word to the Mystics eventually. And if the Shades mean to use this as a weapon of war, it is an even worse idea. In a large city, one worth conquering, there would be many guards and constables, and even Mystics, to hunt it. That is what happens whenever a vampire is desperate enough to attack a city by its own choice. That is why they prey on the weak and the isolated."

"There is more," said Mag, scanning a page. "Something about . . . empowering the vampires. Strengthening them. I cannot entirely understand, but it seems they had some scheme for making the beasts even more fearsome."

"The beast, you mean," I said. "Only one."

Mag stopped short. "I suppose you are right," she said. "Though . . . though they speak of more than one in these pages."

I felt a sensation like ice sliding down my throat and into my gut.

"Mag," I said, my voice coming as a whisper. "How far would this ritual reach? How close would a vampire have to be for the magic to draw it in?"

"Sky above," said Dryleaf. But Mag only stared at me. My words were still working their way through her mind.

"Mag," I said again.

"It says . . . it says many leagues," she told me.

I felt the blood drain from my face. "Lan Shui stands at the feet of the Greatrocks. There is nowhere in Dorsea, and few places in all of Underrealm, where vampires can be found in greater numbers."

"But . . . but vampires never work together," said Mag. "You both said so."

"That is what the stories say," muttered Dryleaf.

"But you should know better than to believe every story you hear, child."

And then in the town above us, the screaming began.

THIRTY-THREE

"Leave me here!" said Dryleaf. "Close the chamber door while you go and help the town."

"We cannot," I said. "They are coming for this place. You are in danger while you remain here. Come, we will hide you upstairs."

We hurried him up to the second floor and made him lock himself in a bedroom. Then Mag and I burst out of the house's front door. In the open air, we could finally place the direction of the screams—north. We flew that way, our boots slapping on the cobblestone streets.

A pallid, hissing form leaped out of the night.

I skidded to a halt, but the vampire had not been attacking me. It fell instead upon a man I had not seen, who had been cowering in a doorway. The man's scream was abruptly cut off as claws sank into his neck, and the vampire bit hard into his throat with its needle teeth.

"No!" cried Mag, flinging herself at the creature. But the vampire, having already taken deep gulps of the man's blood, chittered and fled. It leaped straight up an impossible height, landing on a roof above and vanishing from sight.

I fell to my knees beside the man and threw off my coat. I bunched it up and pressed it to the gaping wound in his neck. He sputtered and gasped, but each desperate attempt at breath only sent a new gush of red cascading down his shirt.

"Mag!" I cried.

"Coming." She ran to me.

"No!" I said. "Go find them. Kill them. Drive them off from the town. I will do what I can for the people. You are the only one who can face the creatures."

She stared down at me, face white as a sheet, eyes filled with fear. And then, even as I watched, the mask came down. The life died in her eyes, and her expression went slack.

Without a word, she turned and ran off into the night.

In mountain lion form, Kaita lurked on a rooftop above me. From her perch, she could see me and Oku battling against another vampire that had come swooping at us. We were hard pressed without Mag there—I fought with a sword in one hand and an arrow in the other, trying to drive the wooden shaft into the creature. Oku snapped and snarled whenever the vampire pressed me too hard, driving it back for only a moment at a time.

At last the vampire decided it had had enough and fled to search for easier prey. It leaped up on the rooftop where Kaita lurked. She ducked back just in time, her black fur melding with the night sky so that I did not see her.

The vampire landed several paces away on the rooftop. It stopped short and turned to her, sniffing. Kaita met its gaze and growled, the deep, rumbling sound shaking the shingles beneath them both.

The vampire sniffed harder and recoiled. Why feast on a mountain cat when there were so many delicious humans nearby? It knew the taste of lion well enough, and it much preferred two-legged prey. It stalked off into the darkness.

Kaita snorted. Then she turned to the corpse lying at her feet. Pantu. The boy's bulging eyes were pointed up towards the moons.

Kaita seized his leg in her wide muzzle. She threw him over the edge of the roof, listening as he landed on the street beside me with a *thud.*

"Sky above," she heard me say. "Pantu. Pantu, are you . . ."

My voice trailed off as I saw his sightless eyes. Kaita smiled in her mind and slunk away.

Mag flew down the streets, searching for her prey. There were screams in all directions, but they rose and faded too quickly for her to get a good sense of where she should go. Only one thing was certain: the Shades had succeeded in their aims, and there was more than one vampire in the town now. From the sound of it, there were at least half a dozen.

The citizens of Lan Shui scrambled and fled in all directions, like chickens who had just found a fox in their henhouse. But no one seemed to know which way to go. Mag saw one group fleeing east collide headlong with another group running west. After some of them slammed into each other and fell to the ground, those still standing kept running the way they had been going. Away from danger, or towards more of it, Mag could not know.

A moment ago, she would have grown frustrated. But her emotions were gone, pushed to the depths of her soul, and only the killer was left. The killer could not afford the thought necessary to care for these people, to be anguished at their terror and their pain. That would be later, when she was herself again.

Finally she heard a scream close by, from the next street over. She turned on the spot and rushed towards the sound. And there, at last, she found her prey.

A vampire crouched over a figure on the ground. A figure in red leather armor. Sinshi, the constable, whose arms still beat feebly at the vampire's shoulder, even as it sucked its meal from his jugular. On the other side of the creature, a man and woman watched in horror from where they sat on the ground. It looked as though Sinshi had pushed them out of the way as the creature attacked. But their terror left them unable to flee, and it would only be a matter of time before the vampire pounced upon them.

If not for Mag.

She ran up to the beast from behind, lunging the last pace. It heard her at the last second and spun—but just a bit too slowly. Her spearhead slashed a deep rent in its side, and it fell back, giving a horrible, guttural screech.

The vampire crouched, hissing and showing its teeth. Mag fell back to defense, her shield up. The vampire began to edge left, trying to circle her, and she did the same, so that they maneuvered around each other. She got herself between the vampire and the bystanders.

"You should be going," Mag said over her shoulder.

The townspeople stared at her for a moment in terror before turning and scrambling away.

The vampire's eyes shifted away from Mag to watch them go. It tried to leap over her to catch them, but Mag predicted the movement. Her spear stabbed upward, the head sinking into the vampire's shoulder. It screeched and landed hard on its side in the street, rolling and coming up in a crouch. It glared at Mag and hissed again. Over its head, she saw the townspeople vanish behind a building.

"Good," she said. "Let us finish it, now."

She leaped to the attack, and the vampire lunged to meet her. Her shield blocked its first swipe, and her spearhead sank into its gut. The vampire screamed as it fell on its back, trying to escape. But Mag followed, thrusting harder on the spear. It pierced flesh and guts, driving through the vampire's back and into the ground below. The skin around the wooden spear haft turned black and wilted, curling back and away from the wound like paper in a flame. The vampire tried to seize the spear—to pull it out, or mayhap to snap it in half. Mag kicked its claws away.

The vampire shuddered and died.

Mag looked up just as Ashta ran into view. The constable's eyes fell upon Sinshi lying dead in the street.

"No!" she cried, falling to her knees beside him. She tilted his head to look into his eyes, but they only stared blankly through her.

"Are you hurt?" said Mag.

Ashta shook, gripping Sinshi's shoulders hard. At last she mastered herself and looked up.

"No."

"Good. I have to go after the others."

"What others?" said Ashta. "They have gone."

Mag paused. She straightened and cocked her head, listening. Lan Shui had gone utterly silent. No more screams, and no more bestial roars.

The fight was over. And deep inside herself, with the ease of long practice, Mag released her trance. Her emotions, her fears, everything came rushing back. For a moment it was overwhelming, and she took a deep breath to maintain her calm. Her shoulders rose and fell, and she was back.

"The wounded will need help," she told Ashta. Even in her own ears, her voice sounded completely different than it had a moment ago. "Whatever you can do, do it. I have to find Albern."

THIRTY-FOUR

DAWN BROKE.

There were many dead strewn about the streets. The constables—those who remained—began to organize the townsfolk to collect the bodies and to heal the wounded. We gathered Dryleaf from the Shades' hideout, returned him to our inn, and went to help the survivors.

Yue found us shortly after the vampires fled. She stopped dead on the street, staring at us, and we met her gaze. She looked beyond weary, swaying on her feet, her eyes blinking too rapidly. It was a far cry from the proud, stocky warrior we had met when we first arrived at the town.

I wondered what she was thinking, in those long moments. Did she blame us for the attack? We had returned to the town full of pride and boasting of victory, but those boasts had proven hollow. Yet we could not have known, any better than Yue could, that the vampires had gathered in numbers.

At last she spoke. "We are collecting the wounded at our station," she said. "If you are not leaving town, then help us bring them."

We did as she asked. That part was easy, for the dead greatly outnumbered the injured.

It was Northwood all over again. I saw the same despair in the face of everyone we passed, the same confusion. Why? Why had this happened to them? They were simple folk. They farmed, and they worked, and they crafted, and they lived their lives. Horror and death had come upon them without warning, without reason. They did not deserve this, and they could scarcely hope to combat it.

When we had fetched all the wounded who had been found in the town, Mag and I stood silent in the street for a while. The night air was cool, and it helped to chill the heat we had worked up with our grisly work. I looked up into the sky, trying to regain a sense of space after spending several hours looking only at dead and dying townsfolk within arm's reach. Mag stared down at her hands.

"Let us get food and something to drink," I said at last.

Mag only nodded. I led her through the streets to our inn. Dryleaf was in the common room, leaning against a wall in the corner, nodding into his chest. I did not want to wake him—the old man had been up most of the night, and he deserved a good rest.

As I went to the barman and ordered breakfast and tea, Mag slumped at a table near the hearth. She stared at her hands the whole time, even as food was brought to us, even as I began to eat. She did not touch her own food. I kept glancing over at her, but she did not meet my gaze even once. Something was weighing on her, that was clear.

Finally I had had enough. "Come on, Mag," I said. "Eat something. And say whatever it is you must say."

She took a bite of the bread on her plate. Then another. Then she started devouring it ravenously, as though her body had only just realized how hungry she was. Her tea was cold by that time, but she drank it down regardless. When she had finished everything on the table before her, she settled back in her chair with a sigh.

"Better?" I said.

"Somewhat," she muttered. Then, to my surprise, she fished into a pouch on her belt and withdrew a copper sliver. She tossed it at me. It gave a heavy *clink* as it landed on the table, and then it rolled across the wood to bump my arm.

"The meal is paid for already," I told her. "Keep your money."

"Look at it, Albern."

Her voice was as solemn as I had ever heard it. Frowning, I scooped up the copper. I looked at it carefully, but I could not see anything amiss. The face of Andriana the Fearless stared up at me.

Then I flipped it over. And still, I looked upon Andriana.

"Ha!" I said. "You see these every once in a while. It gets stamped with the same sign on both sides. I used to have a silver—"

"Latrine duty," said Mag.

I looked at her, not understanding.

"In Northwood, before we rode out. You wanted to go after Loren. I wanted to ride into the Greatrocks. We played latrine duty."

The full weight of what she was saying crashed down upon me. I went very still.

"A coin flip. I keep that copper around as a keepsake, a curiosity. But in that moment, I used it to cheat you. We would not be here if I had not lied. Latrine duty."

I shook my head. "When you make an agreement . . ."

"I stacked the odds," said Mag. "I wish I had not, Albern. I am sorry. You deserve better than—"

"Oh, be quiet," I said. "Honestly, Mag."

She bowed her head, avoiding my gaze. "Of course. I . . . should I leave you alone for a moment?"

"Of course not, you great ass." I laughed. "Latrine duty."

Mag's eyes widened at my laugh. "Are you not upset with me?"

"Am I? I suppose so, a little. But . . ." I sighed and passed a hand over my eyes. "Mag, I . . . I told you much about the Greatrocks. With Loren, I mean, before I came to you in Northwood. But I did not tell you everything, because . . . well, because I was ashamed.

"Loren met me in Strapa. And when she came into my bowyery, she was with a Mystic named Jordel of the family Adair. A finer man I have never met in Underrealm. I could tell they were in some trouble, that they were going somewhere far and doing something important. And I wanted to go with them. Mag, I wanted to go with them so desperately. Yet when I offered my services as a guide, they refused me.

"That piqued my interest, and so I asked around. In no time at all, I discovered that they were hiding their true identity and trying to avoid notice. The Mystics were after them. And so I told the Mystics where they could be found. Soon they were on the run again, fleeing from those who wished to deliver them to the King's justice—and then, who appeared to rescue them, but me. Again I offered my services, and that time they happily took me as their guide."

Mag was looking hard at me. Guilt was still heavy in her eyes. "That is different, Albern. If you had not taken them into the mountains—"

"Jordel would never have discovered the Shades," I told her. "And now Loren will tell the Mystics of the threat, and a great disaster will be averted. I did an evil thing. I betrayed them. And great good came from it. You did nothing nearly so dishonorable. And if we had not come here, Lan Shui would be facing these monsters alone. Instead, they have us. They have you. That means they have a chance."

I pushed back my chair and stood. "If you have done evil against me, I forgive it. That may not entirely assuage your conscience, but if not, that is on your account." I thrust out a hand.

Slowly, Mag rose to her feet. She took my wrist and shook. "Very well," she said quietly. "Thank you."

"You wish to thank me? Give me a week's sleep, a barrel of your finest ale, and figure out some way to kill these vampires before anyone else in Lan Shui gets hurt."

That forced a laugh from her, as I hoped it would. "I cannot help you with the first two. But . . . I may have thought of something when it comes to the vampires."

That took me utterly by surprise. "You have?"

"The Shades' magic summoned them here," she said. "We know that now."

"We do," I said. "And it is an evil like I have never heard tale of, though I know many tales."

"Yet evil may be turned against itself."

I frowned at her. "How do you mean?"

Mag fixed me with a look. "The vampires hunger for the burning blood. And we mean to hunt the vampires."

My eyes widened. "Mag, no."

"Oh yes."

I leaned heavily on the table. "Dark below."

"No, this darkness is within," said Mag. "Within the heart of Lan Shui itself. Let us invite our foes straight into that heart and let the darkness consume them."

THIRTY-FIVE

We went to find Yue before noon. After hearing of the plan, she looked about as convinced as I had been.

"You want to *let* them into the town," she said, as though certain she must have misheard.

"With all the people hidden," said Mag. "No one will be in danger."

"Except whoever stands between the vampires and their goal," said Yue.

"Which will only be us," I said. In truth, I had to force a great deal of confidence into my words—this was Mag's idea, and I was determined to support her, but my fingers kept twitching when I took my attention off them, as though they were desperately trying to flee the impending doom of the rest of my body.

Yue chewed on the inside of her cheek, seemingly unappeased. "Show me," she said at last.

We took her to the Shades' hideout and down the secret staircase to the underground chamber. She stood awestruck in the doorway, looking at the size of it.

"How under the sky did they build this?" she muttered.

"I think they had an alchemist, or more than one," I said. "The people we killed here . . . they have many powerful friends across Underrealm, powerful and evil. I would wager they had whatever resources they required."

We showed her the cauldron and the pit beneath it where the fires had burned. Her expression darkened considerably when we told her of the magestones.

"If magestones are involved, then we should notify the Mystics," she said.

"You have tried to reach them already," Mag pointed out. "And even if you could, how long would it take them to reach us?"

Yue did not seem to have a counterpoint to that. "So your plan," she said slowly, "is to lure the creatures using this cauldron? Can they even smell it from outside?"

"They smelled it from leagues away," I told her. "It is what brought them to Lan Shui in the first place."

"We fight them first on the street outside," said Mag. "They will be focused on an objective, and we should be able to kill some of them as they move towards it. There are only five left."

"Only?" said Yue and I at the same time. It had slipped out of me despite myself.

Recovering quickly, I looked at Yue and gave her a sage nod. "Only."

"But if we need to fall back," Mag pressed on, glaring at me, "we can do so safely. We can fight them in the house above, while they try to figure out a way down into the basement, and if any of them make it to the cauldron, we can attack them while they feed."

"Try and explain, again, how this is better than fighting them at the walls," said Yue, folding her arms.

"What are walls to these beasts?" I said. "They can leap up them in one bound."

"Did you ever serve in a king's army? In a mercenary company?" said Mag.

"No," admitted Yue.

"Then take it from the two of us, who have fought on many battlefields across nine kingdoms," said Mag. "An enemy who dearly wants an objective is easy to manipulate. If you can force them to approach it, you can plan your attack. Our enemies have an advantage in their speed and their strength. But we also have an advantage, for they are little more than animals. We have to out-think them."

There was a long moment of silence while Yue looked slowly between us and the cauldron in the center of the room.

"Very well," she said at last. "But we will take additional precautions."

"Such as what?" I said.

"They must be watched as they enter the town," said Yue. "To make sure they do not deviate from the course you intend them to take. I will not invite them into Lan Shui, only to have them turn aside and rip open the homes of innocent villagers who will be unable to defend themselves."

I glanced at Mag. "Constable, you have seen how quickly the beasts move. Mag and I cannot track them from the walls all the way back to this house quickly enough to try and defend it."

"No, you will remain here," said Yue. "Ashta and I will see to the safety of the town. I am sure some others will want to help, as well."

"Your lives will be in grave danger if you do," said Mag quickly. "You would do better to—"

"No," said Yue, swiping her hand through the air like a knife. "This is my town. You may go through with this plan, but only if you do as I say. We may be at some risk, but we would rather face that danger than let others face it in our stead. And once I tell the townsfolk what you plan to do, I doubt you will be able to keep at least some of them from trying to help. Better to accept the help, if it cannot be turned away, and use it to ensure that as few lives are risked as possible."

Mag could hardly argue with that. "Very well, constable," she said. "I wish you would allow us to face this danger alone. But I thank you nevertheless."

"And I, for one, do not wish to face it alone," I said. "If that matters to anyone, which it does not seem to."

Mag held forth her hand. It took a moment, but Yue grasped her wrist firmly. "Just make sure you kill the things."

"We will," I promised.

The rest of the day was spent in frenzied preparation. Yue and Ashta put word out through the town, and the folk of Lan Shui rushed to secure themselves in their homes. Of those who were physically fit to fight, many volunteered to take up arms against the vampires. Yue took most of these and stationed them throughout the town, to hide with the others and act as guards. If the beasts deviated from the path we had planned for them, these guards would be the first to respond. The rest, mayhap a dozen of the fittest townsfolk, were stationed between the walls and the house—the first line of defense if the vampires should turn aside from their hunt.

We finished our work just in time. The sun lowered in the west, its edge just beginning to slide beneath the top of the land spur. The warm day had begun at last to cool. Someone brought a cold meal to Mag and me at the Shade hideout, and Yue joined us there to eat. We sat on the ground outside the house, scraping the last of the food from our bowls with our fingers. While we ate, I noticed Yue giving us sidelong looks—though she did not seem as suspicious as she might once have been, which encouraged me.

"Is this what you do?" she said, as Mag discarded her bowl on the ground and I gave mine to Oku to lick clean.

"What?" I said, blinking at her.

"The vampires. The ones who used to live here, in this house. Is it your duty to seek out such things and end them? Are you some special sort of . . . of Mystic?"

Mag and I laughed, together, though we probably should not have done. "No, constable," I said. "This is not something we do often—that we have ever done before, in fact."

"What brought you here, then?" she said. "And do not give me the same lies you told when you first arrived. I have placed much faith in you today. I want a real answer."

Mag and I exchanged glances. But truth seemed the only option.

"We come from the town of Northwood, as we said," Mag told her. "Some weeks ago, it was attacked."

Yue's brows rose. "Like here?"

"No," I said. "Not vampires. By an army. They call themselves Shades. The ones who dwelled here were their compatriots." I jerked my thumb at the Shade hideout beside us.

"Who are they?" said Yue, eyeing the building.

"In truth, I know little of their aims, or where they came from," I said. "That boy, Pantu—may he rest in the darkness—he told me they came from Calentin. All I know for certain is that they had a stronghold in the Greatrocks, until a wizard came and drove them out of it. Then they attacked Northwood in great strength and nearly razed it in revenge."

"And when they did, they killed my husband," said Mag softly.

Yue let a long moment of silence pass. "That is an ill thing to hear," she said at last.

Mag pressed on. "There was a weremage. She led their forces in Northwood. She took the form of a lion and killed my Sten. And when they withdrew, she fled west into the Greatrocks. We followed her trail here to Lan Shui. We hoped to find her here, though of course now we know she left this place before we even came."

"Yet you remain," said Yue.

"Of course," said Mag, shrugging. "We are not without a conscience."

I smiled, and Yue appeared to hide a smirk. "Well. You should not have kept all this from me when you arrived," she said.

"I suppose the King's law would say so," I said. "Would you have allowed us in if we had been honest?"

"Do you jest?" said Yue. "Of course not. Yet I suppose, after a fashion, that I am glad you came."

"That is how latrine duty often works," I said.

Yue blinked at me. "What?" she asked, while Mag tried hard to suppress her laughter.

"Nothing."

Stars had begun to appear in the sky above. The moons had not yet risen, but I could almost see the glow of them in the east. I pushed myself to my feet.

"Time is nearly upon us," I said.

"In my experience, time is always upon us, depending on what time you mean." Yue got to her feet and held out her hand a final time. She took Mag's wrist first, and then mine. "Do your best not to get killed tonight."

"We will not," said Mag. "You have made it clear to us how much trouble it is to get rid of bodies."

"Not so much trouble," said Yue. "The vampires will only be acting in self-defense, after all. Does that not excuse any amount of killing?"

I laughed at that. "Keep yourself safe as well tonight, constable."

"I will try."

She took off down the street at a trot, making for the gate where she would stand with the vanguard. Mag and I prepared our weapons and made ready for the night's battle to come.

THIRTY-SIX

THE WOODS AROUND THEM HAD GROWN COLD, AND the fire had begun to burn low. Albern huddled farther under his cloak for warmth.

"Would you mind throwing some more wood on the fire?"

Sun shook herself and rose quickly. "Of course," she said. "Forgive me for not noticing sooner."

"Think nothing of it," said Albern. "I think we both lost ourselves there for a moment."

"I cannot imagine it," said Sun, slowly adding logs to the fire. The flames swelled and crackled, and she relished their sudden warmth. “Sitting there in Lan Shui, knowing the vampires were coming and intending to face them head on. I think I would have died of fright.”

“Well, you must remember that we were hale and hearty youths in those days,” said Albern. “Much as you yourself are now.”

Sun could not help but laugh, though she quickly stifled the sound, which was far too loud in the silent forest. “I do not mean to be rude, but you were already a fair bit older than I am now.”

Albern frowned with mock severity. “I was barely past my fortieth year, thank you kindly.”

“And I have not quite seen my twentieth,” said Sun. “You will forgive me, but that is more than twice as old.”

“Ah, but life’s summer lasts long, and our leaves had not yet begun to brown—only to grey a little bit around the temples.” Albern’s eyes twinkled in the firelight.

“In any case,” said Sun doggedly, “that only proves my point further. You were grown, and warriors as well. I do not think I could sit and wait for such a creature to come for me. The fear would be too great.”

“Oh, I think you have a great deal of courage in you,” said Albern. “And I can tell by your walk and the strength in your arms that you are a warrior in your own right, even if you have not yet been tested.”

Sun could not help the blush that put in her cheeks, though she shook her head to try and dismiss it. "You cannot win an argument with flattery."

"Oh? I seem to recall having done so before." Albern scratched absentmindedly at his stump. "But I do not mean to flatter you. What you have said is the same thing everyone says, until they are thrown headlong into a fight. Some see it coming. Others never do. Either way, they come out the other side a warrior, or they do not come out at all. After you have seen it happen enough times, you tend to pick up a gift for knowing the outcome in advance. I would not say you were a warrior in the making unless I believed it."

A feeling like a cold weight settled in Sun's chest. "I wish I could believe that were true."

Albern gave her a long, searching stare. "Sun, why did you come into my tavern tonight?"

Sun avoided his gaze. "You have not asked me any questions about myself," she said quietly. "You said it did not matter who I was before I walked through that door."

"You do not have to answer," said Albern.

The little clearing settled to silence. For a long moment, Sun planned to do as he suggested, and remain quiet. But then, almost without meaning to, she began to speak.

"Ever since the War of the Necromancer, my family has been dishonored. You know . . . everyone knows how it ended. And most know how we have been viewed for our part in that ending. Now everyone in my family seems obsessed with regaining our honor."

She fell silent for a moment. Albern had not removed his gaze from her. His hood cast shadows over his angular face. "That is not such an evil wish," he said quietly.

"Except that they seem more interested in *having* honor than in *doing* honorable things," said Sun. "They no longer want to be viewed as traitors, as cheats, as faithless scoundrels. Yet none of them seem willing to see *why* we are seen that way. They think they can reclaim their status by building alliances, by strengthening our trade connections, by amassing more power. To me, it seems that such actions are what brought about our dishonor in the first place."

"I would tend to agree with you," said Albern.

"They want me to act like they do," said Sun. "They want me to want what they want. But I . . . I do not. I would rather do good deeds unpraised than receive accolades I know I do not deserve. Does . . . does that make sense?"

"It makes all the sense in the world," said Albern. "And if the opinion of an old man matters to you at all, I think you have the right of it, Sun of the family Valgun." He leaned closer to the climbing flames. "I think I had better carry on. We are nearing the end of the tale."

Sun balked. "We are?"

"Oh yes."

Sun could not help herself; she pouted. "I suppose I have no one to blame but myself," she grumbled. "I had harbored a hope . . . well, you told me you were not giving the tale of your arm, but I thought that might be a ruse. I thought mayhap you were going to surprise me and tell the story I really wanted."

"No, I am afraid I spoke only the truth," said Albern. "And despite what I have told you earlier tonight, it *is* all the truth, though it did not always seem that way."

"What do you mean?" said Sun.

"What I am telling you now is the truth as I know it now," said Albern. "I thought the story was somewhat different when I was living it. And afterwards, I thought it was something else again. Whenever I give you a tale, I try to tell the truest version of it that I know at the time."

"Humph," said Sun, holding her hands out towards the fire. "I still think I would rather read a history book."

"Who are you going to believe?" said Albern, smiling slightly. "Some scholar from your family's court, or the man who lived the tale?"

"If I were to heed a wisdom I have only recently learned, I would not *believe* any of it," said Sun, feeling almost ashamed at how good it felt to say the words.

Albern laughed. "An excellent riposte. But I have only my tale. Shall I finish it?"

Sun nodded.

Just after sundown, Mag and I entered the Shades' hideout and descended to the basement. We rummaged through some of the cabinets along the walls and found several small packets of brown cloth. I untied one to find a collection of black crystals about as large as a finger. Magestones. Oku sniffed at them and growled.

"How many should we use?" I said.

"All of them," said Mag.

I looked at her. "That might burn straight through the bottom of the cauldron."

"I do not think we will have that long before the vampires reach us."

"A heartening thought," I said. "As you wish."

We piled the magestones up under the cauldron and lit them. They caught the sparks easily, like dry leaves, but they burned with a black fire that immediately sucked light from the air. I hastily snatched my hands away from the flames.

"That will do it," I said, edging backwards as waves of heat rippled across my body. "Let us return to the street."

Together we ran up the stairs, weapons in hand, and stopped on the street outside. Mag stuck out a hand, and we gripped wrists.

"Let us become heroes," she said.

"You have been one a long time," I countered. "Tonight I might finally join you."

"Fah." Her grip tightened for a moment. "In earnestness—be careful. If you let yourself die, I may have to kill you."

"And you as well," I said. "Though I suppose you would have to let me."

"I will," she said. "But enough words. Climb, little squirrel."

I headed around the side of the building. Oku started coming after me, but when he noticed Mag holding her position, he paused, looking between the two of us and whining.

"Kip, Oku," I said. "Mag will need you more than I will, I think."

"Kip, is it?" said Mag. "I will remember that when I want to get rid of him."

I frowned at her until, with a disgusted expression, she scratched Oku behind the ears in apology. Then I left her.

Around the side of the house, the roof descended close to the street. I jumped, just catching the edge of it with my fingertips, and hauled myself up. From there I climbed until I was near the roof's peak, where I knelt and readied my bow. I took half the arrows from my quiver and jammed them into the soft wooden shingles of the roof. Another I held loose in my right hand, ready to fire.

The sun had been down for nearly an hour when we heard them.

First there were cries of alarm from the north end of town. The guards on the walls had seen them. We had left the gates open. There was no point in closing them when the vampires could leap over them anyway.

The cries of alarm spread, coming from different directions but always moving south towards us. That was good. It meant the vampires were not stopping for anything, and none of the townsfolk had been drawn into fights. The battle would happen here, in the street in front of the hideout, as we had planned.

And then, at last, we saw them.

Two of the pallid, twisted, screeching creatures burst into sight at once, a distance down the street straight ahead. One had a narrow, jutting jaw and teeth that stuck out from between its lips, and the other had massive arms, thicker than my legs. For half a heartbeat they paused, sniffing at the air.

"Biter," I called down to Mag, pointing to one and then the other, "and Shoulders."

She glared up at me. "They are not pets."

"Oh, come now. Would you not love to take one home?"

The beasts focused on the door of the hideout, and on Mag standing before it. She hefted her spear. Oku bristled and growled.

The vampires screamed with fury and hunger as they charged.

My right hand moved in a blur, nocking, drawing, loosing. They did not expect the first arrow, but my aim was imperfect. The arrowhead nicked Biter in the arm, but no wood pierced its flesh, and it hardly seemed to feel it. After that they kept an eye on me, and they dodged every shot.

In no time they had reached Mag, and a deadly dance started on the street. By Mag's side, Oku snapped and snarled as he tried to catch hold of Shoulders, but it moved too quickly. Mag slashed and weaved, looking for an opening. The vampires kept trying to push past her, attempting to reach the building, but she managed to stop them. Twice when they tried it, she scored a hit with her spearhead, but not deep enough for the wood to penetrate the skin.

In the space of a few moments, I realized I would not be able to get a clean shot from my position on the roof. I scanned the streets all around the building instead—when more vampires came, I would be Mag's first warning. And the other townsfolk—not to mention the constables—should be coming soon, once the rest of the vampires arrived.

But in watching the streets, I forgot the rooftops.

I caught a flash of moonslight on Elf-white skin. That was the only warning I had before the vampire launched itself through the air, flying from the next rooftop onto my own. I managed to catch its wrists and keep its claws from sinking into my chest, but the momentum bowled me over. We tumbled back onto the rooftop, sliding down the wooden shingles, which shook me hard enough to jar my very bones.

At last I managed to tumble, kicking the vampire off me and slowing my headlong descent. I had my sword in hand before I got to my feet, and I fell back into a defensive position. My bow was up near the roof's peak, useless, but I had a few arrows left in my belt quiver. Slowly I drew one, trying not to move suddenly and provoke an attack. The vampire hissed, but it hesitated, studying me through its beady black eyes. A mottled pattern of black spread across its face, outwards from the nose like someone had thrown an ink pellet straight between its eyes.

"Inkstain," I told it. "That is what I will call you."

Inkstain snarled and lunged just as I got the arrow into my hand.

Twice I fended it off with my sword, trying desperately to find a chance to sink the arrow into one of its swiping limbs. It was impossible. The creature's speed was beyond comprehension. The only thing that saved me was that it recognized the danger of the wooden arrow, and that made it cautious in its attacks. I could not begin to understand how Mag managed not only to match them, but beat them. It took all my mind's panicked, animal instincts just to keep me out of reach of its claws.

Then a shingle gave out under Inkstain's feet. It went crashing down, and it grabbed wildly for something to hold onto.

"Something" turned out to be my leg.

We slid down the roof again, and this time we could not stop our descent before we pitched over the edge. I went over first. For one moment I knew weightlessness. My heart felt as though it wanted to pound my guts until they were unconscious. Then I came slamming down on top of a market stall that had been set up against the side of the building. The cloth enveloped me, breaking the fall.

I scrambled out of the tattered, brown fabric just in time. Inkstain came down right where I had been. The market stall collapsed, and the vampire vanished amid the cloth. Its screams redoubled as it thrashed. I saw a clawed hand burst out of the fabric.

Abandoning my sword, I took an arrow in each hand and leaped, plunging them into the flailing mass. Both darts bit flesh, and Inkstain's screams turned from rage to pain. One iron-hard limb smashed into my head, and I fell back onto my rear, my ears ringing.

Fire flashed in my eyes as a torch came sailing through the night. It struck the fabric of the market stall, which caught almost at once. The flames licked and spread, and soon the whole stall was ablaze. Inkstain shrieked and shriveled. What skin I could see blackened and twisted, and soon the cloth stopped moving altogether.

I looked up in shock. Yue stood there, huffing in her armor and with a nasty bruise on one cheek. She extended a hand without speaking, and I took her help to stand.

“Mag needs us,” she said.

“Take me,” I said, and followed her at a dead run towards the front of the building.

THIRTY-SEVEN

WITH THE CRYSTAL CLARITY OF HER BATTLE-TRANCE, Mag saw it when Inkstain bounded over the street to go after me, but Biter and Shoulders kept her too occupied to spare much attention. She trusted me to handle myself, and she kept fighting, kept trying to impale one of the vampires with the wooden haft of her spear. There were only two. She was unlikely to get a better chance.

Then a fresh roar announced the arrival of a third. It sailed through the air, limbs outstretched and rotten teeth bared. On instinct, the other vampires skittered away from it, hissing in anger as it landed between them. The distraction gave Mag a moment to recover, bringing up her shield and facing off against the trio, eyes darting back and forth between them. Oku edged to her side, growling and panting at the same time. The wolfhound was growing weary from trying to keep out of the vampires' grasp.

This new vampire was larger than the others, its limbs even thicker than Shoulders' were, but all in proportion. As it stalked towards her, Biter and Shoulders drew back from it, glancing at it in subservience. They had encountered it before, clearly, and they had not enjoyed the experience.

King. Mag named it in her mind without even thinking. And then, behind her battle-trance, the part of her mind that could still feel had the thought, *I am going to punch Albern.*

Thoughts danced in her mind, far-off music in the calm of her trance. Three vampires before her, and one on the roof. That left one still unaccounted for. And where on earth were the rest of the townspeople? Some of them should have arrived by now, at least.

And then the vampires attacked again, and even her background thoughts vanished.

Her one saving grace against the beasts was that the vampires were clearly unused to fighting together. They were loners, never hunting in packs, and so they had no idea how to approach in a coordinated fashion. For one moment Mag's mind flashed with an image of Victon, her old sergeant, drilling the vampires and teaching them to operate as a unit. If not for the trance, she would have laughed out loud.

Yet the same thing that made them unable to work together also kept her from surprising any of them. When she fought one of them, the other two did not wait idly, thinking their fellow would surely bring her down. They waited for their own chance to fight, and as soon as Mag turned on them, they reacted quickly enough that they almost seemed to be expecting it. She knew she could push herself harder, further, than any human she had met, but if she never managed to bring them down, even her trance would wear out eventually.

Then there came a great commotion from down the street. Mag withdrew by one pace and glanced over the heads of her opponents at the source of the disturbance. King and the other vampires, too, glanced behind to see what was happening.

The final vampire came skidding into the street, crouched on all fours, hissing and spitting. Behind it, from side streets and alleys, came pouring a flood of townsfolk—nearly two dozen of them, and all armed with weapons and torches. Immediately they formed up facing the vampire, thrusting their steel and their flames towards it. The vampire shrieked and swiped at them, but the townsfolk stood strong together, giving it no chance to reach them.

All this Mag saw in a flash, and then she tried

something new. Throwing her arms wide, spear pointing one way and shield another, she gave a battle-roar that shook the walls of the buildings around her.

The attention of Biter, Shoulders, and King snapped back to her at once. Biter jumped forth, matching Mag's pose and scream of defiance. For one heartbeat they faced each other, roaring in hatred, neither willing to back down.

Mag caught just a glimpse of brown fur as Oku saw his chance and lunged. His teeth sank into Biter's throat. It gave a warbling cry and tried to swipe at Oku, but the hound kicked off its chest and swung, avoiding the blow.

Mag's spear pierced Biter's eye and drove all the way through the back of its head.

The vampire's body went slack in an instant. Blackness spread from around the haft of her spear, rippling through the vampire's body until it looked burned.

But with her strike, she had opened herself to an attack. King seized the opportunity, and Mag barely got her shield up in time. The blow was heavy enough to break her arm if she had taken the brunt of it, but Mag managed to turn it. Still, it flung her through the air, and she slammed hard into the side of the Shades' hideout.

Oku darted to her side, snarling and bristling as he turned to face the vampires again. But the vampires could not have cared less about him. Ignoring both

Mag and the hound, they rushed the building's front door and vanished inside. The last vampire, brought to bay by the townsfolk, gave up the fight and joined its fellows, running into the hideout and disappearing from view.

Mag seized Oku's fur and used him to help pull herself up. Oku whined and licked her hand, but Mag was already searching for signs of me. Just then, Yue and I came rushing around the corner of the building. Relief must have been obvious on my face as I ran and embraced her, for Mag gave a cold smile.

"Were you worried about me?" she said tonelessly.

"I should have known better," I said, looking at Biter's corpse. "You got one, then."

"And you? I saw it come for you, but I was distracted."

"I killed it," I told her. "Or rather, *we* did." I motioned towards Yue, who came to us, frowning.

"The others?" she said.

"All inside," said Mag. "Only three left now. It will be harder to fight them in an enclosed space, but I think we can do it."

Yue's eyes widened, and she looked up at the house. "Why risk it? Burn them instead."

Mag looked at me, frowning. "That could work. Unless they escape the flames."

"We will surround the house." Without waiting for another word from us, Yue turned to the townsfolk, who had gathered a few paces away. "Torches! Throw them into the building and onto the roof! Burn it down! And guard it against their escape!"

They obeyed her at once, flinging their torches at the building in great, fiery arcs. Some bounced from the walls or rolled off the roof, but many flew in through open windows or rolled to a stop on the shingles, which began to smoke and smolder. Soon, what looked like a dozen small fires burned through the house. Smoke began to leak out from the windows of both floors.

Yue strode to the front door, which still hung open, and turned to face us. "We three should spread out and guard the easiest exits," she said. "We cannot let them escape. Hopefully the cauldron keeps them busy enough that—"

We had no warning. There was a shattering cry, and then, faster than a blink, pallid, clawed limbs shot out of the doorway. They seized the back of Yue's armor and dragged her into the house before she could even scream.

THIRTY-EIGHT

WE DID NOT STOP TO THINK. WE RUSHED IN AFTER her. It took Oku a moment to brave the flames, but after a few furious barks, he charged in behind us.

By the time we got inside, the vampire had already vanished from the front room. The left and right doors were both open, giving no clue as to where it had gone. Smoke made the room hazy, and the flames licking at the outside of the building lit our way.

"I do not hear her," I said. "Which way do we go?"

"Split up," said Mag, her voice still a monotone. "I can trust you to stay alive if you take Oku with you?"

“We shall see. Oku, tiss.”

The wolfhound ran by my side as I darted to the right and through the door, sword in one hand and an arrow in the other. I did a quick search, looking behind the furniture, but found nothing. Suddenly Oku eyed the door to the next room and started bristling. I heard a sharp cry.

That was good enough for me. I ran and threw my shoulder into the door, and it burst open.

There on the floor lay Yue. Above her crouched a vampire—the final, unnamed one. She had one of its arms by the wrist, barely keeping it away from her face. The other hand was clamped over her shoulder, and the claws were digging into the armor. The vampire hissed and drooled, gobs of its saliva dripping onto Yue’s face, which twisted in pain from the creature’s grip.

Oku snarled and attacked. His teeth penetrated the vampire’s leg before the creature could react. It shrieked and released Yue’s shoulder, but she did not slacken her grip on its other hand.

I shoved my sword through its back. It reared up, screaming in pain, and I jammed my arrow into the back of its neck. Its scream cut off at once, and its free claws scrabbled at its own throat, trying to pluck out the deadly dart. Yue shoved hard, and the vampire fell sideways off her, wide, black eyes spinning in their sockets. As we watched, it curled up on itself, its skin going black.

"Are you all right?" I said, helping Yue to her feet.

"Shoulder, and the smoke," she said, coughing heavily. "But I will survive. Mag?"

"Looking for you as well. We split up."

"That was idiotic."

I raised my eyebrows. "My apologies, constable. We would have consulted you on the rescue plan, were you not the one we planned to rescue." I pulled up my shirt, covering my mouth against the smoke, which was growing ever thicker. Flames were now licking at the edges of the room's window.

Yue ignored my words. "The vampires were going mad," she said. "They were tearing the place apart, trying to get at the chamber beneath the house. But their claws seemed unable to penetrate the floor. I do not know why. It looks like simple wood."

"Enchanted, likely," I said. "Many mysteries, and little time. Come. Let us find Mag."

We ran towards the back of the room, where another door would lead us to the back of the house. I lifted the latch and pulled on the handle.

THOOM

An explosion launched me backwards. I struck Yue, and we both came down hard on the floor. Oku yelped and scuttled away. I pushed up on my elbows, groaning. The back room roared with flames. They had gathered, waiting for a fool to come and open the door, and I had proven to be just such a fool.

“Mag could have been in there,” I grunted, struggling to my feet.

“If she was, she is dead,” said Yue, taking my arm. “But I think she is smarter than that. Come. To the other side of the house. If she lives, she will need us.”

Together we ran back the way I had come, circling around the house the long way.

THIRTY-NINE

When I ran right, Mag went left. She sped through into the second room with the secret entrance to the underground chamber. Half of it was aflame, and the smoke was thick and black.

And there she found the vampires—Shoulders and King, the only two left.

For a heartbeat, the creatures did not seem to notice her. Both were screaming and tearing at the floor, but their claws did not so much as scratch it. That was strange, but Mag had no time to think about it.

The creatures noticed her, and they wheeled around to attack.

She fought only two now, not the three she had faced outside. But the room's small size constrained her. As she dodged and turned, her cloak kept striking the walls and furniture. Pushing the vampires back with a wild swipe, Mag reached up with her shield and undid the clasp. The cloak fell to the floor. That was better, but not enough to give her the advantage. Her spear strikes had to be somewhat restrained, or she risked striking the walls and knocking herself off balance.

Mag switched her strategy, pressing in closer and using the spear more as a staff. It brought her within reach of the vampires' claws, and she had to block them both with the spear haft and the shield. But with a clever twist, she managed a solid kick into Shoulders' chest.

Shoulders flew away, tumbling over the back of a chair that had caught on fire. The flames erupted across the vampire's skin almost instantly, and it shrieked and tried to bat at them even as its back slammed into the tapestry on the wall.

The vampire was so busy with the flames, it did not see Mag launch herself through the air. Her spear impaled it through the chest and sank deep into the wall behind. The wood and flames spread through Shoulders together, and it died with black blood dribbling from its jaws.

Too late, Mag realized that she had punched a hole

straight through the door that led to the underground chamber. She turned, wrenching her spear from the wall and the corpse. King stood there in the center of the room, its head back, sniffing at the air.

It turned on her, its black eyes narrowing to slits.

Mag tried to spear it as it flew through the air towards her, but it caught the spear in one hand and threw her aside with the other. Its claws sank into the wooden wall, and it ripped the door from its hinges, throwing it into the flames on the other side of the room. With a rending screech, it vanished into the shadows of the stairwell.

Yue and I burst into the room just as Mag was getting to her feet. Yue had one arm over my shoulders, and her other hand held the wound near her neck. Oku whined as he ran to Mag and licked her hand.

"One left," said Mag. "It got in."

She wasted no more words, but ran down the stairwell after the thing. Oku gave a bark and ran after her.

"Leave it, Mag!" I cried. "Let the flames finish it!"

"A little late for that," growled Yue.

"Dark take her," I mumbled. "I will get you to the front and then get her out of the cavern."

"No time," said Yue. "I am coming. You both came in here for me." She pushed off of me and drew her short sword in one hand, hefting her cudgel in the other.

"We have no time to argue, but let us pretend I did," I told her. "Come, if you cannot be stopped."

Just inside the doorway was a torch on the wall. I took it and lit it from the flames at the edge of the room before running down the stairs, Yue just behind me. We reached the bottom to see Mag and Oku locked in combat with King. But its proximity to the magestone-infused blood seemed to have given the creature a new surge of strength. Even as I tried to work out how to enter the fight, it sent Oku flying with a kick and swiped at Mag so savagely that she was forced several steps back.

Before any of us could react, the vampire rushed to the cauldron and stooped over the side, plunging its face into the blood.

We all watched, struck dumb and paralyzed with horror, as King threw its head back and roared. The roar turned deep, guttural, until I could feel it shaking and vibrating within my chest. The vampire's pallid skin began to darken, a deep crimson spreading through it as long-dry veins refilled. The red suffused all of its body from top to bottom, and the skin rippled as bones shifted and rearranged themselves beneath. Then the creature shrieked, and my heart leaped, for it sounded like a cry of pain. But then ridges of bone sprang out through the skin, running down its back and arms, with huge spikes protruding from the elbows. All the while, the vampire's body continued to grow, until it stood now at least three heads taller than me, even hunched over as it was.

Yue and I were frozen in horror, but Mag had kept

her wits about her. As the transformation neared completion, Mag brought back her arm and heaved her spear straight into King's now-massive back.

King whirled and held up a hand. It did not catch the spear. It let the weapon pass straight through its flesh. The spear shuddered to a stop halfway through the claw, its wood coming to rest deep in the vampire's flesh.

The vampire scowled down at the wound. Then it dragged the spear the rest of the way through and flung it, contemptuously, at Mag's feet.

For a heartbeat we hesitated, waiting for the wood to poison the vampire, to send it cowering to its knees.

Nothing happened, except that the hole in the vampire's hand began to seal itself shut.

"Dark take it," muttered Mag. She stooped to pick up her spear, ignoring the black blood that coated its length.

"This was the aim of the ritual," I said. "The documents spoke of strengthening the vampires somehow."

"How do we kill it?" said Yue. "I thought wood was poison to these things."

"It used to be," said Mag. "Mayhap fire will still do the trick."

"We could retreat," said Yue. "The building is burning. This thing will burn with it."

I looked at King. It had stooped over the cauldron again to take another deep draught. "This chamber will not burn. The floorboards are enchanted. And even if it begins to, I think the creature will burst out before it perishes."

As if King could understand my words, its head snapped up towards the ceiling for a moment. Slowly it turned its gaze upon us. Black eyes shone with hate.

"I think it heard you," Yue pointed out mildly.

"I have my torch," I muttered. "If I can get an opening, I can throw it at the vampire, and we will hope it catches."

"Yue should get one, too, and quickly," said Mag. King had begun to stalk closer.

Yue pulled a torch from the wall and lit it with the flames of mine. "Spread out," I said.

I edged right, Yue left, and Mag stood in the middle with Oku. King, seeing us split up, stopped moving, crouched low, and swiveled its head back and forth to keep an eye on all of us.

"Do it as soon as you can," said Mag suddenly, and then she threw herself at the vampire. Oku was only a half-pace behind.

They danced around each other in the center of the room. But Mag could no longer hold her own against the thing. Whereas before she had held against the vampires' strength and somewhat outmatched them in speed, now she was like a man fighting a tiger. She and King traded blows twice in the blink of an eye, but then the vampire's claws slammed into Mag's shield, and she fell on her back. Instantly she rolled, coming up on her feet again, but the vampire was just behind her. This time its claws raked her scale shirt, and she was thrown away again.

Yue and I charged, torches high. But the vampire turned on us and swiped. Yue dropped to the ground to avoid it, but I was too slow. I felt its putrid claws bite into the flesh of my arm, and I cried out with pain.

Before it could follow up, Mag was there again, her spear thrusting, but each time the thing dodged or turned aside her blows with claws as long as my hands. That gave me the time I needed to scramble away from the fight, now cradling my shoulder. I backed away from the spinning, screeching creature and caught Yue's eye from across the room.

"I will try to give you another opening," I called out to her.

"Never mind that," she said. "We have to distract it."

And then she ran for the cauldron.

I cried out a warning before I could stop myself. The vampire heard, drove Mag off with a wild swipe, and turned just in time to see Yue seize the edge of the cauldron. She heaved, trying to upend it.

The vampire roared and launched itself at her. Yue spun on the spot, thrusting her torch up straight into its face. The creature recoiled, but only for a moment. Then it seized the end of the torch in one clawed hand. It shrieked, its black eyes going wide. But it tightened its grip, digging its claws into its own flesh as it completely enveloped the flames with its hand. Its whole body shuddered, spiny ridges jumping back and forth like mountains in an earthquake.

The flames guttered out. The vampire hissed straight into Yue's face, pained, but very much alive.

"Ah," said Yue.

The vampire scooped her up, its clawed fingers wrapping all the way around her torso, and flung her bodily across the room.

CRACK

She struck the wall, slid to the floor, and was still.

"Yue!" I cried. I tried to dart around King, to run to her, but it spun at the sound of my voice. One limb lashed out. I avoided the claws, but the palm struck me like a bear's paw. I, too, flew into the wall, and my head struck it so hard I nearly blacked out straight away.

"Albern!" cried Mag. "The blood!"

I tried to look at her, tried to focus in a world that was suddenly swimming and hazy. She had reached the cauldron, just as Yue had. But Yue's distraction, and mine, had given her the time she needed.

She heaved. It did not look as if she should have been able to move the giant iron bowl. But Mag knew leverage—knew how to get more out of the human body than anyone had a right to expect.

The cauldron upended. The blood flooded over the stone floor, splashing all across it, crashing against the vampire's legs like the ocean against rocks, soaking its lower body in black liquid.

The vampire screamed in livid fury. But it was too focused on the blood to try and claim vengeance against Mag. It fell to its knees, trying desperately to lap up the blood on the ground, pressing its nose and tongue into the stones.

"The blood!" cried Mag again. "With your torch, you idiot!"

Her voice dragged my attention back from King. I frowned at her. The blood? Yue had already tried that. She might be dead. My torch?

I looked down. I still held my torch in my hand, where it burned brightly. When the vampire had struck me, I had dropped my sword, but somehow I had held onto my stupid torch.

Stupid torch. Why should I care about it. The vampire had put Yue's flame out. Fire had caused pain, yes, but it had not killed the thing.

Then Mag was there, kneeling over me, snatching the torch out of my hand. "Honestly, I have to do everything," she said mildly.

And then she flung the torch into the blood that soaked the floor.

It caught at once, like lamp oil. Black flames rippled out across the stones, consuming all the blood in a flash. It rushed up King's arms and legs, its torso, all covered in the black liquid. The creature's screams were terrible. It writhed, but that only sent it splashing through more blood, through more flame. The darkfire consumed it, its body bubbling and popping, sick, hot, wet spurts of fat and gristle sizzling across the room, splashing in the flaming blood, sending it flying up in little sparks.

"Come on," said Mag. She hauled me to my feet and helped me across the room, careful to give the flames a wide berth. We found Yue collapsed at the bottom of the opposite wall.

"Is she alive?" I said.

"We have to hope so," said Mag. "But I cannot carry you anymore, for I will need your help with her."

I took my arm from Mag's shoulders, and between the two of us we hauled Yue up. She did not stir or groan, but I did not have the time to check for breath or a heartbeat. We merely held her between us, her arms across our shoulders, the way we had hauled so many wounded fellows from battlefields in our youth.

The stairs were difficult to navigate, carrying Yue as we were. When we reached the top, we saw that we had almost been too late. The whole house was consumed in flames, so thick that we almost could not push through them to reach the street again. But we managed it, bursting out through the flames to the shock of the many frightened onlookers, most of whom had to have assumed we were dead already. Oku gave great leaps as he bounded around us, baying with joy and terror.

"Back!" I said. "Someone get me water!"

We laid Yue down between us, and I fumbled with the straps of her armor. Ashta appeared, helping me. We got Yue's armor off, and I pressed my head to her chest, listening desperately, trying to feel the rise and fall of her breath.

And then at last . . .

Pa-pump. Pa-pump.

"Get. Off me," groaned Yue.

I fell back on my rear, closing my eyes and heaving a deep sigh of relief. "Thank the sky."

"Here, Sergeant," said Ashta, relief nearly causing her to drop the waterskin. "Drink this."

"Lift her head," said Mag wryly, "or she will drown instead of burning alive."

She had fetched her singed cloak from the house on our way out, and now she fashioned it into a pillow for Yue. The constable drank deep of Ashta's water, until finally she pushed it away, sputtering and coughing.

"Are you all right?" I asked her.

"I am alive," she said. "That is more than I think I should expect. The vampire?"

"We killed it," I told her. "Something we could not have done without you."

"I am not proud to have been mere bait, but I suppose I am the only one who had the courage for it," said Yue.

"Certainly, it is something I have never volunteered for," I told her.

Yue snorted. "Of course not." Then her countenance grew stern, and she held my gaze. "In all earnestness, thank you for your help. And, I suppose, for saving my life."

"Oh, constable," I said, grinning at her. "You cannot think we did that for you. I have it on the very best authority that corpses are simply a nightmare to take care of. The paperwork alone."

Her brows drew together. "I could still arrest you. Both of you."

I patted her shoulder gently. "You are welcome to try."

Some of the townsfolk who had skill at healing had been summoned, and they came forwards to care for her now. I stood and went to Mag's side. Oku was with her, but she paid him no attention. She had turned from us, and now she stood surveying the Shades' hideout as it burned. Some of the townsfolk had set up a watering line, passing buckets from hand to hand and dousing the nearby buildings to ensure they did not catch alight. But the flames seemed to be self-contained, and there was no wind. The night's danger looked to be well and truly over.

"The blood," I said. Mag did not look at me, so I pressed on. "How did you know about the blood?"

"We all should have known," she said lightly, free from the battle-trance. "From the moment we read their notes. The process infused the blood with magestone essence, remember? I have never seen a substance that catches fire more easily than magestone."

I shook my head. "It was a guess. You risked all our lives on that strategy."

"It was the only idea we had," said Mag. Then at last she turned to me, and a wide grin was plastered across her face. "And what are you complaining for? It worked."

I laughed at that. "I cannot argue with you there."

Wordlessly we embraced, clutching each other tight in the light and warmth of the flames. And in that moment, for one brief instance, I felt as though Mag—the old Mag, the one I had known since we were both young—held me in her arms, and that she would never leave my side again.

FORTY

THE FIRE WAS PUT OUT EVENTUALLY, BUT LONG AFTER we had already gone to bed. We tried to stay up and help the townsfolk, but they insisted we return to our inn and rest. Ashta, who Yue had deputized until she had recovered, was particularly insistent. When we finally returned to the inn, Dryleaf was nowhere to be seen. We were too tired to search for him that night, and went straight to bed.

We woke the next morning well past dawn. In fact, when I looked out the tiny window of our room, it looked as if even noon had passed us by. It is possible there were some parts of my body that did not hurt, but I could not have told you what they were. Every motion made me groan like an old man.

Mag, sky bless her, seemed fine. She moved lightly on her feet, and there was no sign of ache or pain within her. I saw no bruises on her skin, and of course, as you can imagine, there were no cuts or scrapes, either. I shook my head at it more than once, as we readied ourselves to emerge from our room. Even vampires, inhumanly strong beasts though they were, had been unable to injure Mag in any lasting way. She had been part of my life for more years now than she had not. Yet not even age, it seemed, had proven able to catch her in its inevitable grasp.

When we made our way at last to the common room, we found Dryleaf sitting by the fire, in the very same place he had been when first we met him. I crossed the room to speak with him while Mag went to settle our account with the innkeeper. Dryleaf seemed to recognize the gait of my footsteps, for he tilted his head up eagerly, his milky eyes staring just over my left shoulder.

"I hear you have become heroes," he said.

"Some seem to think so, yes," I told him. "But we were only two among many who fought bravely last night."

"Yes," said Dryleaf, his bushy brows dancing as

he nodded. “Yue suffered some injury, I hear, but it sounds as though she will make a full and speedy recovery.”

“That is good,” I said. “She stood bravely against the monsters last night.”

Dryleaf’s shoulders rose and fell, as though with a sigh, but he made no sound. “And I suppose you have seen to your purpose here in Lan Shui, then. Will you be leaving town?”

“We will,” I said. “We have business elsewhere.”

“Most people do, when they come to visit Lan Shui,” he said. “Yet a place may be a way-stop, and still people make for it when occasion arises.”

“I thought I would ask—if you do not mind—would you accompany us this morning?” I said. “We want to visit Yue before we go, and I know you are fond of her. And I would appreciate your company.”

Dryleaf got up so fast, I was afraid he would hurt himself. “It would be my great pleasure,” he said. “And for my part, I give my word to keep your pace and not impose a moment’s delay. Now let us go and meet with Mag, for if my ears do not deceive me, I think she is having some sort of trouble with the innkeeper.”

I took Dryleaf’s arm and led him towards Mag. The old man had been correct. Mag was engaged in a heated argument with the innkeeper as we came up, though the innkeeper himself only met her angry words with a beatific smile, which he turned on me as I drew up to the bar.

Mag whirled on the two of us. "Ah, good," she said. "Dryleaf. Help me convince this idiot that he does not know how to run a business."

"Before I try, I would rather hear the details of the situation," said Dryleaf diplomatically.

"Mag, what under the sky is going on?" I said.

"This man," said Mag, thrusting a finger at the innkeeper's face—the innkeeper's vacant smile widened—"will not take my money."

"No, I will not," agreed the innkeeper, his massive mustache jumping as he sniffed.

"We stayed here for *days,* you ox!" cried Mag. "Take our money!"

Instead of answering, the innkeeper reached into a purse at his belt, produced two pennies, and laid them on the pile of coins that lay on the bar in front of him. The pile seemed somewhat larger than it should have been, considering the time we had spent in Lan Shui.

"And he *will not* stop doing that!" said Mag, sounding quite ready to throttle the man.

"No, I will not," said the innkeeper, sounding absolutely delighted.

"Listen, friend," I said. "No one appreciates your generosity more than we do. But you cannot survive on good deeds and well wishes alone. Take some of our coin."

The innkeeper answered only with another two pennies laid on the pile.

"Stop telling him to take money," growled Mag,

who seemed to wish to ignore the fact that she had just done the same thing. "It only makes him give us more."

"I think you should leave," said Dryleaf. "It seems an untenable situation for the two of you, unless you wish to rob the poor man blind."

The innkeeper nodded gaily, as though he had never heard truer words.

"But we *are* robbing him blind," said Mag. "I used to own an inn myself, you know. And I am—well, in all honesty, I am insulted on his behalf."

To my surprise, Dryleaf put his hands on his hips and scowled in Mag's direction. "If you do not wish for people to give you gifts, to say nothing of praise, then I would cease your frankly ridiculous habit of running around and saving them from danger. Many people in the nine kingdoms see this as the only natural reaction to such a thing."

"I did not come here to save anyone," grumbled Mag, avoiding looking at either Dryleaf or the innkeeper. "And so be it, if they are too foolish to take my money—*put them back.*" She snatched the pile of silver away from the innkeeper, who had been reaching for another pair of pennies from his purse.

We beat a hasty retreat from the inn and out into the street, Mag scowling, Dryleaf chuckling mightily, and me trying to restrain myself from joining him. Mag was still trying to cram the coins into her purse several streets later—the innkeeper had given her quite a lot of them. But we both stopped short as we saw Liu standing there before us.

The boy was not alone. Next to him was the man who had taken him in when we had brought him back to Lan Shui. I had never learned his name. But beside them both sat Oku. The dog grinned up at us, tongue lolling from its mouth as it panted in the heat of the day.

"Liu," said Mag, crouching at once to speak with him at eye-level. "How are you?"

"I am well," he said. "You killed the monsters?"

"We helped," I told him. "Many in the town fought them together."

"I am glad," said Liu. "I am glad they are dead."

Mag looked a little sad at that. But she reached out and ruffled his hair. "We have to be going now, but we know we leave Lan Shui under your protection. You will watch out for all these people for us, will you not? Many of them are not very smart. They will need you."

Liu smiled at that. "Of course. I am going to be a constable one day."

"I think you will be a great one."

"I think Oku should go with you," said Liu.

I took a step forwards. "Liu, that is very kind of you," I said. "But he is your hound. This is his home."

"His home was in the mountains," said Liu. "So was mine. But I think he needs to go and protect other people's homes now. That is what you are going to do."

"Let him stay and protect you," I said.

Liu's eyes began to well with tears, and his cheeks flushed. "I am safe now. You killed the monsters. But there may be other monsters out there. I want to know that you are safe, too."

Mag had moved behind the boy, and she was giving me a scowl he could not see. And in my mind, that settled the matter. I gave Liu a warm smile.

"Then it would be our pleasure to take him along with us."

Mag barely stifled a groan. But she plastered a smile on her face as Liu turned and hugged her legs. Then the boy went to Oku and clutched at his dark brown fur.

"Take care of them," he said. "Mayhap I will see you when we are both older."

"We will make sure to come and visit," I said. "Thank you, Liu."

"Fare well," said Mag. She gave the boy another tight hug and then headed north. I followed her, Dryleaf on my arm. Oku took two tentative steps after us, but then he stopped and looked back at Liu.

"Kip, boy," said Liu. "Go with them."

Oku looked at us, and his mouth snapped shut. He looked back at Liu and whined.

"Oku, tiss," I said.

The hound met my gaze. He ran back to Liu and licked his face twice. Liu laughed and gave the dog another hug. Then Oku ran after me, trotting at my heels. Just before we turned the corner out of sight, he gave one last glance back at Liu. Then the boy was gone.

I had forgotten the way to the constables' station, so we followed Dryleaf's directions to find it. A sharp knock produced Constable Ashta in short order, and she ushered us in to visit Yue. The sergeant had been laid upon a wide, soft bed in the back room of the station, where she was propped up on many pillows. She appeared to have been dozing when we arrived, but her eyes snapped open as we entered. She shifted herself so as to appear more upright. As we came to her bedside, she surveyed us with stern, uncompromising eyes.

"You lot are off, then?" she said brusquely.

"We are," said Mag. "But we wanted to ensure you were well taken care of."

"Of course I am," said Yue. "And entirely unsurprised to see you scuttling off after having made so much trouble."

I chuckled. "Yes, but at least we leave you with our apologies. That must be worth something."

"Hardly," said Yue. "But actually, there is one matter that must be tended to before you sally off. By the King's law, there is a bounty on vampires. Any killed and turned in to the law are worth five gold weights each. You have killed seven while you have been here. I never learned my numbers very well, so let us call it forty weights."

Mag gave a loud, frustrated groan and turned to

me. "Darkness take all these people. Do they not realize that coins are worth *money?* Why are they so eager to be rid of them?" But then her eyes lit up with an idea, and she whirled back to Yue. "No! Keep the coins. Use them in our name, to support those who lost homes and loved ones to the vampires' attack. And start with that *absolute* fool of an innkeeper whose custom we took. Will you do that for us?"

"Lan Shui has more than enough helping hands to take care of those who are bereaved," said Yue. "And I am afraid the King's law is quite clear about the terms of the bounty."

"Sky above, you—I will not—this—" Mag ended in a sputter, thrusting a finger at Yue. "I am not taking your gold. So unless you mean to get out of that bed this instant and *pursue* me out of town to hide a coin purse in my saddlebags, I am afraid you must be disappointed. Albern, I am taking my leave. Say your farewells, and then let us ride on from this haven of woodenheads." She stalked out of the room, only pausing for a moment at the door to turn and give Yue a final "I am glad you will recover" before vanishing.

I stepped up beside Yue with a smile. As I did, Ashta passed Mag on the way in. She stared after Mag, who had stormed off in a huff, and shook her head as the door slammed shut behind her.

"You shoved the purse in her saddlebag?" said Yue.

"I did, Sergeant," said Ashta. "And judging by the look on her face, I am glad she did not see it."

"Despite her admonishment," I said to Yue, "Mag herself has never been good at holding on to coin. I hope you will forgive her rash words."

"If she follows the King's law, I will," said Yue, arching an eyebrow.

"Thank you, constable. Though you know, you helped us kill two of the beasts."

"Yet constables are exempt from the bounty," said Yue.

"That seems unjust," I said.

"I do not write the laws," she said. "I only enforce them."

I placed a hand on her shoulder, squeezing her through the thick bandages she had there. "And I think you do excellently at it. Fare well, constable. I am sorry to have disturbed the peace of your people."

"Things are better now than they were when you arrived, I suppose," said Yue, meeting my gaze. "If you ever draw near to Lan Shui again, I would not mind if you visited us. You did not get to see many of the town's more attractive features. This bed, for example, is quite comfortable when it is not holding a convalescent."

I do not mind telling you that my cheeks went absolutely wine-dark with color. From his place by the door, Dryleaf gave a conspicuous cough, and Ashta became suddenly very interested in something out the window.

"I . . . I am sure it is," I said finally. "Mayhap I will take you up on your offer, if ever I return this way."

"You would be fortunate to," said Yue with a snort. Then her eyes slid past me to Dryleaf. "Still your giggling, old man. I have not forgotten the help you gave to these people when they were still strangers. I have my eye on you."

"And it is only that fact that lets me feel safe when I lay my head down at night," said Dryleaf, bowing. "I am glad you are well, Yue."

"Of course you are," said Yue. "Well, enough of both of you. I have been ordered to rest well in order to speed my recovery, and I always listen to my healer."

"That is a lie," whispered Dryleaf, as we beat our hasty retreat. "She is one of the most obstinate patients in the nine lands. The healers have told me so. I think she was as stunned by her words to you as you were, and wanted an excuse to kick us out."

We returned to the inn, where we began to ready our horses for travel. Foolhoof looked at me as suspiciously as ever, while Mist, of course, easily took the blanket, bit, and bridle as Mag put them on. Dryleaf sat on a little wooden stool near the front of the stable, a gentle smile plastered on his face. It looked forced.

"Mag," I said quietly, stepping close to her for a moment. "Do you think the innkeeper has any spare horses for sale?"

"Any innkeeper worth their salt does, and he is too much of a fool to be worth that much," said Mag irritably. But she glanced around the stable. "No, in truth, I think he does. There are too many horses here for the number of guests I have seen in the common room, at least. Why do you ask?"

I glanced over my shoulder at Dryleaf, sitting by the stable's front door, and then met Mag's gaze. I raised my eyebrows. She pursed her lips and looked at the old man, considering. At last she looked back at me and nodded.

I left my horse for a moment and went to the old man, sitting beside him on the bench at the front of the stable. "Dryleaf," I said. "I have been thinking much about what you said."

"Hm?" said Dryleaf, shaking himself as though he had been pulled from deep thought. "I have said many things."

"I mean about how you came to be in Lan Shui."

Dryleaf sighed. "Oh? Have you?"

"I have," I said. "And I thought—though you may have no interest in such a scheme—I thought you *could* come with us, if you so desired. We have no plans to visit the Birchwood Forest. But we might go there one day."

For the second time that day, Dryleaf moved with the shocking speed of a much younger man. He leaped to his feet, hands trembling, and I saw tears well up in his cloudy eyes.

"I . . . if you took me with you, I would—I swear I would be no burden, and I would—"

"Sky above, man, of course I know that," I said. "You have forgotten more leagues of travel than I have ever ridden. And for my part, I would be happy to have your wisdom at our side, and I swear we would keep you safe. And something tells me we may have tasks ahead of us for which we will require your help."

"Anything," said Dryleaf. "If my old bones can do it, consider it done."

"Very well. I have your first task for you." I pulled out the purse Yue had given me. "Go and see the innkeeper, and purchase yourself a horse. I think he would refuse to take any of our coin, but I think he might take yours."

Dryleaf let out a laugh that almost turned into a sob, shaking his head. "Even your first task for me is a gift. I am in your debt, Albern of the family Telfer, and I will not forget it."

"You will not have time to," I assured him. "Before long, the hardness of the road and the open fields upon which we make our beds will have reminded you of why you abandoned them for comfort and safety. But while you are seized with this madness, I will take advantage of it."

"How very shrewd of you," said Dryleaf. "But now excuse me—I must purchase myself a horse."

The business was done before we had finished saddling our mounts, and soon the three of us rode out of the stable, Oku trotting along beside our horses. As we passed through the streets, townsfolk waved and wished us well—especially Mag. She rode high in her saddle, her back straight. Her eyes were fixed on the road ahead, the way they had been when we rode into Lan Shui. But now she turned her sight upon the people who called out to her, and smiled at them, and wished them well.

And I was proud to ride by her side, as we made north for Calentin.

For home.

FORTY-ONE

"A GOOD TALE," SAID SUN, AS ALBERN'S VOICE TRAILED away to nothing. "A good tale, and well told."

Albern did not answer her for a moment. He stared at the fire between them, the flames dancing in his eyes, his arm across the top of his knee, and his fingers hanging idly before his face. For a moment he resembled nothing so much as a statue, a warding figure placed in the woods to guard them from death and darkness, and to provide comfort to any traveler who came his way—comfort, but no help.

Finally he stirred and looked at Sun across the fire.

He stared at her for a moment, as though he were hearing her words again in his mind, and then he smiled. "I recognize the words of praise that were customary in your family's court, and I thank you for them."

"Now tell me about your arm."

Albern laughed. "No. Not yet. That is the *end* of the story—or the only ending most people care about. But endings are useless if you do not know where things began. The journey, the whole of it, is what a story is all about. In this small tale I have just told you, imagine how much drier it would have been if I had just told you about Lan Shui and fighting the vampires, without telling you about Northwood first. Imagine how little you would have cared about Northwood if you had not known about Sten."

It was a fair enough point. But the spell of the old man's tale was wearing off now, and it left her feeling cold and alone in the woods, despite the fire and Albern's presence. "Well then, I suppose we had better—"

"Quiet," rasped Albern, so suddenly that Sun obeyed without question.

The old man rose, and from his belt he drew a sword—old, battered, but well sharpened and polished. Sun got to her feet as well, though she did not know why. Without thinking, she drew an arrow and fitted it to the string of Albern's bow, peering out into the night beside him. She had not heard whatever had alerted him, but now she could feel it. The woods were too quiet, and there was a presence. Something was out there, watching them.

"What is it?" she whispered. "A wolf?"

"Not a wolf," said Albern.

And then a creature of nightmares bounded into the firelight. Man-sized and man-shaped, but horribly twisted and bent. It landed on all fours, and there it crouched, hissing at them. Pallid, white skin. Hands that ended in claws as long as Sun's fingers, and a mouth full of pointed teeth.

Sun might have had difficulty identifying it, if she had not heard it mentioned so often already that night.

Vampire, her mind screamed.

And then it roared as it attacked.

First it leaped for Sun, but Albern gave a great cry and jumped in between them. His wild, swinging sword drove the creature back a pace or two, and Albern sidestepped to draw it farther from the fire.

Sun's whole body had gone rigid, but then she realized what Albern was doing. He was stepping aside so that she would have a clear shot. With that thought, her body seemed to move of its own accord. The bow came up, she drew, and she sighted down the arrow.

Albern gave a cry and swiped at the vampire. It lunged to the side, arms wide. And Sun loosed.

With everything Albern had told her that night, she fully expected the vampire to dodge her shot. But to her surprise, it pierced the vampire straight through the wrist. The creature screamed—a terrible, ear-shattering noise that threatened to deafen her, especially in the deep silence of the woods.

The vampire wrenched the arrow out of its limb. The edges of the wound began to turn black. It whirled on her, hissing, but Albern attacked, sword flashing in the firelight.

With a shriek, the vampire leaped off into the woods and the darkness.

The clearing settled again to silence. And as it did, Sun realized that *now* she was shaking, *now* she was quivering and breathing so hard that she did not think she would be able to stand for more than a few heartbeats. The bow clattered from her hand to the ground, and suddenly she was sitting, though she had made no move to lower herself. Her tailbone hurt, but it was a dull, distant sort of pain.

"What . . . sky above, what was that?" she gasped, though she was not truly speaking to anyone.

"Too bad, is what it was," said Albern. "I had hoped we could kill the thing, but it got away. Ah, well. They tend to do that, as I have told you already tonight. And the wound will fester—if it does not die from the infection, it will at least be easier to finish off."

"That was a vampire!"

"Of course it was."

Sun looked at him, eyes wide. "You *knew?* You *knew* that creature was coming?"

"Why, yes," said Albern. "That is why we came out here. And was I not right? You are a warrior true. I can tell. I can always tell. Even back then, I could tell, and I am better at it now."

"But I—but you met me in a tavern by chance!" said Sun, rising shakily to her feet. "What would you have done if I had not come? You could not have faced that thing alone!"

Albern smiled at her, gently and with a little sadness in his eyes. "We met in the tavern, but not by chance. This is the thirteenth town you have visited on your family's trip, Sun. The sixth one was the first time you slipped away from the caravan. You have done it again in every town since. You have been looking for something."

"You . . . you were following me?"

"Sky, no," said Albern. "But you have been seen, and many remarked on it as something strange. The rumor of you reached my ears, and I determined to find you tonight. The constable? He helped me. When Tunsha signaled to the tavern with his ring, he was also telling the constable that all was well and his job was done."

"Then you tricked me," said Sun. "You led me along on a scheme."

"I did," said Albern. "I think you needed me to. But it is done now. And if I was wrong, then you can go. You can return to your family, whom you despise, and go along with their plots, which you disdain."

Sun was standing again. She had no more memory of rising than she had had of sitting down. "Or?"

Albern cocked an eyebrow. "Or what?"

"You make it sound as though I have another choice. I could go home. Or . . . ?"

"Or you could come with me, and I could tell you another story."

She looked away from him. "Where are you going?"

"Lan Shui."

"The town where—"

Albern nodded. "The town from the tale, yes."

"What are you doing there?"

"I am visiting a friend," said Albern. "And then I am taking care of some business. It is somewhat akin to our business tonight, but until I have your answer, I do not think I will tell you any more."

"How do you mean to fight another monster like that one if I do *not* come with you?" said Sun.

Albern smiled at her, gently and with a little sadness in his eyes. "You were here, in the right place at the right time, tonight. But if you had not come, someone else would have. And if no one shows up, I can hunt someone down. But tonight it was you, and I am glad. You may believe whatever you wish, Sun, but I told you. I no longer believe in chance as I did when I was your age."

"I . . . I still do not understand," said Sun.

"What?" said Albern, spreading his arm wide. "Ask me anything you wish, and I shall do my best to explain."

A thousand questions whirled in her mind, but none of them seemed like the right one. She tossed them aside one by one, until at last she had the question she truly wanted to ask—the only one, really, she *could* ask.

"Should we go after it?" she said, looking Albern in the eye. "If it escapes, we may regret it."

"Well, we may," said Albern, suddenly cagey. "But we may regret it even more deeply if we pursue it in the woods by moonslight. We do not have a warrior like Mag at our side, and I have my doubts about battling the beast twice in one night."

"Oh, but once was fine," said Sun, shaking her head.

"For a young one like that, yes," said Albern. When she gave him a look, he nodded. "Yes, very young. I would not have brought you out here to fight a creature like the ones Mag and I faced. They were old, very old, nearly as old as the bones of the hills whence they came. I doubt the one we saw tonight is much older than I am."

"That is quite old," said Sun.

Albern's mouth twisted. "Always ready with a barb. I admire that. In any case, you said you wanted to do good things more than you wanted accolades. Well, you have done a very good thing tonight, though I doubt anyone shall ever hear of it. Return to your family if you wish."

So saying, he strode to her and took his bow from

her hands. In an instant, he had unstrung it and stowed the string in a pouch at his belt, and then he set off through the trees towards the place where he had left his horse. Sun, for the second time that night, found herself staring after the old bowyer, dumbstruck. Just before he vanished from sight, she ran after him.

"Wait!" she cried. "What if I *do* want to come with you?"

Albern stopped and looked back at her, squinting in the moonslight. "You seemed quite angry, and so I gave the cause up for lost."

"I *am* quite angry."

He shrugged. "Well, then. You can find your way back to town, can you not? You know where the road is—just there. I do not think you will meet any more dangers in the forest tonight, but I could give you my sword, if you wish. Morled should still be there, if you hurry, and I do not doubt that she would be glad to see you."

Sun looked off through the trees. There, far in the distance, she could just make out the lights of the town: a soft, fiery glow over the top of a hill, that poured through the trees in little shafts.

It had been a long time. Half the night. Her retainers would be nearly frantic, and Mother and Father would have been alerted that she was missing by this point.

But she could still go to them. She could go on through the rest of their tour of Dorsea, and then return home to Dulmun. She could carry on with only the memory of this one little adventure.

She looked at Albern instead.

"I want to come with you."

With one hand on his saddle, Albern regarded her. "Are you certain?"

"Yes."

"Why?"

Sun lifted her chin. "Is my company unwelcome?"

"You will have a hard time turning back if you go on with me tonight," said Albern. "So I would like you to be very sure of your choice before you make it."

"I do not hate my family," she said. "Yet for a long time, I have not been able to say that I love them, either, and I think their feelings are the same towards me. In my kingdom, parents adopt children often, and those children are treated just the same as if the parents had bedded to make them. You need not share your family's blood to love them—yet neither must you love them simply because you share blood. I am not desperate to escape them, and I would not die if I remained. Yet I need a better purpose in my life than that. I need something more to pull me through each day than the thought that things could be worse."

She took another step towards Albern, and now they were eye-to-eye. "You are a trickster. I do not like that. I do not like being led along a path I cannot see beneath my feet. But tonight, you and I did a good thing. I want to come with you, if you can promise that we will do more good in the nine kingdoms. I want to come with you, if you promise not to trick me into doing the right thing, but trust me to make the right decision."

Albern gave her a long, careful look before answering. "I can promise both those things," he said quietly. "One last time. Are you sure?"

"I am sure," said Sun, and she realized it was true. She did not want to go home. The whole time she had been in this strange, foreign kingdom, she had been looking for some escape—some way to leave, and never have to return. Now that she had found such a chance, she would not turn her back on it.

"I am sure," she said again. "The beginning of the story has been good. I want to hear the rest of it."

Albern smiled his widest grin yet. "And I would be happy to tell it to you. Come on, then. Let us get moving. The road is long, and it always grows darker before revealing at last the sun."

"As you say," said Sun. "But as we go, please, carry on."

Slowly, Albern nodded. "Until the tale's true end."

KEEP READING

You have begun the Tales of the Wanderer. But as Albern and Mag ride from Lan Shui towards Calentin, many questions remain.

Why does Kaita hate Mag? What does she have planned for the Wanderer in Albern's homeland of Calentin? And what else do the Shades have planned for the nine kingdoms of Underrealm?

Find out in *Stone Heart,* the next book in the Tales of the Wanderer. Get it here:

Underrealm.net/TOW2

AUTHOR'S NOTE

In these Author's Notes, I like to tell you something special about the book you've just read, or what was going through my head while I was writing it.

Instead, today I just want to tell you that this book was a pain in my ass.

I didn't finish it. I defeated it.

I also think it might be the best Underrealm book I've written so far.

If you enjoyed it—and I hope you did—please know that it came at the expense of a lot of energy and frustration.

But having kicked its teeth in, I'm much better prepared for the next one.

That's all I have to say. Until next time, dearest denizen of Underrealm.

Garrett Robinson,
July 2018

CONNECT ONLINE

DISCORD

Discord is a free voice and text chat engine for gamers, geeks—and for readers like you. Legacy Books has a Discord server that we think is pretty awesome. You can chat with Garrett Robinson and ALL the authors of Underrealm, as well as many other readers just like you:

Underrealm.net/Discord

YOUTUBE

Catch up with me weekly (when I'm not directing a film or having a baby). You can watch my YouTube channel where I talk about art, science, life, my books, and the world.

But not cats.

Never cats.

GarrettBRobinson.com/yt

THE BOOKS OF UNDERREALM

THE NIGHTBLADE EPIC

NIGHTBLADE

MYSTIC

DARKFIRE

SHADEBORN

WEREMAGE

YERRIN

THE ACADEMY JOURNALS

THE ALCHEMIST'S TOUCH

THE MINDMAGE'S WRATH

THE FIREMAGE'S VENGEANCE

THE TALES OF THE WANDERER

BLOOD LUST

STONE HEART

HELL SKIN

THE BOOKS OF UNDERREALM

CHRONOLOGICAL ORDER

NIGHTBLADE

MYSTIC

DARKFIRE

SHADEBORN

BLOOD LUST

THE ALCHEMIST'S TOUCH

WEREMAGE

THE MINDMAGE'S WRATH

STONE HEART

THE FIREMAGE'S VENGEANCE

HELL SKIN

YERRIN

ABOUT THE AUTHOR

Garrett Robinson was born and raised in Los Angeles. The son of an author/painter father and a violinist/singer mother, no one was surprised when he grew up to be an artist.

After blooding himself in the independent film industry, he self-published his first book in 2012 and swiftly followed it with a stream of others, publishing more than two million words by 2014. Within months he topped numerous Amazon bestseller lists. Now he spends his time writing books and directing films.

A passionate fantasy author, his most popular books are the novels of Underrealm, including The Nightblade Epic and The Academy Journals series.

However, he has delved into many other genres. Some works are for adult audiences only, such as *Non Zombie* and *Hit Girls,* but he has also published popular books for younger readers, including The Realm Keepers series and *The Ninjabread Man*, co-authored with Z.C. Bolger.

Garrett lives in Oregon with his wife Meghan, his children Dawn, Luke, and Desmond, and his dog Chewbacca.

Garrett can be found on:

BLOG: garrettbrobinson.com/blog
EMAIL: garrett@garrettbrobinson.com
TWITTER: twitter.com/garrettauthor
FACEBOOK: facebook.com/garrettbrobinson

EPILOGUE

You did not think I forgot about Kaita, did you?

She was there, in Lan Shui, observing the three of us as we rode forth on horseback, Oku trotting beside us.

Kaita still mourned the deaths of Dellek and the other Shades. And for the sake of petty revenge, she wished the vampires had claimed more lives before Mag and I had destroyed them. But she had realized that we would never ride north for Calentin until the threat to Lan Shui had been ended, and so she had let it happen without interfering. And now, things were mostly going according to her plan again.

All except the old man. "Dryleaf," he called himself. Kaita had not predicted him, and she feared there might be more to him than there appeared. So she had taken the form of a few of the folk of Lan Shui, and she had gone poking about, trying to see if the old man had some hidden agenda that had caused him to take up with us.

She had discovered nothing. It seemed he had joined up with us by sheer luck (if you believe in luck). Ever since he had arrived in Lan Shui, he had taken no interest whatsoever in the great events of Underrealm. He was a fixture of the town, an elder who gave advice when he could and sang songs when he could not.

Indeed, the only thing Kaita had managed to learn was that he had not always been known as Dryleaf. Long ago, when he first came to Lan Shui, he had gone by another name, though the old one sounded just as nonsensical to Kaita.

After all, who ever heard of an old peddler named Bracken?

www.ingramcontent.com/pod-product-compliance
Lightning Source LLC
Chambersburg PA
CBHW030810310726
48980CB00006B/442/J

* 9 7 8 1 9 4 1 0 7 6 5 3 8 *